Penguin Books
The Great Dethriffe

C. D. B. Bryan is the author of one previous
novel, *P. S. Wilkinson*. Mr Bryan lives with his
wife and child in Connecticut.

Penguin Books Ltd, Harmondsworth,
Middlesex, England
Penguin Books Australia Ltd, Ringwood,
Victoria, Australia
Penguin Books (N.Z.) Ltd. 182–190 Wairau Road,
Auckland 10, New Zealand

First published in the U.S.A. 1972
First published in Great Britain by W. H. Allen 1972
Published in Penguin Books 1974

Made and printed in Great Britain by
C. Nicholls & Company Ltd
Set in Linotype Juliana

C. D. B. Bryan

The Great Dethriffe

Penguin Books

to Katharine B. O'Hara and St George Bryan II, with love

Alfred's
Book

After all is there not much more mystery in the relations of man to man than we generally recognise? None of us can truly assert that he really knows someone else, even if he has lived with him for years.

Of that which constitutes our inner life, we can impart even to those most intimate with us only fragments, the whole we cannot give, nor would they be able to comprehend it.

We wander through this life together in a semi-darkness in which none of us can distinguish exactly the features of his neighbor, only from time to time, through some experience that we have of our companion, or through some remark that he passes, he stands for a moment close to us, as though illuminated by a flash of lightning. Then we see him as he really is.

After that we again walk on together in the darkness, perhaps for a long time, and try in vain to make out our fellow traveler's features.

– Albert Schweitzer

If the volume or the tone of the work can lead one to believe that the author is attempting a sum, hasten to point out to him that he is face to face with the opposite attempt, that of an implacable *subtraction*.

– 'Morelli'
in Julio Cortázar's HOPSCOTCH

Chapter One

When I was twenty-five I fell in love for the first time with a married woman. She was Teddy Baldwin, a New York high fashion model whom I met at a cocktail party given by George Dethriffe, a friend of mine since childhood. The party was in honour of Alice Townsend who never appeared.

About three months after the party, George Dethriffe and Alice Townsend were married; I sold my first short story to a very good magazine; and Teddy Baldwin, upon learning that she was being sent to Rome to do location shots for a fashion magazine, asked me to go with her. We arrived in Rome on Sunday, 10 December 1961, two weeks after George and Alice Dethriffe arrived in Florence on their honeymoon.

Ordinarily Teddy left our hotel before sunrise so that she would be on location when the morning light was right and I would go back to sleep until awakened by that incredible din of motorcycles, buses, scooters, automobiles, bells, horns, whistles, squeals, curses, howls and shouts and the crashing together of pots, pans, lids, kettles and pails. And then wrapping myself in the blanket for warmth, I would cross to our window, fling open the shutters and be confronted almost nose to nose by the elderly lady who so impassively examined me from her window sill opposite. As far as I could tell she never left that window. Even though the temperature hovered near freezing she remained like some fleshy gargoyle overlooking our street. And sometimes an old man would appear at the window next to hers who would crowd his sill with potted cactus plants that remained until the shadows fell again. He bore a haunting resemblance to some of the later busts of Caesar, the ones which show his face etched and melancholy, lips turned down at the corners, cheeks drawn and hollow, the jaw almost thin.

On those mornings Teddy worked, I strolled around. Even though I had never been to Rome I experienced, as I suppose does every traveller to that city, a flood of memories whenever I rounded a corner and suddenly came upon a fountain or an obelisk, a façade or a statue so absolutely familiar that the air would grow still about me.

I would take long walks down to the Tiber stopping at a fruit stall to buy a blood orange or an apple, and then perhaps cross the Ponte S. Angelo with its statues of St Peter and St Paul and the ten angels looking every bit as chilled by the blustering wind as me. Then on to Hadrian's tomb, the battered brick of the Castel S. Angelo the colour of dried blood, crowned by the baroque sculpted archangel Michael sheathing his sword. And from there down the broad Mussolinied Via della Conciliazone to the Piazza S. Pietro with Bernini's lobster claw colonnades supporting one hundred and forty saints who bore so dismaying a resemblance to cheerleaders exhorting pilgrims to piety.

I was in a tourist frenzy those first days. I wanted to see everything. Teddy was bored by ruins. I was addicted to them.

The morning of our tenth day in Rome, Teddy did not have to be on location and we walked together to American Express to pick up our mail and in my case hopefully a dividend cheque or two. But my mail consisted only of an unfamiliar pale blue envelope postmarked La Spezia. And while Teddy went to the counter to cash some Traveller's Cheques, I opened my letter and saw it was from George Dethriffe.

Dear Alfred:

Alice is thriving in this atmosphere. She says she *adores* Florence, *adores* the Uffizi, *adores* the Bargello and *adores* the Italians who are attracted to her blondeness like moths to a flame. Am stunned by the facility with which American women adopt Italian expressions! All of Alice's sentences start with *Mio Dio* and *Ecco* and I'm left saying *Che sera, sera*. I can now speak just enough Italian to ask a question, the answer to which I stand no chance of understanding.

We have been 'touring' but will definitely be back in Florence the weekend before Christmas and will be staying at the Grand on the Piazza Ognissanti. We would like you to spend Christmas with us. I have reserved a room for you next to ours overlooking the Arno, starting Friday, the 22nd. I will not accept no as an answer. I will pay all and would ask only that you accept my largesse as a Christmas present contribution to the arts. I am hungry for conversation with you. I not only urge you to come, my old friend, I beg you to come. I am enclosing train schedules and addresses where to reach us.

I was folding the letter and stuffing it back into its envelope when Teddy returned.

'Did you get all the money you need?' I asked her.

'Never!' Teddy laughed. 'Who was your letter from?'

'George,' I said. 'George Dethriffe. He wants me to come up to Florence this week-end to spend Christmas with him and Alice.'

'On their honeymoon?'

'Well, they'll have been over here almost a month by then so it isn't as though I were crashing their wedding night.'

'Are you going to go?'

'I've never been to Florence,' I said. 'Did you know my mother went to school there?'

'In Florence? Why?'

'I don't know. In those days young ladies spent their junior years in Florence.'

'Did she let the hair grow in her armpits?'

'My mother never grew any hair under her arms. In fact she never grew hair on her legs. She never – the only hair she had was on her head, long golden ringlets. My mother was a saintly woman. She –'

'She sounds like a Mouseketeer,' Teddy said.

'A *what*?'

'A Mouseketeer, you remember,' she said. 'Annette Funicello and all the rest? M, I, C,' she sang, 'K, E, Y, ... M, O, U, S, E. Don't you remember that?'

'Vaguely.'

'Well, a Mouseketeer, a girl Mouseketeer was always so clean and wholesome, cute and sparkly, that you just knew she never had to go to the bathroom. Walt Disney wouldn't let her.' Teddy looked at me for a moment, 'Well, he wouldn't, Alfred. I hear he was a terrible tyrant. No Mouseketeer was ever permitted to go to the bathroom. Because if you had to go to the bathroom, it meant there was something *unclean* inside you. And everyone knows that a Mouseketeer is clean and wholesome through and through. Three times whiter and brighter than any other children. Not only that, but they didn't have armpits either. They had *under arms.*'

'Armpits,' I sighed, shaking my head. 'Here we are in the city of popes and kings and all you can talk about are armpits.'

'The Pope has armpits.'

'The Pope most certainly does not. He has under arms.'

'I don't think you should be offended by armpits, Alfred. Everybody has one – two, in fact, in case one should break down. Even you, even you, Alfred, have armpits. You must learn to face up to that fact. Squarely. As your doctor and your friend – I want you to think of me as your friend, too, Alfred,' she said, patting my arm, 'and not just as your doctor. I'm telling you this for your own good. Even I have armpits.'

I took her elbow and propelled her down the stairs and out on to the street toward the Piazza di Spagna.

'And sometimes,' Teddy continued, 'sometimes late at night, when the city is sleeping, I go to my window, turn on all the lights, pull up the shade and expose my armpits to whatever pervert wanders by. I just raise my arms shamelessly, shamelessly and let them look. Where are you taking me?'

'To the Babington Tea Room.'

'That's nice,' she said. 'Anyway, some night, Alfred, I'd like to show them to you.'

'One at a time?'

'If you'd like. In fact,' she said, 'if you'd like to go back to our room I could show one of them to you right now.'

'It does seem a bit early for tea,' I said 'And as my doctor you know the value of bed rest.'

'But I want you to think of me as a friend, Alfred,' she said. 'Can't you forget for a moment that I'm a doctor?'

'I could, I suppose. It's just that you're always wearing that big damn mirror on your forehead.'

Teddy pantomimed removing the headband and mirror. 'There!' she said. 'Now you can see me as I really am. A woman driven by a woman's needs, tormented by a woman's desires.'

'My God, Doctor, you never told me you're a *woman*! Why, Doctor, without that, without that mirror you're ... you're *beautiful!*'

Teddy and I stood there in the bright winter morning at the base of the Spanish Steps laughing at each other, and then we turned around, went back to our hotel, closed the shutters, and made love.

'Was it good for you?' Teddy asked.

'It was good,' I said. 'Truly good, Pilar.'

'Truly? And the earth moved, *Americano*?'

'Half of Iran slid into the sea,' I smiled.

'Alfred?'

'Yes?'

'Are you going to spend Christmas with George?'

'Yes. I think so,' I said. 'Why?'

'When will you be leaving?'

'Friday afternoon,' I said. 'You'll be gone by then, won't you?'

'Yes,' she said. 'I have to leave that morning.'

'I don't want you to go,' I said.

'I don't either.'

'Do you have to go back?'

'Yes. Christmas is a very big deal to Alex.' She turned my head toward her. 'Alfred?'

'Yes?'

'Would you marry me?' Teddy asked.

'If what?'

'If nothing. I love you.'

'I love you, too,' I said. 'And yes, I would marry you.'

'But what?'

'But you're already married,' I said. 'That and the fact that every now and then, in spite of everything you've done, I cannot help myself and quite involuntarily I find myself thinking of you as my doctor.'

Teddy giggled and pushed her nose against my jaw, then suddenly sat up. 'God, I'm starving!'

'Me too. Where are they doing the photography this afternoon?'

'The Colosseum. What time is it? I have to be there at two-thirty.'

I looked over at the clock on the bedside table. 'It's a little after one. We'd better get going. I saw what looks like a nice restaurant we could go to that's not far from the Colosseum and the Forum.'

'Anyplace,' she said. 'I'm starved.'

We got up and dressed, and Teddy opened the shutters and waved at the gargoyle lady across the way and the gargoyle lady just stared back. So Teddy beckoned me over to the window beside her and pointed at me, then placed both her hands over her heart and pantomimed a huge sigh. And I put my arm around Teddy's shoulder and we leaned our foreheads together as though we were in one of those three-pictures-for-a-quarter booths. Teddy did a little tap-dance and shuffle, waved good-bye, and we left our room, rode the ancient, shuddering, spark-spitting elevator down to the lobby and out we went into the street.

A waiter with a folded copy of *L'Umanità* tucked under his arm led us to a small table beneath great loops of fishnets, and using his newspaper as a whisk broom, cleared the crumbs away, tucked the paper back under his arm, bent down to make two little tugs at the red and white tablecloth, then leaned back in resignation and infinite weariness to take our order.

During lunch Teddy and I talked about what it would be like to be married to each other, the sort of house we would live in, where we would like it to be. I wanted to live on a farm and Teddy wanted to live by the ocean. And we tried to think of where we could find a farm overlooking the sea. And she asked me whether I thought we would be happily married and I told her of course we would, isn't everybody? And then Teddy asked me what I thought George Dethriffe was really like, and I laughed because how is it possible to know anybody that well.

'But you know him better than I do,' Teddy insisted, 'so try. Tell me.'

'But I don't really know, Teddy. I think I've always thought of George as being more symbolic than actual. More symptomatic, if you know what I mean.'

'I don't have the foggiest idea what you mean,' she said. 'Why do you always use such big words with me?'

'Well, I just mean – I don't know – he's, I think simply that George Dethriffe is the only one of my contemporaries whom I feel confident would behave as a gentleman no matter what.'

'I'm not entirely sure that that isn't the worst thing you could say about him,' Teddy said.

'Well, I didn't mean it that way,' I said. 'I meant it as a compliment.'

'I know you did, but still, it's an awful thing to say. Do you remember the first night we met? – You've got a piece of onion on your chin – We were sitting in George's living room on those sofas and I told you that I thought George was one of the few real gentlemen I'd ever met?'

I nodded.

'Are you angry with me?' Teddy asked.

'No, why?'

'You're not speaking to me.'

'I've been too busy eating.' I laughed. 'Do you want coffee or dessert?'

'Coffee,' Teddy said. '*Decaffeinato, per favore.*'

'*Sì, signora,*' I said.

'*Grazie tanto.*'

'*Prego,*' I said. When the waiter came back I asked for two coffees, whatever they use for Sanka.

'Why didn't you ask for them in Italian?' Teddy asked me.

'Because I would have outraged the waiter, embarrassed you and humiliated myself.'

'Well,' Teddy said, 'that's one of the differences between you and George, Alfred. You're both gentlemen, but you get embarrassed by it and George doesn't.'

'Well, if I seem embarrassed by it, it's because I'm really not a gentleman at all.'

'What makes you think you're not?'

'My cheque-book,' I said. 'I can't afford to be.'

'But you told me before that money has nothing to do with it.'

'It doesn't, once you have enough money so that it has nothing to do with it.'

'What about about your inheritance? Those trusts?'

'The trusts don't become mine until I'm thirty, and as for the inheritance, that's a long way off. Besides, the trusts are capital. I don't like to touch it. And, well, I've had to dip into the money occasionally, but I've tried not to do that often. I don't know if I can ever make any money writing, and I feel an obligation to leave something at least to my children when and if I ever have any.'

'You'll have lovely children,' Teddy said. 'I wish we –'

The waiter suddenly appeared with the cheque and became intimately involved with my figuring of a tip plus the service charge. I evidently tipped him enough because he became all smiles and pleasantries about Rome, the weather and President Kennedy.

'What time is it, now?' Teddy asked me as we left the restaurant.

'Almost two,' I said. 'We can cut right through the Forum.' At the Piazza Venezia I pointed at the huge white wedding cake of the monument to Victor Emmanuel II and the Palazzo Venezia beyond it. 'Do you see that balcony over there?'

'What about it?'

'That's where Mussolini made his speeches from. I can remember photographs of him standing up there, his arms stretched out – did you know the whites showed all around his eyes?'

'What did Mussolini say?'

'He said, "Romans, today the seven forty-three express from Milano arrived on time," and they all cheered like hell and bombed the Ethiopians.'

'Why'd they do that?'

'Bomb the Ethiopians? For practice.'

'Be serious,' Teddy said.

'I am serious.'

'But that's *awful*!' Teddy said. 'Look, I don't think we have time to go through the Forum, let's just keep on straight down the street here to the Colosseum.'

'Don't you want to see the Forum?'

'I've seen it,' Teddy said, and when she caught my look she added, 'I know, I *know*, but to me a ruin is a ruin.'

'Is a ruin,' I smiled. 'George Dethriffe is a George Dethriffe is a George Dethriffe.'

'He seems like a ruin in a way,' Teddy said. 'Like a – like one of those columns that stand all alone in the Forum. He seems so distant ... so detached, is that the word I'm looking for? He's not snobbish or anything like that, it's just that he seems so untouchable – like one of those columns when everything else around them is in ruins. In spite of everything George is still there, you know.'

I tried to explain to Teddy that I didn't think that George Dethriffe would ever be completely free of others' misconceptions about him. At times, in fact, I know he encouraged these misconceptions because there was a certain chameleon quality about George which enabled him to blend into whatever 'character' was expected of him. He did not do it out of self-preservation, or to retain privacy, although that no doubt entered into it; instead, I think he did it out of an unwillingness to displease the other person. I suppose the point I was trying to make for Teddy was simply that George Dethriffe wasn't aloof at all. He was really very nice.

'He is nice,' Teddy agreed. 'And so are you.'

'No, I'm not,' I said. 'If I were nice, I wouldn't be here. Nice guys don't go to Rome with married women.'

'What does that make me?' Teddy asked very quietly.

'You? You were nice enough to invite me, to want me here with you.'

'But, I'm a married woman as you pointed out.'

'Yes you are,' I said. 'And you're the nicest married woman I've ever known.'

'But you don't think I'm a – a whatever it's called, an Evil woman, do you?'

'Of course not. And nobody else knows we're here together, so ...'

'So that makes it all right?'

'It makes it all right with me. How did we get on the subject of contemporary morality, anyway?'

'You brought it up,' said Teddy. 'You said that you weren't nice because you were in Rome with a married woman.'

'Well, what I meant was according to –'

'– contemporary morality.'

'– contemporary morality, I'm not nice. But I don't feel the slightest trace of guilt. In fact, until I stupidly brought up this subject, I was willing to bet that I was the happiest man in Rome. I was so happy because I was having such a nice time with you and I was thinking about how after you're through modelling, we can go somewhere and get something to drink, in fact a lot of things to drink and maybe do some Christmas shopping or go to the Via Veneto and look at people or go to a Lex Barker movie or whatever it is you might like to do.'

'We'd better hurry then,' Teddy said. 'I really have to be at the Colosseum on time – and you can spare me all your Colosseum jokes right now.'

'Why don't you come up to Florence with me?'

'Do you mean that?' Teddy asked. She had stopped dead and held me back. 'I mean, you're serious aren't you? You really mean that?'

'Why are you so surprised?'

'I don't know,' Teddy said. 'Maybe it's because I think you do know what it would mean if I went up to Florence with you. It would mean first of all not showing up in New York when I'm supposed to.'

'I know.'

'And so you must also know what that would mean,' Teddy said. She was looking at me intently, nervously. 'I'm not just thinking about the bookings they would have to cancel, the loss of money. They'd only crucify me for that. But what about Alex? You know Alex would come here right away. He'd take the first flight. What do you intend – what would you want me to do about Alex? Leave a message for him that I'm going to Florence with you? Tell him Merry Christmas, I want a divorce? If I did go to Florence with you it would mean giving up Alex and maybe getting fired by the agency.'

'The agency would never fire you. You're ne of their top models,' I said. 'Even if they did, you're so much in demand another agency would take you on right away. You could probably even – all you'd have to do is send word that you'd picked up some Roman virus and –'

'– And no one would ever know, is that it? I wouldn't even have to give up Alex, right? ... Ohhh, Alfred,' she said, shaking her head sadly, 'ohhh, Alfred ...'

'I love you, Teddy,' I said.

'Do you?' she asked.

'You know I do, Teddy,' I said. 'I'm sorry I ...'

'For what?' she asked. 'Why are you sorry? Because you know you hurt me? Because you know I'm not good enough for you?'

'Oh for Chrissake, Teddy! ... That's not it at all, you know that.'

'I'm just some silly little middle-class model, right? Models are supposed to be stupid, right? Just a pretty little face, right?' She was crying now, her head lowered and her hands to her cheeks. 'Models aren't supposed to have any feelings, right?' she asked.

'Teddy, please. Please, Teddy.' I held my hand out to her.

'I'm not going to make a scene,' she said, pushing my hand away.

'Teddy, I love you, I really do.'

'Then why? Why, Alfred? Why don't you want to marry me? Why are you even making me ask you this? Why do you hurt me so much?'

'I didn't mean to. I didn't know, Teddy, I thought you were happy –'

'Oh goddam it, Alfred, how can you be so stupid! You call yourself, you think of yourself as a writer, how can you be so stupid!' She pushed herself back from me. 'Don't you know anything about women? Did all those years cooped up with other little boys in prep schools, all those goddam aristocratic little brick prep schools, didn't you learn anything? Don't you even know that what a woman wants most of all is to be married to someone who loves her? Or is that too middle class? Maybe you think of love differently. But I thought you loved me. I really thought you did.'

'But I do!'

'You don't even know what love means, Alfred! And I know, I *know* you're a writer and what a cliché that is, but I don't care. You don't even know what love means, because if you did, you'd never have done this to me. If you really loved me you'd know that – oh, goddam it, why do I always, *always* get myself in such messes?'

'Teddy, Teddy ...'

'If you, if you so much as once more tell me that you love me, I'll – I'll hit you with my purse. I'm not kidding.'

'But I do love you.'

'Then why don't you *do* something about it?' she asked. She was no longer crying.

'Like marry you? How could I ask you that now? Is that what you want?'

'*Yes*, goddam it! – I mean, NO! I don't want to marry you. I don't want you to marry me. I couldn't now anyway. I don't, all I want, all I ever wanted was for you just to *ask* me to marry you. Don't you see? Don't you understand? You-never-even-gave-me-the-chance-to-say-no –' She started walking again, walking away from me, and I had to hurry to catch up.

'Teddy, will you marry me?'

'No!' she said, not pausing at all. 'No, a thousand times no.'

'Teddy, please.' I pulled her arm to stop her. The Colosseum loomed before us. 'Please, Teddy.'

'No, Alfred,' Teddy said. She was rummaging through her canvas tote bag for a Kleenex.

'I mean it, Teddy,' I said. 'I'm not just asking you to marry me to be nice.'

'To be nice! To *be nice!*' Teddy looked at me in wonder and in rage. 'No, no thank you, Alfred. No, thank you very much. But I'm already married, as you were nice enough to point out. And you did not feel nice being here with me. And being nice worries you, but it shouldn't, Alfred. Because you, you have not been very nice. Not very nice at all. And I'm telling you this,' she said with just the faintest of smiles, 'I'm telling you this, Alfred, not as your doctor, or your friend. I'm telling you this as a woman.'

'I know.'

'Do you?'

'Of course I do, Teddy. How do you think I feel?'

'I don't care how you feel,' she said. 'I just know that I feel awful.'

'I feel awful, too,' I said.

'I feel *more* awful.'

'I feel pretty damned awful.'

'So what are we going to do now?'

'Well, you're going to go get photographed and I'm, I don't know what I'm going to do. Go down to the Forum I guess, wander around until I find some sword to impale myself upon. Or, if you'd like, I could go to the Colosseum with you and throw myself to the lions.'

'There aren't any. Just cats. How can you make jokes at a time like this?'

'Because I'm too ashamed of myself not to,' I said.

Teddy just looked at me for a long time. 'I think you really mean that. I think maybe for the first time you've been absolutely honest. Welcome home, Alfred Moulton,' she said gently. 'Welcome to the living, breathing, here-today world.' She stood on tiptoes and kissed me and I held on to her as tightly as I could.

'I love you, Teddy.'

'And I you. Damn it, Alfred, in spite of it all, I still love you. I really do. You're absolutely hopeless and so am I. And you don't have to marry me, I mean that. I'm going to say something to you which may sound cruel, but I don't mean it that way. I won't marry you because you're too young for me. I don't mean immature, although God knows you're that, too, but so is everyone else at our age. You're too young, which is different from being immature.'

'Will you meet me after the Colosseum?'

'Of course. You're the only friend I have in Rome.' Teddy laughed. 'Some friend you turned out to be.' She pulled her mirror out of her tote bag and looked at her eyes. 'God, they look like our Michelin guide with all the roads leading to my pupils.'

'Tell the photographer the cold made your eyes water,' I said. 'How long will you be?'

'Two hours, maybe a little more. Where will you be?'

'In the Forum with the other ghosts. It's about two-thirty now, so you'd better get going. I'll meet you at the ruins of the temple of the Vestal Virgins, I can't think of any more appropriate place. It's the little round one.'

'Will you do me a favour while you're in The Forum?'

'Sure, what?'

'Don't join the ghosts. Don't change back into the Alfred Moulton who wanted to marry me out of niceness – I know you don't think you meant it that way, but you did. You were doing me a favour. You were offering to be my husband as a favour. I'll meet you at the Vestal Virgins or wherever and whenever you want, just so long as the Alfred Moulton I'm meeting is the one who is being honest, not just being nice.'

'Okay,' I said.

She gave me a light kiss on the cheek. 'See you in a couple of hours, okay?'

'Please, please do.'

'I will. *Ciao*,' she said and trotted off to the Colosseum.

'*Ciao*, Teddy.'

Chapter Two

I watched Teddy disappear beneath one of the arches, and then I turned and walked back up the Via dei Fori Imperiali and bought an admission ticket to the Forum.

I followed the ramp down into the ruins, and walked upon the black paving slabs of the ancient Sacra Via, the massive arch of Septimius Severus over my left shoulder, the majestic standing columns of the Temple of Saturn behind me. This was one of the moments I had most looked forward to, that moment during which I would be alone at what was once imperial Rome. I sat looking up the Sacra Via to the Arch of Titus and waited for my imagination to supply me Horace hurrying down to the Forum with his Bore. Where were Cicero's rowdy crowds, elbows flailing, togas lifted slightly so as not to impede their steps? Where were the priests and augurs in their red-hemmed togas stained, perhaps, by a recent sacrifice? Where were the senators in their purple-bordered *togae praetextae*, their red shoes, scurrying to their seats in the Senate House?

Where was a victorious general in the purple he was permitted to wear in celebration? Where were his fellow officers of the Legion? No litters bore rich men by. No heralds marked the approach of Caesar. No orators stood on the Rostra. There were no quarrels in the market place. No ghosts. There was not even the steady drip, drip, drip of the water clocks to mark that time had passed and was passing still. There was only the winter wind gusting candy wrappers through the empty ruins. And so I opened George's letter again to look at the train schedules.

There was an express to Florence early Friday afternoon that I could catch and I made a note of its departure time in my pocket diary just beneath the note I had made at some point in the past that tomorrow, Thursday, 21 December, was the twenty-first anniversary of F. Scott Fitzgerald's death. And I knew I'd been wrong, that the ghosts were not gone after all, that one ghost still remained and that he had died not in Rome but in Hollywood.

There is a story that very few mourners attended F. Scott Fitzgerald's funeral, that it rained that bleak December day in 1940 as it had rained upon Jay Gatsby's, and that someone (in an interview somewhere Dorothy Parker said it was she) was there to comment, 'The poor son of a bitch.'

It doesn't matter whether the story is actual or apocryphal. What was important to me about Fitzgerald was the myth. And when one was used to dealing with myths, one seldom let truth stand in the way.

There are two F. Scott Fitzgeralds.

There is the real, the Carl Van Vechten photographed Fitzgerald, who stands middle-aged and ghostly pale in a favourite tweed jacket, the ends of his thick knitted, striped tie slightly askew. Fitzgerald is smiling the tremulous smile one holds too long while the photographer doggedly adjusts and readjusts the focus. His fingertips have strayed to fiddle with a button low on his Brooks Brothers shirt and he is leaning to one side to duck the bright sun. Fitzgerald's eyes are kind; he seems more at ease than the smile would suggest. His eyes show a willingness to stand still as a favour for as long as is necessary.

And then there is the mythical Fitzgerald: the young, golden distillation of Antibes twilights, of travelling home from schools in curtained Pullman sleeper cars, of champagne and hip flasks, of John Held, Jr, woodcuts of flappers and coonskins, of open limousines and hydroplanes; a Fitzgerald who is forever more Gatsby then Carraway, whose shirts were not simply Brooks Brothers button-down whites, but rather like Gatsby's 'shirts with stripes and scrolls and plaids in coral and apple green and lavender and faint orange', shirts whose optimism Daisy Buchanan and an entire generation of her daughters might cry over. This was my Fitzgerald.

When I thought of Fitzgerald, I thought of him as being young – younger in fact, than my age now. He was forever suntanned, happy and in love with Zelda. He was forever in love with New York City, too. In my imagination he was joyfully flirting with its towers and canyons, abandoning himself to that guileless romanticism Midwesterners have for our city. And New York responded. Just for Fitzgerald the orchestra played all night on the St Regis roof; Central Park was green and inviting; the bud vases in the horse-drawn hansoms outside the Plaza were filled with flowers. The jazz was hot. The chorus line bold. Plate glass became crystal. Street lights became diamonds. And the rich were still different from you and from me.

Even though I knew the years of my parents' youth were never so exciting as Fitzgerald made them appear, and even though I knew how few of that era's survivors honestly believed that the way Fitzgerald wrote it was the way that some of them somewhere had lived it, still so many of my parents' friends and so many of my own friends were devoting so awesome a portion of their energies toward the retention of that style, the sustaining of that myth, that I wanted to believe not only for their sake but for my own as well that *it might just be possible* to prolong over decades all the joy of that frozen, crystalline moment that the water drops from the Plaza Hotel fountain first splashed down upon the very young and evening-clothed Scott and Zelda Fitzgerald.

'You just don't know what it was like then,' I have been told. 'There was such gaiety ... so much excitement! We had such fun ... my God, there were some marvellous people!'

There was – *We had* – *There were* – past tenses all, but the past has always dominated the present for me. I was brought up with the past, marinated in ancestral anecdotes and memorabilia. The houses in which I was raised were filled with their spoor: chairs they sat on, beds they gave birth in, crystal they toasted with, silver they served from, portraits they sat for, books commissioned by them, rugs they walked upon, tapestries they wove. And what, after all, was I but a collection of their parts: the tallness of my father's side of the family, my maternal grandmother's eyes, my grandfather's ear, my great uncle's colouring, my mother's laugh. As expected, I was sent to their schools where I was taught their legacies and when in the history books they talked about slave owners and shipbuilders, bankers and judges, politicians and soldiers, hell, I *knew* some of them. I've drunk from their cups. In fact, when I was an undergraduate at Yale, I attended the one-hundredth birthday party of my great, great aunt who, as a little girl, had not only spoken with General Robert E. Lee, but who, with the impudence of youth, had chided J. E. B. Stuart for the garish plume he wore on his hat. How can I forget a past which goes back to the ancestor who so testily noted in our family Bible that 'whereas 1765 has seen the Savannah River overflow mightily its banks, the year will probably best be remembered for that detestable Act of Parliament, the Stamp Act'. How can anyone ignore a past when it so clearly continues to exist? Why else the gold ring on the little finger of the left hand with the family crest? One cannot so easily dismiss tradition. It is our inheritance and our albatross. For what was my trip to Rome with Teddy but a celebration of the sort of impulse which creates family anecdotes? Had not my great-great-uncle Robert shot the gun out of Senator Robertson's hand? Had not my great-aunt Samantha run off with a Jesuit priest? Had not my own father, posing as King Saud's eldest son, the Crown Prince, dazzled and duped New York and Hollywood society for two weeks? What does it matter that I wasn't even born when my mother and father and all their brothers and sisters chartered a DC-3 and hired a jazz band to play without pause all the way down to Lexington for the running of the 1926 Kentucky Derby? I know all about that just as I know about Uncle Randall, who on that flight bailed out somewhere over West Virginia and not only made it on time to the race, but bet $500 on Bubbling Over, the horse that won. And later on that same summer did not my mother and father on the Riviera meet the Scott Fitzgeralds at a dinner given by Gerald and Sara Murphy at their Villa America?

And so, as I sat there on my crumbling piece of Roman stone recalling Teddy Baldwin's 'welcome to the living, breathing, here-today world', I realized that I didn't have the slightest idea of what she was talking about. How could a *here-today* world exist without reference to a past? How could it presume to compare with the excitement and glitter of the Fitzgerald era?

You see, even knowing that the Roaring Twenties gave way to the Depression, that the Fitzgerald era was a harmless hoax, a 'let's pretend' perpetuated by writers and ballyhoo men, nevertheless the years had become for me what they had only pretended to have been for its survivors. The twenties were important to me because they were the years of my parents' youth. The last years of Style. My father was born in 1899, my mother in 1903. She was twenty-nine when she had my older brother, thirty-three when she'd had me. And my father was thirty-seven years older than me forever. Therefore they seemed much older than my friends' parents; their youth held that much more of a mystery and glamour. The War to End All Wars had been fought and won. Bankers drove Pierce Arrows, bootleggers churned about Long Island Sound in mahogany-hulled inboard motor launches. It was still Boom time on Wall Street. The family still owned land. They still had money. There were banjos in the big bands and the flappers flapped thigh-high through balloons. Now just some yellowed clipping tucked away in an attic scrapbook, but still to me the unforgettable image of my parents' *then*: young and lean as wolves, confidently stalking across a page in *Vanity Fair*.

My youth was the Second World War, the Return to Normalcy, the Army-McCarthy Hearings, the Korean War, the Eisenhower Administration. And so without any stylish era to call my own I had become an heir to a previous generation's myth, content to keep up appearances until something grander came along. And I never felt alone. Instead, I felt my contemporaries mirrored all about me as if in some Busby Berkeley Hollywood extravaganza. White tied, white tailed, white top-hatted, white gloved, white-faced – thousands of us with our hands poised over thousands of piano keyboards, thousands of aloof smiles frozen upon our thousands of clean-shaven faces. It was as though we had all been sitting there waiting for our cue, waiting for our generation to be called on stage, waiting politely we products of the Fifties, waiting to be asked to begin. And we waited. And I would have waited forever had not Teddy's 'welcome to the living, breathing here-today world' made me aware that we weren't going to be needed after all, that we were, in fact, a mothball fleet. And even though I wasn't sure I knew what she meant, at least as I thought about her honesty, her unselfconsciousness, her willingness to risk embarrassment, I began to have some insight into how different her world was from mine and how different she was from what I had permitted myself to become. And I didn't much like it.

You see, I knew I had hurt Teddy Baldwin, a girl I professed to love, far more than I could have had I meant to do so deliberately. And because I did not feel remorse so much as I felt an impatience that her distress might interfere with the pleasure we were having, and because I knew that my conscience bothered me only slightly, and because I knew that I should have been shamed by my cold-bloodedness and that, in fact, I was not, a certain icy detachment settled like some protective bell jar about me. And it was this detachment which I recognized and identified for the first time as my enemy.

It was this detachment which I had always had about myself and everything around me which I had erroneously believed essential to Good Writing, essential to the Craft. (Which was not, in my case, a craft at all but rather a self-indulgent affectation masquerading as a calling.) And I saw for the first time that this detachment was what would always eliminate any chance I might have of ever amounting to anything more than a reporter, a voyeur, a cataloguer of customs doomed forever to being more sociologist than sympathetic. And it is in an attempt to destroy what yet remains of that damned detachment that I confess that during that long, cold afternoon I spent down in the Roman Forum, I was still more concerned and interested in salvaging my self-respect than Teddy's. Do not mistake my self-concern for conceit. At twenty-five I did not think of myself as an individual at all!

I never thought of myself as anything more than a crude barometer which might reflect the atmospheric changes about me. During those moments when my conformity most depressed me I used to console myself that whatever value I might have as a writer lay not in my being any different from my contemporaries, but rather in my being so very typical of them. I saw myself as having much the same obligations as a successful secret agent: not only did I need not be any different from those around me, but I *could not* be any different. For to have been different would have led to my discovery and therefore dismissal from their ranks. My assignment was to tunnel from within. If I were successful, if I could articulate why something meant so much to me, then my value and rewards lay in being able to explain why it meant so much to those like me. *I* was not supposed to exist. *I* was to be synonymous with *we*.

Well, as *we* circled and rapped upon the bell jar which had descended upon that other Alfred Moulton, we knew that we had just hurt a very sweet and lovely and nice girl very badly, who had nevertheless welcomed us to 'the living, breathing, here-today world'. And we wondered why instead of worrying about her, we were worrying about being left out, of not being a part of the world to which she belonged. And the more I thought about it the more I realized that until now there had never before been a world to which I had wanted to belong. Except for the world of the Fitzgerald era and that was turning out to be nothing more than a nostalgia for a period I had never experienced.

And so, as I waited for Teddy among the toppled columns, the decayed plinths, the cracked paving stones of imperial Rome with the icy wind gusting candy wrappers about my feet, the chill I felt was the chill of death – not my own, but that of the era whose style I had adopted and celebrated as my own, knowing it was not only impractical, but obsolete. And so, of course, were we: George Dethriffe, Alice Townsend Dethriffe and me. Like the three lone columns of the Temple of Castor and Pollux.

And not far away stood the single, graceful column dedicated to Phocas, a disappointing emperor.

I come to bury Fitzgerald, not to praise him.

Chapter Three

It was a quarter past five. I took a deep breath and stamped my feet in an attempt to get some circulation started. Teddy should have been back by now. My head was beginning to ache from the cold and too many cigarettes, so I decided to leave the Forum to wait for Teddy by the Colosseum.

I walked back along the black paving slabs of the Sacra Via, past the crumbling stones of the Basilica of Julius Caesar toward the Arch of Septimius Severus and the exit. At the top of the ramp I paused for one long last look at those three tall, graceful columns. They were beautiful. In the gathering dusk they possessed a dignity that reconstruction of the Temple of Castor and Pollux would only obscure. And I knew I would not have liked them half so much had they not been in ruin.

I couldn't find Teddy in the Colosseum, and I was fairly certain that I would have seen her had we passed along the way. But, perhaps because of the cold or the failing light, the models had moved on to a different location. If that were the case, then I thought the wisest thing was for me to go back to our hotel room and wait for her there.

I waited all night.

And the next day.

And the day after that.

And on the third day the desk clerk told me that a special delivery letter had been placed in my room. I didn't even wait for the elevator. Instead, I ran up the stairs two at a time and burst through my door. The letter, postmarked from New York City, was from Teddy.

Dearest Alfred:

I was so afraid. I still am and always will be, I suppose. We finished at the Colosseum early, and when I walked back to meet you at the Forum I saw you from above and I was scared to see you.

You have always been so much smarter, better educated than me. Your background and your family are so different from my own. I was always afraid of saying something stupid or doing something stupid in front of you and I was becoming so self-conscious that I wasn't having any fun. Even though I loved you very much it scared me at times to be with you. I couldn't be myself. I kept trying to be what I hoped you wanted me to be. And so when I saw you in the Forum – and you looked so at peace, as though you belonged there – I didn't dare see you. I just picked up my passport, went out to the airport and got on the first plane coming here I could. I didn't even dare go up to our room because it would have been so filled with you.

You could always argue better than me. I didn't dare say anything to you. You never got angry, you'd just get more and more distant and filled with facts which I could never change because I have never been able to distinguish between what were facts and what I just knew was true. And I didn't dare talk to you because I knew you could talk me into staying and I knew that if I stayed it would be wrong. If I stayed you would think you ought to marry me. And no matter what you might say, or think, I knew you never wanted to marry me. Not me, really.

And I *am* married. And I'm not very strong. But I have the terrible feeling that what I have here with Alex is all that I'm entitled to. So could you send me my luggage? I told Alex the airlines had misplaced it.

I did love you. I still do. I'm just not very strong. So please don't try to make me change my mind. Don't call or write me when you get back, *please*? I ask you this not only as your friend, but as your doctor. I'm crying now, so I'm going to stop.

Teddy

For a long time I just sat on the edge of the bed with Teddy's letter in my hand. I read it over and over again. At first I thought Teddy had made some mistake, that this letter hadn't been intended for me at all – how could it have been? The person she had written about wasn't anything like me. How could she think that that person she had run away from in her letter bore any resemblance to me? What about all the laughter we had shared?

But of course it was me. And for all our laughter I hadn't given her much fun.

I did go up to Florence for Christmas. I'd say I had a pretty good time – not very good, but good enough. There is something that happens to American men and women in Europe. Somehow the men seem more vulnerable. They lose their sense of identity, who and what they are; and they lose their sense of territory. I have always felt uneasy about being in an unfamiliar land, a little afraid. Since I do not understand the language I become, not suspicious, but more cautious. On the other hand, women seem to become stronger in Europe. Perhaps they realize that they have more in common with their husbands once they remove their husbands from their territory. They share the same uncertainties, but the women have greater familiarity with uncertainties, the men are more familiar with ritual. Certainly Alice seemed stronger.

On Tuesday, the day after Christmas, having spent part of the afternoon in the Uffizi's glassed-in gallery of Roman statues which overlooks the Arno, we wandered into a British pub called St George and the Dragon and we seated ourselves at a small table against the red velvet-lined wall. Across from us a group of languid young men seated on the high bar stools were conversing in an excited mixture of Italian punctuated by American slang and English punctuated by Italian slang.

For some reason George and I got on the subject of aristocracy. Our discussion was partially prompted by our viewing of the Roman statuary and partially, I think, it was my own attempt to exorcise and rationalize the painfulness of Teddy's departure. At any rate class distinction is a topic that makes me intensely uncomfortable. Whenever I feel myself about to say something even remotely class-conscious, I cringe as though in anticipation of a pig-bladder clout from behind. Be that as it may, George is an old enough friend so that I felt I might at least ask him whether he believed there was such a thing as an American aristocracy or whether, almost by definition, no such thing could exist.

'Of course it exists,' George said. 'It exists in every country that permits the concept to exist. And America not only permits it, but encourages it. For one thing look at the canonization of the Kennedys that is going on in the press. Another thing is how else can you explain the proliferation of society columnists?'

'But they write about café society,' I protested. 'And the jet set. You certainly don't consider them aristocracy, do you?'

'They overlap from time to time,' George answered.

'What are you talking about?' Alice asked him.

'I'm trying to talk about aristocracy,' George said.

'And who is aristocracy?' Alice asked.

'That's what I've been trying to explain,' George said. 'Right now, they're the people who are trying to support worthy projects. Generally they're functioning as protective agents, guardians of taste, conservation of land, whole towns, that sort of work. And the usual amount of art museums and ballets. And I think even though they're trying to do their work quietly, as unobtrusively as possible, it sometimes is impossible not to get into the papers, especially when someone buys an entire island and turns it over to the government as a park.'

'Tell me, George,' Alice said, leaning forward slightly, 'do you consider yourself aristocracy?'

'Of course not.'

'Not even a part of it, secretly?' she asked him.

'What are the requirements for aristocracy?' I asked, changing the subject as quickly as possible.

'George hasn't answered my question,' Alice said.

'Well, first of all there are two requirements,' George said. 'Three things, really. Taste, time and money – not in that order. The major requirement is money. Lots of it. It doesn't matter who makes it or how he made it, because whoever first makes it is *nouveau riche* and not aristocracy.'

'All right,' I said, 'so the first requirement is old money.'

'That's the first two,' George said. 'That includes the time element. Several generations must retain and hopefully increase the money. A minimum of three generations are required. The second must be assimilated into the culture, become accepted by society as such. And then –'

'George, you surprise me,' Alice interrupted. 'I never would have expected you thought so much about it.'

'I haven't thought so much about it,' he said.

'You mean you've always known it?' Alice asked. 'It was something your nanny whispered in your ear?' She was smiling, but it was the sort of smile one might expect to find on the face of a snake.

'Why are you taking this so personally?' George asked her.

'And just what the hell do you mean by that?' Alice asked.

'What I mean, Alice, is that you are incapable of listening to conversations which in any way touch upon social distinctions without becoming personally involved. You always feel as though in some way judgement is being passed on you. That you're being excluded. All that has been happening is that Alfred asked me a question and I've been trying my best to answer him.'

'Why's it so important to Alfred?' Alice asked.

'Ask him,' George said.

'Because,' I said, 'I'm interested in George's opinions on it.'

'Well you pump George all you want, but I don't understand how hearsay can help much. As George said, the first requirement is money and —'

'And George is paying for my hotel room here,' I said. 'The second requirement is time. So why don't you just give us time to finish this conversation, hmm?'

'You really hate me, don't you?' Alice said with startling vehemence. 'You really hate me because you don't think George should have married me and —'

'— Oh for Chrissake,' I said.

'— and you're jealous, aren't you? Aren't you?' she repeated more loudly, and the two men in the bar stools nearest us turned to listen.

'Alice,' George said gently, 'be quiet.'

'Maybe you and Alfred should have married,' she said.

'Alice, we're all very tired,' I said. 'Why don't you and George go on back to the hotel. I'll wander around a bit and follow later on. There's no sense in arguing about something we don't really give a damn about. So why don't we just cut it short and go.'

'Why?' Alice asked. 'Don't go. I'll leave and you both can stay. You'd be much happier that way, wouldn't you?' She placed her hand on George's arm. 'You stay,' she said. 'It's a perfect place, and you can have good old available Alfred for company, okay?'

'Look, Alice,' I said, 'I don't want to get into the middle of any family arguments. Why don't you and George just head on back and I'll meet you later.'

'See, sweetie?' she said to George. 'Alfred wants us to go. We could go back to the hotel and go to bed. You'd like that, wouldn't you, George?'

'I'll tell you what I'd really like,' George said very quietly, 'I'd like you to shut the hell up. Alfred has been a friend of mine for a great many years, and you, Alice, Alfred is also a friend of yours, and it seems to me, Alice, that you need every friend you can get. If I were you, I'd —'

'Alfred isn't any friend of mine,' she said, 'or of yours. The only reason why Alfred Moulton pays any attention to me is because I'm your wife. And the only reason why he has anything to do with you is because you're good for his book. He probably loves to see us fight — don't you, Alfred?'

'Leave me out of this, please,' I said. 'Just go on pretending I'm not here.'

'You can almost see him taking notes,' Alice told George. 'Alfred would love nothing better than for us to put on a really good show. But making a scene would offend your delicate sensibilities, wouldn't it, George? You're much too well bred to ever make a scene, aren't you, George?'

'Alice,' George said with great weariness, 'be a good girl and be quiet, please.'

'Oh you son of a bitch!' she said. 'What do I have to do before you acknowledge I exist?'

'Alice, you exist,' George said. 'You never fail to make your presence known. Like the moon and the tides, like death and taxes, you are here. Now be a good girl and be quiet so that Alfred and I —'

'— So that you two, ahh-rist-o-crahts can talk. If Alfred is so aristocratic, why isn't he rich?'

'Alice,' I asked, 'are you getting your period?'

'Shit!' she snorted. 'That's your answer to everything. If a woman gets angry or, or overwrought it's –'

'"Overwrought"?' I said. 'My God, where did you find that word?'

'In a pig's ass,' she said, pushing her chair back from the table. 'What a sweet pair you two are. Really. I'm going back to the hotel.'

'Fine,' George said.

'Are you coming?' she asked him.

'No. Not now. In a while,' he said, 'when I feel like it.'

'Then what about you, Alfred?' she asked me. 'Would you like to come back to the hotel with me?'

'Leave Alfred out of it,' George said.

'I asked Alfred,' she said. 'Let him answer.'

'To tell you the truth, Alice –' I began.

'By all means tell me the truth.'

'All right,' I said, 'if you'd like me to walk you back to the hotel, I'd be happy to. On the other hand, we could all walk back together and George and I, if he wants, could continue this talk in the hotel bar.'

'Good. Good idea,' George said, and stood up too. The waiter came over immediately, and I paid the bill. As George and Alice walked out the door, one of the young men on the bar stools swivelled to face me and in a very precise English accent he said, 'Most awful bitch, isn't she?'

'Isn't everybody?' I said.

The next day in the hotel lobby while George was off on some errand, Alice apologized. 'I don't know why at times I say those awful things. I love George so very much and I know he loves me and at times I seem to try to deliberately hurt him. I always seem to do these things in front of you and –'

'Well,' I interrupted, 'you don't –'

'No, let me finish,' she said. 'Please, Alfred. I didn't want you to come to Florence. That's why yesterday I wanted George to come back to the hotel with me. Not to make love, but just so that I could get him away from you.'

'But why, Alice?' I asked her. 'What have I done?'

'Do you know why George wanted you to come? He said, George said, it was because he just wanted somebody to talk to. How do you think that makes me feel? Why can't he talk to me?'

'But he can. He does.'

'He doesn't say anything ... I wanted our honeymoon to be so nice, so romantic...' She shook her head sadly. 'And it was, until George knew you were coming. You have a very strong effect on George – on people. You make them do things they wouldn't do otherwise. I don't know how or why, but you seem to start things.'

'Oh, come on ...'

'No, I mean it! You have a very strong effect on George. He thinks you're planning to write about him, and it's changed him. It has. It really has, Alfred, so stop shaking your head. Now if he thinks of anything to say or do he wants to save it until you're around. He doesn't want to say or do it with me.'

'That's nonsense!' I said. 'Come on, Alice, you don't really believe that, do you? You don't believe I came up here just to write about you, do you?'

'You don't care about us,' she said. 'You just watch and take secret notes. I know how paranoid that sounds, but you make me paranoid. You really do! Do you know what George said to me last night just before we went to sleep?'

'I'm surprised you don't think I was listening at the keyhole,' I smiled.

'It isn't funny!' Alice said. 'George told me that we would have to think of lots of colourful things to do while you were with us. *Colourful things*. Those were his exact words. Like ice skating on the Arno. Or renting a Rolls for a winter picnic somehow. You've actually got him thinking this way.'

'Well, so what? That sounds like fun.'

'Ohh, Alfred, please ...' she said. 'A long time ago we were friends, you said you loved me even though you didn't really mean it, I know. But if you're still my friend at all, please go away. Please. Go back to New York or somewhere. Just let George and me alone. Would you do that for me?'

'Of course,' I said.

'And you won't tell George what I said?'

'No, I won't say anything. I'll just tell him it was time for me to go back. To get a job.'

'Really? You'll go?'

Her face was so pathetically hopeful I said, 'I'll go tomorrow. As soon as I can.'

'And you don't hate me, really, do you?' Alice looked at me with those soft silver-grey eyes, her long blonde hair a gentle wave around her neck.

'I never have hated you,' I said. 'I've known you far too long for that.'

'That's a good line,' she said, and all the warmth fled from her eyes. 'You ought to use that in your book.'

'I didn't mean it as a good line,' I said.

'I know what you meant. You don't have to explain. You don't hate me, but you don't like me very much. But you, Alfred, of all people, of all George's friends, should understand what it's like not to have money any more. To be totally dependent upon someone else's generosity for everything – and George has given me everything, far more than I would ever ask for –'

'But you sound as though you resent him for that.'

'Should I be grateful? Am I supposed to spend the rest of my life tugging the brim of my cap and saying, "God Bless You, Kind Sir?" Are you grateful that he's paying for your stay here?'

'Of course I am,' I said.

'You don't resent him for having money when you don't?'

'Why should I?'

'Balls!' Alice said. 'We're two of a kind, you and me. We know what it's like to have money, to be able to buy anything you want. To be free. Don't tell me not having money doesn't bother you.'

'Of course it bothers me, but I might earn some someday and –'

'And you'll also inherit some. You, at least, can look forward to that. But I don't even have that. All I've got is what George gives me.'

'What would you do if you had your own money?' I asked her.

'I don't know,' Alice said. 'Go somewhere.'

'With George?'

'Sure, why not?'

'Well, you don't sound very enthusiastic.'

'I don't get enthusiastic about fantasies,' Alice said. 'You know, Alfred, I'll tell you something which I suppose I shouldn't. But it's something I've been thinking about a great deal anyway. We've known each other for a long time and when I was a débutante in New York and going to a different party every night but meeting the same old people over and over again, I used to really love being with you. And – let me finish – we were comfortable together, weren't we?'

'I thought so,' I said. 'I certainly loved being with you.'

'Well, I used to think that someday I might even marry you.'

'Me?' I asked, astonished.

'Sure, why not? In those days anything was possible. You weren't the only one, of course. But if you remember what débutante parties were for, what they used to be for, it wasn't so unlikely as you may think that I would think in those terms. All young girls think about whom they might marry, don't young men?'

'Not at the age you're talking about.'

'You never thought what it might be like to be married to me?'

'Not when we were going to debutante parties,' I said.

'What did you think about?' she asked, then added, 'As if I didn't know. Let me ask you something, and I'd like an honest answer. Would you go to bed with me now?'

'Right now? Or now that you're married to George?'

'Now that I'm married to George,' she laughed. 'Certainly I don't mean here in the lobby.'

'I don't know, Alice, but I suppose an absolutely honest answer would be, given the proper circumstances I would go to bed with you, yes.'

'In spite of the fact that I'm George's wife?'

'Well, you asked me to be honest. I don't think if we went to bed with each other I'd be making love to George's wife, I'd be making love to you, if that distinction makes any sense, and why shouldn't it since this discussion is purely academic – it is academic, isn't it?'

'Is it?' Alice asked.

'For the time being,' I said. 'I'm leaving tomorrow.'

'I know and, well – nothing, I guess.'

'You weren't going to tell me that you'll miss me, were you?'

'No, I was going to say that I'm glad you're not angry with me. I hoped you'd understand that it was nothing personal.'

'I'm afraid I don't understand you, Alice. What, then, is it if it's not personal?'

'Let's just call it an instinct for self-preservation.' Alice smiled. 'As one shark to another.' She looked around the lobby. 'I wonder where George is. He should be back by now . . .'

'He'll be back.'

'Maybe when we get back to New York and get settled – did George tell you? We're thinking of moving to the country.'

'Where?'

'We haven't decided, but once we get settled, perhaps you can come up for a weekend.'

'Was that an invitation? One shark to another?'

'Not sharks, Alfred, friends,' Alice said, then smiled. 'We are friends, you and I. We understand each other.'

'You mean, I assume, that we're very much alike.'

'Oh look,' Alice said, and she waved, 'here comes George now.'

Chapter Four

I have known George Dethriffe since I was nine years old. Actually, I suppose I could say I have known him all my life since in an old photograph album of my mother's there is a snapshot of George and me in a sandbox captioned, 'Hobe Sound, January 1937.' We are both almost one year old, and are sitting in that peculiarly noodle-jointed manner infants have, hydrocephalic heads bobbing at the end of wrist-wide necks, George is hitting me in the foot with a small tin shovel, and I appear to be eating sand. I don't remember anything of George Dethriffe during that period, nor do I remember anything of Hobe Sound. Frankly, I don't remember much about anything until I was at least five. Looking through the family album I can see that my parents went to Hobe Sound for at least three more years. There is one final Hobe Sound photograph of my older brother, Walker, my father and myself (then four years old) leaning against the sweeping fender of a Duesenberg roadster. My father is standing with his weight on his right foot, his left foot crossing his right at the ankle, one hand on hip, the other palm supporting him on the fender. Walker and I are attempting to copy the pose, and we seemed to have achieved an uneasy status somewhere between the Lafayette Escadrille and the Marx Brothers. In the background of the photograph is a sign, 'Jupiter Island Club', where we stayed. The Duesenberg was not ours. My father later, years later, told me the photograph was taken as a gag – the point of which has long since been forgotten. But I believe I remember that automobile. It was a beautiful machine.

My grandmother used to make a curious semantic distinction: any automobile in the Ford, Chevrolet, Dodge, Plymouth, De Soto category was called by her a *car*; Buicks, Lincolns, Packards,

La Salles and Cadillacs were *motors*. The Duesenbergs, Rolls Royces, Pierce Arrows and other more exotic automobiles were *motorcars*. I think this was an absolutely unconscious grading of quality on her part since she really had very little interest in automobiles. One other semantic note about my grandmother (and, one supposes, her friends): she would use *motor* as a verb. 'I must motor into town.' How I loved the way she spoke. 'Have the motor put in the garage,' she would say, pronouncing it *gahrahj*. She had a marvellously rich New York voice, an accent bred of strawberries and English nannies. She died when I was barely into my teens. I remember, though, she had a tendency to type her grandchildren according to their interests: My brother, Walker, was interested in books, and I was the grandchild who was interested in automobiles. My cousin, Philip, liked old aeroplanes. Cousin Page liked horses, and so on. I remember sitting with her one afternoon and hearing her say, 'Do you know, Alfred, no one nice drives a Cadillac any more.'

Anyway, I think I remember that Duesenberg. I believe it was tan, with dark brown fenders and trim. But perhaps all I remember is that fading photograph. The Duesenberg belonged to the Dethriffes.

George Dethriffe's great-grandfather amassed his fortune in land. Old Dethriffe owned what is now Dethriffe County in upper New York State, plus a three block square of downtown New York City, plus fifteen per cent of the Erie Railroad, and he probably could have owned the state capital, but he didn't need to. His son-in-law was Governor. George's great-grandfather began to sell land at the turn of the century and managed to untimely invest enough of the proceeds to lose a considerable amount in the 1907 panic. George's grandfather held on to the property that remained, recouped a decent portion of the losses, suffered little during the Depression, thought Roosevelt *nouveau riche*, and quite possibly 'a pawn of the Jewish interests'. George's grandfather's estate was valued at 23.8 million dollars at his death – before taxes – and was to be divided equally among George's father and four uncles. The Internal Revenue Act of 1936 reduced their inheritance to just over $850,000 apiece. By this time Dethriffe & Co. was out of real estate and into investment banking.

My friend, George Dethriffe, was born at the Doctor's Hospital in New York City on 9 January 1936, and was brought up in New York City except for summers at Southampton and winters on Hobe Sound.

George and I were sent off to boarding school in 1946. We arrived during the mid-term. George was ten; I was still nine. We went to the Napier Boarding School in Napier, Georgia, a small school that had sprung up around a once-fashionable fox-hunting and polo-playing winter resort. George and I were new boys in the fourth grade. Our whole class never had more than nine boys in it.

Christmas vacations were longer at Napier Boarding School than at most regular preparatory schools. This was because there was no spring vacation at Napier. The students, or at least the ninety per cent majority who were boarders, came from Pennsylvania, Delaware, New Jersey, New York and Connecticut. We would travel to and from school in a private railway car with Miss Scott, the school nurse, as chaperone. The boys got off at Wilmington, Thirtieth Street Station, North Philadelphia, and when finally we pulled into Pennsylvania Station in New York, our car would be more than two-thirds empty, and we would stand around and pat each other's backs, wish each other Merry Christmas and pretend George Dethriffe had been taken off at Trenton. Then we'd walk off the train with our little grey blazers with the gold piping, brass buttons, and school crest on the breast pocket.

I don't remember ever seeing anyone actually meet George at the station. As the rest of us would leave with our parents, or in some cases, chauffeurs, I would see George standing by himself between two enormous suitcases. He would assure me and my parents that his mother would be there soon, and then he would reach inside his jacket to pull up his sleeves so that his hands would show beneath those huge French cuffs.

Most of the boys in our class were from divorced families, and maybe custody problems were alleviated by having the child away at school nine months of the year. George's parents and my parents weren't divorced, and there were two other boys in our class whose parents were still married. Four out of nine. And I can remember the afternoon when one of the remaining four told us his parents were getting a divorce, and our entire class signed a letter one of us had written begging them not to.

None of us at Napier believed we were sent there for a better education. Napier's academic rating was appalling. Out of the nine in my class only one graduated from college the year he was supposed to. The rest of us lost a year along the way. Napier was a school for rich men's sons, for gentlemen, and no more. It survived not because it provided the students with an education, but because it provided them with a home.

After Napier, George Dethriffe went to Groton as had his father and grandfather, and as had, to his grandfather's eternal chagrin, Franklin Delano Roosevelt. In March 1953, when George was a junior at Groton, his father died.

The funeral was held on a Saturday afternoon. Mr Dethriffe had died the previous Thursday evening at his club, The Brook. He died in the library and it was evidently several hours before anyone noticed. No fuss, no bother, no scenes, everything was quiet. George's father was buried in the family plot on some hideous Long Island cemetery. Afterwards, George and his mother drove back to the apartment at 810 Park Avenue and had dinner.

I know that George loved his father, but I would be surprised if they had had a very personal relationship. During the few weekends I stayed with George in his family's apartment, I can't remember George and his father ever joking, or even speaking much with one another. They would nod to each other, exchange a few remarks, smile as two gentlemen might upon meeting at the magazine rack at their club. It was as though very early in their relationship they had reached an agreement about each other, and this *entente cordiale* would remain fixed no matter how long the father had had to live. They honoured one another, but it was less than that. They took each other so much for granted that they never bothered to learn anything more about each other. Mr Dethriffe was the Father. George was the Son. Father. Son. Fathers love Sons. Sons love Fathers.

Prior to his father's death, George had favoured going from Groton on to Princeton. Instead he went to Harvard, in honour of his father.

'It's the sort of thing Dad would have done,' George told me. He did not mean this as maliciously as it sounded. Instead, he said it with a little smile and a shrug as if in admission of the 'Like Father, like Son' relationship which simply didn't exist at all. George favoured his mother.

George's Harvard years were undistinguished. He rowed, but never well enough to make the first boat. He joined the Fly even though his father and grandfather had been Porcellian, but George declined membership because Porcellian would not elect a friend of his. He graduated from Harvard in 1958, spent the summer in Southampton and that fall was sent into the Army for six months at Fort Dix. When he was released from active duty, he went downtown to Dethriffe & Co., and asked whether he might have a job. Of course he was given one.

George moved into his mother's apartment. He was not being paid much while serving what amounted to his apprenticeship. The income which he derived from his father's estate, he reinvested. That income amounted to about $650 a month, and had he wished to he could have lived quite comfortably without touching the $80 a week he made as salary. However, his mother had a maid and cook, his laundry and dry cleaning went out with his mother's, she got him theatre tickets through the Colony Club and bought him lunch at the Passy. He played squash after work with friends at the Racquet. Played poker occasionally at the Knickerbocker. He continued to read an enormous amount; but since 810 Park had a good library, he stayed home. George lived with his mother for three years.

This, then, was the George Dethriffe I knew at age twenty-five. Admittedly, I did not know George very well. We had grown up together. We had known each other all our lives; but, as might be suspected, tended to think of each other in generalities. To me, George was someone who lived in New York, who wintered at Hobe, summered at Southampton. I thought of him in terms of activities such as debutante parties, sailboat races, squash matches. I knew he bought his suits at Brooks Brothers and later at Tripler's. I knew his measurements were on file at A. T. Harris where we all rented our cutaways for weddings. We had prep school and college backgrounds in common. I associated him with his parents' Duesenberg and later the Packards, Mercedes Benzes and, after his father's death, his mother's Rolls Royce. I am aware that what I have listed are things and places, and they are not so much peculiar to George as they are typical of any George of similar background growing up in New York City. The reader might have learned just as much had I passed around George's old scrapbook and photograph album. I wish it were possible for me to have done so.

I was still in Washington on the newspaper when George Dethriffe sat down next to Alice Townsend at a dinner party. George fell in love with her that night and she, in turn, set about to change him to suit her image.

Because clothing was important to Alice, she made it important to George. Gone were the Tripler suits, he affected now more British tailoring. Fitted jackets, higher vents, tighter trousers. He wore English shoes, Peal or Church. A flower in his buttonhole. George had always had taste, and with Alice to urge him, he dressed more boldly. But the boldness took a strange turn. There was something deliberately dated about George's clothing, as though the wide ties, the high detachable collars, the waistcoat with the heavy gold chain were patterned after some excellent gentlemen's tailoring firm's 1925 inventory. George began to dress as though he anticipated being asked, like Alice, to model. Only, unlike Alice, George would have to be posed on the running board of a Type 41 Bugatti Royale, or, at the very least, a boat-tailed Auburn Speedster, and there would no doubt be a lawn party in the background, flowered hats, white flannels and blue blazers, suntanned fawn-eyed ladies in bright-coloured dresses, wicker picnic baskets, napkin wrapped wine bottles in silver coolers, croquet and badminton; and farther back, beyond the stone summer cottage, and supervised by nannies, lovely children in sailor suits would be stick guiding toy sailboats along the edge of the lake.

If George Dethriffe appeared in costume it was interesting to me that the masquerade was such a success. It was not until I attended my first of those astonishing parties given by George in his penthouse apartment, that I realized why he was so successful.

Chapter Five

I don't know how well George Dethriffe knew Alice Townsend before he fell in love with her. He might have seen her during school dances and joint glee club concerts, or summers around Southampton. He might have noticed her name or seen her photographs in the society pages. I can remember several débutante dinners at which George, myself and Alice were present, but not very many. George might have seen Alice's photograph in *Town and Country* – not especially a mark in her favour, but it probably meant something to her then. I know George remembered the Irving Penn photograph in *Vogue* taken when Alice was sixteen. It was quite famous, Alice was given the entire page. She was posed with her body three-quarter profile but with her face turned directly toward the camera. She appeared to be nude. Obviously she had not posed nude, but the photograph displaying the tops of her breasts, her bare shoulders, her long neck and incredible face gave an impression of nakedness. I say 'incredible' because I remember the photograph, too; and it was incredible to me that at sixteen any girl could be so beautiful. All the bone structure which would make Alice a strikingly lovely woman was there, but her cheeks were still covered by the softest patina of youth.

Alice's eyebrows were dark, far darker than her sun-bleached hair, and her eyebrows appeared so finely drawn as to have been etched. She did not pout, as was the fashion among sixteen-year-olds of a later day, nor did she smile. Instead, she looked out from that page with silver-grey eyes of such intensity that I can remember touching the page in wonder. She would not have been so lovely, however, were it not for the birthmark high on her left cheekbone. The birthmark, a deep violet-coloured tiny blur somehow made Alice seem more beautiful. The flaw made her more vulnerable.

Irving Penn posed Alice so that the birthmark showed. Alice never liked the photograph because of this. Before George and Alice were married, when George asked her for a copy of the photograph, she gave him one with the birthmark air-brushed out.

I did not meet Alice until she was eighteen and a débutante. I was twenty and a senior at Yale. Alice was presented first at the Winander Autumn Ball (which even then more symbolically than actually launched the New York débutante season). and I was her escort at the tea dance given in her honour at the Colony Club. I was her escort not because we were romantically involved, but because we shared a minor incident which Alice felt had been a major embarrassment. Several evenings before her tea dance, a young man who was to have taken Alice to a party got stranded by a blizzard and was unable to get into New York. Alice's mother called my mother (they knew each other very well, but I had never seen much of Mrs Townsend) and asked if I would pick up Alice. I was ushered into the Townsends' apartment by a coloured maid wearing a black uniform with a starched white lace collar. The Ambassador and Mrs Townsend were having cocktails, and Mrs Townsend said I was beginning to look more and more like my grandmother – a curious remark, I felt. It made me feel I needed a haircut, which I no doubt did. The Ambassador sat large and pink-jowled in his evening jacket under which he wore the scarlet vest of the Century Association. He also wore monogrammed needlepoint evening slippers and called me boy the entire time.

'My God, boy,' he said at one point, 'if Harvard was good enough for your father and grandfather before him, it certainly would have been good enough for you!'

I was trying to explain to him that (a) I was unable to get into Harvard and that (b) my father went to the University of Virginia, when Alice made her entrance. (Several years later George told me that never during their marriage did Alice simply enter a room. There always seemed to be some sort of production involved: invisible lighting cues, cameras dollying back, wardrobe mistresses scurrying around beyond the set.) Alice was wearing a metallic grey strapless evening gown which was tightly fitted over her bust and hips. Her hair was swept upward and back and held by a diamond tiara, and her bare neck and shoulders reminded me so strongly of that *Vogue* photograph that I approached her with the same sense of wonder with which I had approached her photograph three years before.

Alice wore no jewellery other than the tiara, and a minimum of make-up. I helped her into her evening coat, an embroidered silk, and in the elevator down and during the taxi ride to the Plaza I babbled like a schoolboy.

The dinner at the Plaza Hotel was given in the Rendezvous Room (since replaced by Trader Vic's) and as we walked down the deep red-carpeted stairway past those curious sconces — I vaguely remember some sort of arms coming out of the walls which held candelabra. Just those arms, joined to the wall at the elbow. We could see that there already was a large number of young people whom we saw at the other dinners, the other dances, whom we had gone to school and college with. I walked behind Alice to help her out of her coat and as she stepped away I saw the stain and dropped the coat back over her shoulders.

'What is it, Alfred?' she asked. 'What's the matter?'

I took Alice's arm and led her away from the others. 'Your period,' I whispered.

'My what? — Oh God!'

We hurried back up the stairs and out of the hotel.

'Did it — was it awful?' she asked me.

I opened the door to the taxi, then slid in beside her. 'No. It wasn't awful at all.'

'But did everybody see?'

'I don't think anyone could have. I was behind you and your coat wasn't off for more than a second.'

During the ride back uptown to the Townsends' apartment Alice kept touching her fingertips to her lips. 'I feel so stupid,' she said. 'I should have known. I thought I was just tired. I should have kept track. Counted.'

'Hey, hey, it doesn't matter.' I took Alice's hand. 'No one but me saw, and God didn't strike me blind.'

She squeezed my hand tightly. 'I'm so sorry,' she said.

'We can go back to the dinner after you change.'

'We couldn't possibly make it before the dinner started. And I'd feel so rude coming in that late.'

'Then we won't go to the dinner at all. We can pick up a sandwich at your apartment and go on to the dance.'

'But what can I wear?'

'You must have other evening dresses.'

She thought for a moment, 'I don't think any of them are back from the cleaner.'

We were riding in one of those old De Soto taxicabs, the ones with the tinted plexiglass skylights. And as the taxicab turned into Alice's block, she let go of my hand and I was amused that she might think her father would see us holding hands from seventeen floors above. I paid the driver and followed Alice into her building. On the way up to the apartment, Alice leaned against the mahogany back wall of the elevator. She turned to me and smiled slightly, 'Poor you.'

'Poor me? Why?'

'What if I don't have anything to wear?'

'Then we won't go to the dance.'

'But what shall we do?' she asked.

I can remember the look on the elevator operator's face that evening as though it were today. He said, 'The Ambassador and Mrs Townsend have gone out for the evening.'

'We'll think of something,' I said.

We did. We went to see Alec Guinness in *The Bridge on the River Kwai*.

(Ten or so years ago, with only the merest scientific awareness and understanding of the biological reasons behind a woman's menstrual cycle, I naïvely believed that the man's role during menstruation was to behave as a sophisticated and compassionate bystander. I viewed my function with absolute detachment as an attempt to diminish any embarrassment Alice might feel by re-assuring her that her menstruation and resulting stain was quite natural, inconsequential and somehow endearingly female. By adopting such an attitude I hoped to convince Alice that the incident had made no difference to me; and, therefore, my continuing presence rather than serve as a reminder of her embarrassment, might serve as assurance of the incident's

53

insignificance. I was successful for, as I mentioned, Alice asked me to escort her to the Colony Club tea dance given that winter in her honour. And, as I also mentioned, that was ten or so years ago.

The intervening years have shown me how naïve I was to have believed it possible for a male to remain detached about menstruation and to consider it as simply a biological process. Menstrual periods have gripped me in emotional hammer locks. Menstruation has been Armageddon and Divine Absolution and all the circles and stations in between. Like the Mesquakie Indian, who scatters and harvests his seeds by moon cycles, I have measured my yield in menstrual cycles. I have known women who are totally incapacitated by their periods, who lie legs up on a wall, gulping gin and Darvons. I have known women whose response to menstruation is embarrassment or martyrdom or earthmother pride or lumberjack indifference. I have known the relief of a clockwork period, the anxiety of a late period, the bafflement of the skipped period. I have experienced the joy of a missed period which presaged the pregnancy of my wife, and the horror of the missed period which presaged the pregnancy of a woman not my wife. I have known the agony of the miscarriage when pregnancy seemed assured, and the reprieve of the miscarriage when the pregnancy was unwanted. For the past ten or so years I have been threatened and forgiven, punished and rewarded, battered and becalmed by menstrual periods. No longer do I look upon menstruation as a simple biological occurrence. Instead, I look upon it as I look upon an impending thunderstorm. Safe and warm though I feel within the shelter of my happy marriage, I yet respectfully and cautiously mark the storm clouds building. And when my wife turns on me with darkening brow and lightning bitchery, I comfort myself that these welcome rains provide relief. And pray the storm will soon pass.)

I saw Alice quite often that winter. There were those who thought Alice and I were going together or a couple or whatever the phrase for it was then, but we weren't. Alice was, as I've pointed out, an extraordinarily beautiful young woman; but she also had many of the resulting problems and insecurities. She didn't believe that any young man was interested in anything more than going to bed with her. Or she felt the young man wanted her as some sort of hunting trophy. She felt no one was interested in finding out how smart she was, boys were interested only in showing her how smart they were. And, evidently, young man after young man, disarmed and unnerved by Alice's beauty, fought back with sarcasm and rudeness in an attempt to restore his standing. Relationships among young men and women, sequestered as we were nine months of the year in school, were difficult enough without the additional strain of distortion and misunderstanding. Circumstances force these shallow relationships. And Alice, I think, was every bit as predatory as her young men. Once during a lull at a dinner party, she passed me her charm bracelet and ticked off the club emblems and fraternity pins her boyfriends had given her as though she were counting scalps. It was quite chilling.

But, perhaps because of her period, perhaps because her family knew my family or whatever the reason, I was Alice's escort to those dances because we were comfortable together. We both liked to duck out of the dances to go to movies, or down to the Village. I liked Alice. She was great fun to be with. And God knows I was flattered by all the other young men and women who thought I was making it with her. Sure, after we would return to her parents' apartment we would perform the standard meaningless amount of necking – a couple of suffocatingly long French kisses and a few gropes at her clothed breasts. But it was always more ritual than sensual. Like some benign eunuch, I never got any further than that. The one evening that I took Alice out to dinner and, over the wine, told her that I loved her in the hope that such an admission would lead to an evening more sensual than ritual, I created instead an awkwardness between us. I had turned our friendship toward something neither of us wanted. I had become *serious* and, subsequently, a problem.

Someone else took Alice to the next dance.

And although I thought often of asking Alice up to Yale for a week-end, I never did, partly because I knew she would refuse, and largely because I was involved with a girl with whom I was habitually (and copiously) spending the week-end in bed.

After graduation I went directly into the Navy OCS program,

was assigned as an Ensign to a destroyer, and I did not see Alice again for three years, the fall of 1961.

The summer following her début, Alice Townsend toured Europe with a plumpish friend named Karen Weaver. In Naples they met twin brothers, who had sailed across the Atlantic with their father on his yacht. The twin brothers and their father asked Alice and Karen to join them for a cruise up the Italian Riviera. The cruise was to take two days; but the yacht's auxiliary engine failed the first night, there was no wind and they drifted off course. Seventy-two hours later they were spotted by the U.S.S. *Forrest Sherman*, a destroyer at that time on manoeuvres with the Sixth Fleet. The destroyer radioed their position to the Italian Coast Guard, or whatever, and they were towed back into Naples. Their recovery would have received minor coverage had it not been for the *paparazzi* who noticed the abrupt manner in which Alice and Karen left the yacht, the obvious bruises on the twin brothers and their anger and disgust with their father. Alice and Karen rented a little Fiat and fled. The brothers booked separate flights – one for Paris, the other for London – and the father sold the yacht at a substantial profit to an Italian motion picture director. Alice did not talk about what had happened on the yacht; but plump Karen was not the least reticent and the story I heard, third-hand at least by the time it reached me was that the father had ordered the brothers off the yacht after they had first sabotaged the radios and then the engine so that they would have more time for Alice to choose between them, how all along it had been the father who was after Alice, how Alice had politely refused the man's marriage proposal (his wife in Westport received this news with mixed emotions) and finally, how the Italian police had had to forcibly detain Mr So-and-so at the border to give Alice and Karen time to get away.

The man continued to pester Alice even after she had returned to Vassar. Karen insisted that the man had never been encouraged by Alice, and this was probably true if only because Alice was at that time involved with an associate professor in the English department who was subsequently dismissed on the grounds that he had not sufficiently published.

Alice quit Vassar her junior year and somehow popped up in Hollywood. I read in Leonard Lyons she had been picked by Billy Wilder for a new comedy. Evidently something didn't work out because Pamela Tiffin appeared in the actual movie, and Alice returned East. She was in Washington, D.C. at about the same time I was there, and she took a job working for the Kennedy for President campaign headquarters. I had a job with the Washington *Daily News* covering nightclubs, or what passes for nightclubs in Washington, and I met several girls of Alice's age who were working for Kennedy (including a lovely and delightful trio nicknamed 'Fiddle, Faddle and Phyllis' who went on to work in the White House when Kennedy was elected). But I saw little of their group unless I ran into them at a bar or the Carriage House.

I did do one favour for Alice. An item crossed my desk reporting she had been arrested for drag racing at two-thirty one morning on a deserted stretch of the George Washington parkway. Because I wore a tie, the night editor thought I was 'society' and he wanted to know if I knew her. I said I didn't, and no connection was made between Alice and the Ambassador. She appeared before a Virginia judge the next day, was fined three hundred dollars, and had her licence suspended for a year. So she sold her car (a Triumph TR-3), and quit her job with Kennedy, returned to New York City, lasted about six months as a researcher for *Time*, worked for a few months in a Madison Avenue art gallery, then decided to attend the New School.

There was never any real scandal which Alice's behaviour initiated. She was a lovely and colourful young woman and gossip prone. She made good copy in a time when far less attractive and intelligent young women were hiring press agents to get them attention. Alice never needed to pose nude in *Harper's Bazaar*, she never needed to be photographed at El Morocco with the Duke of Baroda or in a discothèque with Andy Warhol. When she appeared in a fashion magazine she was paid for it. And she did it to get a good price on her clothes. Clothes were important to Alice, and she wore them well. As the *maître de* of a very good room in a very good New York City hotel once told me, 'Miss Townsend *dresses* the room.' And Alice was seen in many of the best rooms until the business about her father came up.

A government investigation revealed that during her father's ambassadorship to a small Latin American country, he had 'conspired to misuse and misdirect U.S. Government funds' by channelling the aid into companies in that country in which he owned interests. Two months before the hearings Ambassador Townsend died of a heart attack. The obituaries (at least in the *New York Times*) played down the scandal and played up the tributes from other grand old statesmen.

Later, Alice told George how one morning, shortly after her father's death, her mother had assembled the three children in her New York City apartment bedroom. Mrs Townsend was sitting up in bed, a breakfast tray on her lap. She had finished her grapefruit and was eating shirred eggs and protein toast with marmalade as she told them there was practically no more money, that their father's handling of their money had been, 'at best, imprudent', and that it would be wise if the daughters married soon, and married money. Mrs Townsend further added, as she sipped her coffee, that whatever resources they had were to be concentrated upon the continuance of young Packard's education. (Packard had just been accepted at the Harvard Business School.) And that it would not do at all to draw attention to the family's financial plight.

The scandal never materialized. The hearings were cancelled. The curious satisfied themselves that no irregularities had been established; it had all been a misunderstanding. And wasn't it a shame that it had occured just before the grand old Ambassador's death? Just so long as the Townsend daughters could marry money, and Packard was hired by a respectable firm, and just so long as Mrs Townsend – after a suitable period of mourning – could marry again someone of standing, no one could know that the Townsend family had suffered any difficulties at all.

What is so extraordinary to me is that this all sounds like a scene out of some polite eighteenth-century novel. It sounds that way to me now; but when I was a part of it, it all seemed quite Mete and Propere.

Several years ago, a friend of mine who is with a law firm in

Beverly Hills came East and told me over cocktails about an amazing evening he had recently been through. He and six other bachelors, ranging in age from twenty-eight to fifty-five, were invited to a black tie dinner given by a recently widowed lady. No other ladies were invited. The lady, in her early forties, and the seven gentlemen in their evening clothes, were served an excellent dinner with excellent wines, and following dinner the gentlemen were given some of her late husband's excellent cognac and pre-Castro Cuban cigars. They were then asked one at a time to step into the library. When it became my friend's turn, he entered and seated himself, as requested, in one of the soft, deep leather chairs by the fire. The lady remained standing, facing him in the centre of the room. She was wearing a full-length, high-necked, loose-fitting evening gown. When my friend had made himself comfortable, she began :

'Frederick, as you know, Paul left me very well provided for.' As she spoke, she began to unbutton her evening gown, starting at the throat and continuing down. 'I am a woman of certain means. And I am a mother. Young Paul, junior needs a man around. Although I am, perhaps, a dozen years older than you, you can see that I am not an *old* woman.' At this point she opened her gown and held it away from her body. She was wearing nothing underneath it. 'I do not intend to waste that youth I have left,' she said, and then closed the gown and began to button it back up. 'I asked you to come tonight because I do not wish to remain unmarried for long. I am not asking you to marry me, I am merely asking you to consider that I have position, wealth, contacts, a certain intelligence, all of which I am willing to share and –' She paused and smiled somewhat sardonically, '– and, fifty per cent of which you will become legally entitled to upon our marriage under California law.'

'Should you feel that a relationship leading to marriage would be mutually advantageous, then, after a suitable period of time, I will expect you to call upon me. I ask you not to say anything to anyone about this, nor do I wish you to say anything to me at this time.'

The lady nodded slightly and my friend stood up. She held out her hand for him to shake and said, 'Thank you so much for coming this evening, Frederick, it was lovely seeing you. Please express my warmest affection to your dear mother and father.' She released his hand and said, 'Would you be good enough to ask Lawrence Cahill to step in, please?'

The lady evidently made the same speech to all seven men; and one of them subsequently married her. That was several years ago.

To me, one of the most curious aspects of this story was that my friend was unable to tell me what the Beverly Hills lady's body looked like.

'But didn't you *look* at her?' I asked him.

'Well, yes, I suppose so. She had a pretty good figure, I guess. I looked mostly at her eyes.'

'Her eyes? ... Well, what did her eyes look like?'

'What do you mean? They were blue, I think. I mean they were normal. Like her voice. In fact the funny thing about the whole damned thing was that it seemed so – as if what she was doing *was* perfectly normal, you know?'

'But Freddy, when you looked at her eyes, where was *she* looking?'

'What do you mean?'

'I mean where was she looking? Was she looking at you? Was she looking down at herself? Over your shoulder? How did she look? Was she embarrassed? Frightened? Was she excited? What did she look like?'

'Alfred,' he said, 'I really don't remember. To tell you the truth, I was the one who was embarrassed. I mean, my God, there was a friend of my mother's undressing in front of me, and I didn't know where to look. I mean, if I looked at her, I felt that would embarrass her, too. Listen, Alfred, I didn't mean to get involved in a long story, I just thought it might be something which would interest you, you being a writer and all.'

Well, as a 'writer and all' I am not entirely convinced that the story about the Beverly Hills lady belongs in this book, and yet I cannot bring myself to leave it out. Call it instinct or a hunch or whatever, I believe the anecdote is less of a digression than it seems. It indicates to me, at least, something about the difference between the lady in Beverly Hills and Mrs Townsend, Alice's mother. For example, no matter how urgently Mrs Townsend wished or needed to remarry, she never would have offered herself as blatantly as did the lady in Beverly Hills. It wasn't the disrobing in front of seven men that would have prevented her; she was prevented by the chance of someone talking, of having her friends find out that she so urgently desired to remarry. Does that make any sense? It is all right to want something, but it is not all right to want something too much. Mrs Townsend would never have risked the humiliation of having her friends find out she wanted anything – be it remarriage or a Renoir – *that* much.

This recantation of avarice is not only true of Mrs Townsend and her contemporaries, but hopelessly true of me and many of my contemporaries: the Fourth Generation, properly schooled and clothed, socially acceptable ladies and gentlemen, who, having been taught never to talk about *m, o, n, e, y*, are not only embarrassed by money, but seem as in my case totally incapable of earning it. Perhaps somewhere along the line of dark, weathered shingle summer resorts, or at some brick and ivied preparatory school, at some point after a lost set of tennis, a too many faults horse-show, a fumbled end zone pass, a missed buoy sailing race, some parent or some coach or some pro somewhere told us once too often that it wasn't important to win or lose, but how we played the game. And we believed him. We accepted this to the extent that it is often difficult for us to differentiate between and evaluate the significance of the games we are called on to play. I suppose the point I am trying to make here is that even though the power, the talent, the great fortunes were gone by the time George and Alice came of age, the demand for *style* yet remained. One was taught to behave in such-and-such a manner whether one had money or not. There was a standard one was expected to uphold, and *m, o, n, e, y* had nothing to do with it.

Frankly, when George married Alice, he thought she had money. A lot of it. And frankly, Alice thought the same was true for George.

Imagine their surprise.

Chapter Six

George Dethriffe lived in the Adler, a massive grey stone building that stands twin-towered and twenty stories tall on Fifth Avenue three blocks up from The Plaza. The grey awning with the brown trim projects out from the wide double doorway to the kerb; its canvas is clean and taut. As I rounded the corner of Sixty-second Street and walked beneath the awning that crisp autumnal evening of my first party at George's, the doorman shifted smoothly to block my entrance.

'Can I be of any assistance?' he asked me.

His politeness startled me as much as the abrupt precision with which he had placed himself between me and the entrance. I told him my name and that George Dethriffe was expecting me.

'Mr Dethriffe asked that you go right up,' the doorman said. His white gloves reflected in the brass plate as he swung open the door. 'That will be the penthouse, sir. The elevator operator will direct you.'

I crossed the black and white checked marble lobby between two huge gilt-framed mirrors. Beneath each mirror was a richly glowing mahogany sideboard, supporting a large vase of cut hot-house flowers. The elderly white-haired elevator operator wore a neatly tailored grey uniform with brown trim. There was just the smallest trace of brass polish on his white cotton gloves.

'Mr Dethriffe's apartment?' he asked, as he slid shut the grille and swung down the wooden lever.

'Yes, please.'

'That will be penthouse A, sir.'

There was no jerk, only the most gentle rising sensation.

'Have many guests arrived?' I asked.

'A few. It's still early,' he replied. 'Mr Dethriffe's guests generally arrive following dinner. At all hours,' he added, and then, turning to me, he said, 'But we're instructed not to let anyone up after two in the morning.'

'It sounds as though Mr Dethriffe keeps you busy.'

'Oh yes, but he's a fine young gentleman. He's never any trouble.'

The elevator halted and the operator said, 'Excuse me,' and reached across to slide back the heavy door then waited as I rang George's apartment. A moment later George Dethriffe, in patent leather pumps, the palest grey flannel trousers, a navy-blue, six-buttoned, double-breasted blazer, opened the door and said, 'Alfred, my old friend, how good of you to come.' He leaned past my shoulder and said, 'Thank you Charles, you needn't wait. Murphy will keep an eye on the guests when they pass the front door.'

'Very well, Mr Dethriffe,' the old man said.

'Come in, Alfred. Come in!' George said. 'You've never been here, have you? My new place. I want you to tell me what you think of it.'

We had been standing in a short hallway, then he turned and led me into the living-room. 'Do you like it?' George Dethriffe's living-room was at least forty feet long and twenty feet wide, and the ceiling was two floors above us. Midway between where we were standing and the opposite wall, a bartender stood behind a linen-covered dining-room table setting up bottles and glasses. The fiddleback, leather-cushioned dining-room chairs had been placed against the wall. Opposite us, a wrought-iron staircase rose against the far wall up to a balcony which ran the width of the living-room, then crossed over us and followed the wall along the depth of the room until the balustrade butted into the far wall next to the three tall Gothic arched and leaded pane windows. The pale blue reversed *fortuni* curtains were drawn open, and through the windows in the gathering dusk, one could dimly perceive the brighter lights of Central Park.

It was, as I mentioned, autumn and somewhat chilly. The fireplace was alive with crackling butterwood. At right angles to, and on either side of the fire-place were two modestly-sized deep-cushioned sofas covered in a bright linen print. Above the fire-place hung a Chagall.

'It was my mother's,' George said when he saw me looking at it. 'She never liked it. It used to hang in the living room at Southampton. Perhaps you remember it.'

'No, I don't think so.'

'Well, it was bright – is bright. I'm not wild about it either, but until I buy a painting I like better, I'll let it hang.'

I looked around the room. 'The elevator operator said you had other guests –?'

'They're in the library,' George said. 'I wanted to talk to you alone for a while. Let me get you a drink. What are you having?'

'A Martini would be fine.'

George walked over to the bartender and I stayed examining the room. An old green-leather topped and dark wood desk stood in one corner, softly lit by a brass student's lamp with double, red-glass shades. A baby grand piano was canted slightly off centre from the Gothic windows. On the piano were at least a dozen varying-sized silver-framed photographs of George's family, friends' weddings, dogs and horses. There were small cherrywood tables next to soft, stuffed white linen chairs, a needle-pointed backgammon table, a mahogany gate-leg table with magazines, books and more silver-framed photographs. A white, deep-piled rug had been laid on the dark wooden floor, and the contrast was so startling that the rug appeared to levitate.

George returned with our drinks and motioned for me to sit in one of the sofas by the fireplace. George sat in the other. He raised his glass towards me and said 'Good to have you back, my friend, welcome.'

'It's nice to be back,' I said, returning the toast. 'Your apartment is very impressive.'

'Ah yes – "impressive" – good. That's a good word for it,' George said. He stood up and walked over to the mantle and made an unnecessary adjustment on the Chagall, then turned back to me. 'Be honest, Alfred. You don't think it's too – too lavish? Too ostentatious?'

'No, I don't think it's ostentatious,' I said, then added, laughing, 'On the other hand it certainly isn't monastic. I'd say it looks very nice indeed.'

'Good,' George said, then he returned to the sofa and sat down.

'The reason I wanted us to talk alone for a moment before I introduced you to the other guests is – well, there are two reasons, actually, but one of them is simply that you're one of my best friends and I haven't seen you in a long time. I'm so glad you called me yesterday. When did you get back to New York?'

'Yesterday.'

'Are you going to stay here now? I mean have you left Washington for good?'

'I think so,' I said. 'It's pretty much a one-factory town and since I'm trying to write and since most of the publishers, editors, agents and so forth are here in New York, it didn't make much sense to me to stay down there. And, well, there are other reasons for wanting to be closer to New York ...'

'Your brother?'

'I want to see him,' I said.

'Well, this brings us to my second reason. Where are you staying now?'

'Tonight? At the Yale Club. I'm going to stay there until I can find an apartment.'

'Then you haven't made any plans for one yet?'

'I haven't even started to look.'

'Good, good.' George said. 'My second reason, my proposition is this: how would you like to live here with me?'

'Live here with you?' I repeated stupidly.

'I'd pay the maintenance, of course, but I'd expect you to pay your share of whatever else.'

'Well, I don't know, George ...'

'But you said you liked the apartment.'

'Of course I like the apartment,' I said, thinking of the dim one-and-a-half-room apartment I could afford. 'But why do you want me to live here? Wouldn't I get in the way?'

'Don't be absurd. You're my friend,' he said. 'I think it would be great fun. You'd have your own room, you could be alone as much as you like. Do your own writing. I'd be at the office most of the day and –' George was interrupted by the most beautiful girl I had ever seen, who appeared out of the library and told him that he was wanted on the telephone.

'It's Alice,' the girl said. 'She said it was important and that she wants to talk to you.'

'Okay, I'll take it in the bedroom upstairs.' He stood up. 'Think over my offer, Alfred ...' And then he introduced me to the girl who had given him the message and moved away.

And that was how I met Teddy Baldwin.

While George was on the telephone, Teddy and I made small talk. I learned that she appeared predominantly in the younger-age fashion magazines, more *Mademoiselle* and *Glamour* than *Harper's Bazaar* or *Vogue*. She was twenty-four, admitted to being twenty-one and looked eighteen. She had just come back from Majorca, she told me, and had I ever read any Robert Graves? And she asked me how I knew George, and I told her that we had grown up together, gone to school together. Then, she wanted to know, why hadn't she seen me before since she went to all of George's parties. And I told her that I had been living in Washington.

'Are you married?'

'Me?' I asked, astonished. 'No. Why?'

'I am,' she said. And when she saw me glance at the bare ring finger on her left hand, she added, 'I am. Really! Absolutely. Licence. Preacher. Vows and all. I just don't always wear the ring.' She leaned forward to peek into the library. 'Actually my husband is here tonight. Would you like to meet him? He's an architect.'

'I would, later. I told George I'd wait for him.'

'To talk about that offer?' Teddy asked. 'Was that about the boxer?'

'What boxer?' I asked.

'George is trying to get everyone to invest in some heavy-weight fighter named "King" Johnson. He's coloured. I met him at George's last party.'

'Have you been to many of George's parties?'

'I've been to about a half-dozen of them. I just met George this past summer. We were using this place as a location. A whisky ad – a lot of beautiful people clustered around Peter Duchin at the piano. George came back from the office just as we were finishing. He and Peter were old friends somehow, and George invited us to stay for cocktails. I did, but Peter had to get ready for work and most of the others left with him. We all wanted George to be in the whisky picture too, but he wouldn't do it. I think if Alice had asked him to he might have – do you know Alice Townsend?'

'I haven't seen her in about three years or so. A very lovely girl. Was that Alice who just called?'

'George is really gone on her,' Teddy said.

'Is Alice really gone on George?'

'The only thing Alice really is, is fucked up,' Teddy said, then added, 'pardon my language, but that's the way she is.'

'How do you mean?'

'As though she's about to have a nervous breakdown is the way I mean – do you have a cigarette?'

I stood up and gave Teddy a cigarette, then lit it for her. She held the cigarette above her cupped palm, her thumb and three fingers supporting the cigarette as though she were Akim Tamiroff playing a Czarist executioner. 'You know, of course, that George wants to marry her.'

'Does she want to marry him?' I asked.

'She doesn't know what she wants,' Teddy said.

'Who doesn't know what she wants?' George asked, as he approached us.

'A friend of mine. A model,' Teddy said. 'A big company's been after her to sign an exclusive with them and she doesn't know whether to do it or not.'

'Oh,' George said. 'Well, that's one business I know nothing about.' Then to me he said, 'That was Alice Townsend. She said she didn't think she would be able to come tonight. I told her you had just walked in, and she sent you her love and hopes to see you soon.'

'I'm sorry she couldn't come,' I said.

'I am, too,' George said and then abruptly snapped his fingers, and snapped them again three or four times in sharp succession. 'Well ... Well! Why don't we go into the library, Teddy? Will you join us?' To me. 'I think you know some of the guests already, Alfred. And the others, well, you'll have time to meet them as they arrive.'

There were about five couples in the library, some seated in the deep, red-leather chairs grouped about the fire and the others standing by the dark, panelled walls where lovely, old hunting prints hung. The greens in the prints had faded, the reds become pink, the misty colours broken only by sudden, startling patches of white: a boot top, a horse's rolling eye, a distant fence. To the right, as we had entered, were doors leading out on to the terrace. On either side of the fireplace were the bookcases with row upon row of leather-bound books. The poets were in green Moroccan leather, the playwrights in burgundy red; the historians wore blue, biographers black, essayists purple. It was obvious that the books had been bound within the past twenty-five years and, once bound, used solely for display. It was also obvious that with the exception of the collected works of Henry James, John Galsworthy and Edith Wharton, not one of the library's authors had witnessed the twentieth century.

'So you're a writer,' Teddy Baldwin's husband was saying to me.

'I hope to be,' I said.

'Alfred? Alfred?' George called to me. 'Pull out the Wordsworth. I want you to see something.'

I looked for the book in the shelves.

'It's near you on the bottom,' George said. He moved over to me. 'About four books in from the right. That's it. Pull it out.'

There were two thick volumes and as I pulled out the first, the second slid out along with it and I saw that the volumes had been glued together. When I opened the book I discovered that the pages had been hollowed out to contain a revolver. There was a rounded impression for the barrel, then a deeper cut for the cylinder, the trigger guard and grip. There was even a lined and hollowed-out case for cartridges. But the book was empty.

'Don't you think that's interesting?' George asked.

'Where's the revolver?'

'It never had one. But have you ever seen a volume hollowed out so – so specifically?'

'Are all these books fake?' I asked him. 'Hide-outs and secret panels for playing-cards, daggers, dice and the like?'

George laughed and shook his head. 'No, that's the only one.

In fact you'll find that in the other books even the pages have been cut. Uncle Robert used to give me a volume or two each Christmas. From as long back as I can remember. He still does. I can remember hating them as presents for a time. I'd open them up Christmas morning and moan, "Oh God, a *book*!" and then my father would whisk them away saying, "You'll appreciate them when you're older" ... I thought they were dirty books, the way they were locked up.'

'Dirty books?' Teddy asked. 'Where?'

Teddy's husband patted her hand and said, 'Our little darling has always found fantasy more engaging than fact.'

'Ohhhh, Alex,' Teddy said. 'Please ... Please, not tonight.'

I had moved towards George but he had disappeared, and when I turned back to the model, she had disappeared, too.

'So you're a writer,' her husband repeated.

As it turned out, those few words in the library were the last George and I had an opportunity to exchange until hours later when the party broke up. Other than the couples I had met in the library, I believe I was one of the few persons actually invited to the party. People showed up at George's parties without invitations, at the cocktail parties anyway. The dinners were by invitation only.

That first party I attended was typical of George's parties, I learned. From approximately nine-thirty on, an increasing stream of guests would flow into the penthouse, eddy around the bar, and wash through to the library. The women in their bright cocktail dresses clustered like tropical fish around reefs of furniture as the men, in their dinner jackets or dark suits cut through them like sharks. There was always movement and colour, bubbles of conversation would surface over the din, voices would recede and be lost in the undertow just as some new voice or laughter would break. As that first evening progressed, it became evident that George's party was The Party to go to that night. So in They came. And effortlessly gliding among them all was George Dethriffe, smiling, exchanging nods or shrugs, listening and laughing happily then moving on.

At midnight a girl from an Off-Broadway revue which had closed the evening before, sat down by the piano and began to play her guitar. She sat with her back to the windows and played and sang for at least an hour, then put down her guitar and wandered away. Later, a young man picked up the guitar, some-one else played the piano, and soon couples began to dance. The men held the women lightly and they spun in tight circles. The women leaned back against the supporting arms of their men and laughed, ducked forward to hear some more, and laughed again. I could watch them from where I sat in the library, again trapped by the model's husband, Alex, who was by this time very drunk.

'Do you have any idea what it's like to be married to Teddy?' he whispered to me. 'Do you have *any* idea what it's like to be married to a girl who made eighty thousand dollars last year? Eight – eighteee thow-thow-san dollars –?'

'What does she do with all her money?' I asked.

'*Our* money,' he said fiercely. 'That's what's so goddam smart about old Teddy. She invests it.' Alex gripped my arm. 'Trusts. She sets up trusts all over. A trust for me. A trust for her. A trust for unborn children.' He let go of my arm. 'She's a smart girl, an' don't you forget it.'

'I'm sure she is,' I said.

'She *is*!' he said. 'That's what I've been trying to *tell* you.' Alex leaned forward and gripped my arm again. 'Listen,' he whispered, then looked beyond me balefully. 'I was just telling our friend here how smart you are,' he said.

Teddy looked at me, then back at her husband. 'Why don't you let me take "our friend" away for a moment,' she said. 'He should mix. This is the first of George's parties he's been to and there's someone here I want him to meet.'

'Who's to meet?' Alex asked. 'Some old people saying the same old things.'

'Alex, darling,' Teddy said. 'You're repeating yourself.' She held out her hand towards me and pulled me away.

I stood up and said, 'Excuse me, Alex.'

'Sure,' he said with a little wave of dismissal.

Teddy led me into the living-room. 'I'm sorry,' she said, 'he really can be such a bore when he drinks.'

'Not at all,' I said.

'Don't *you* be a bore, too,' she laughed.

'Who did you want me to meet?'

'Me!' she said.

I stayed with Teddy until the party broke up. We laughed and talked and danced when we wanted to hold each other and it was nice and warm and relaxed until Alex emerged from the library to claim her. By that time, however, Teddy and I had agreed to meet the next afternoon at the zoo, and I returned her to him without regret.

By four that morning George Dethriffe and I were alone in the library. He stood before the fireplace, pushing around the butt ends of logs atop the glowing coals until a feeble fire started up again. I mixed us fresh drinks and carried them back from the silent butler tray with the cut-glass decanters to our leather chairs by the fire. We sat down and were silent, felt comfortable in our silence and then I broke the silence by saying that it had been quite a party.

'Have a good time?' George asked me.

'Very.'

'I'm sorry Alice couldn't come,' George said. 'I told you she sent her love, didn't I?'

'Yes, yes you did. Thank you very much.'

'You know, Alfred? She's such a lovely girl – a wonderful girl. I really am so sorry she couldn't come for so many reasons. When she can't come – when she doesn't come to these parties, the whole thing seems like such a stupid waste.'

'What whole thing?'

'The whole party,' George said. He slid out of his pumps and placed his heels on the leather pig. 'Christ Almighty, Alfred, you know what a bore these parties can be. I only give them because of Alice.' He saw my bewilderment and began to explain, 'Alice loves parties. She was brought up on parties. You remember when she was a deb and what fun she was, what fun she had. She was always so alive, remember?'

'Yes, but isn't she alive now?'

'Not in the same way,' George said.

'Well, maybe we're getting older. Our idea of fun, of being alive, changes.'

'Well, yes, of course I know that,' George said, 'but Alice is different. She's not like the other girls we grew up with. There was always something special about Alice, that's why I throw these parties for her.'

'Even the ones she doesn't make it to?'

'Even the ones she doesn't make it to,' George said. 'She likes knowing they were given. She likes knowing she was missed.'

'George, excuse me, but what are you talking about?'

'I couldn't even count the people who asked me where Alice was tonight,' he said. 'Everyone missed her. I asked her to marry me. You knew that, didn't you?'

'I knew you wanted to,' I said, 'What did she say?'

'She said she wanted time...' George rattled the ice in his glass. We both fell silent again. I was staring, somewhat embarrassedly into the fire; George looked down at his feet. 'If I could just get her to slow down, stop running for a while ... You know, Alfred, it's funny, she's so scared of being bored. Marriage doesn't need to be a bore. I keep telling her that.'

'And you keep throwing these parties,' I said.

'And I keep throwing these parties.'

'When did you ask Alice to marry you?' I asked.

'Last year. The first night I saw her,' he said. 'At a dinner party. It was the first time I had seen her since she was a debutante. We were seated next to each other at the dinner. I don't even remember what it was we talked about. All I know is that by the end of dinner I knew I wanted Alice to be my wife. She was the first woman I ever felt that way about. I never thought it could happen that way, but it did.'

'Love at first sight?' I smiled.

'More than that,' George said and laughed. 'It was marriage at first sight. I knew that this was it, and I asked her to marry me.'

'And she said, "Give me time."'

'Well, no, actually she sort of laughed at me.'

'I don't blame her,' I said.

We were both silent again until George asked me if I had made up my mind about his offer. I told him I would like very much to move in at least for a trial period, and if it didn't work out, then nothing lost.

'Done. Good. Fine,' George said. 'I want to give a lot more parties. You have a lot of interesting friends, ask some of them to the parties. I know Alice would enjoy meeting them as much as I would.' It was at this point that George started talking to me about Alice, how she had changed his life, how she had encouraged him to move out of his mother's apartment, how she had influenced his dress, his manner, his behaviour. And throughout what he was telling me, I had the uneasy feeling I had been through it before, not exactly a *déjà vu*, just an awareness that it had happened somewhere before, but not to me. I tuned in and out of George's reminiscences about his first meetings with Alice, trying to pin down where I had heard this when my glance fell upon his leather-bound books and I suddenly remembered George saying, 'Even the pages have been cut,' and I almost shouted, '*Gatsby!*' interrupting George in mid-sentence. He looked startled and I said, '*Jay Gatsby!* That's it! *The Great Gatsby!* F. Scott Fitzgerald and all the rest!'

'All the rest of what?'

'This whole conversation. This whole evening. Everything. I'd had the feeling all night long I'd been through it before and now, George, I know where it was. This is the sort of evening I might have expected at Jay Gatsby's!'

George smiled, 'Alice told me she thought I was like Gatsby the first evening I met her.'

And there it was.

I looked at my friend, George Dethriffe, sitting in the leather chair across from me, his heels resting on the leather pig, the crystal glass of amber whisky held lazily in his long thin fingers. He was returning my gaze with a bright, guileless, almost boyish smile of pleasure. A beautiful and exciting woman had told my friend that he was like a character out of F. Scott Fitzgerald. Alice Townsend had convinced George Dethriffe that he, too, was young and exciting and handsome. And he was so pleased I had recognized his role, his fantasy, the myth to which he had succumbed, that I could not bring myself to tell him that it was all wrong. Yet, I must have known then as I do now, that the more you extend someone's illusions, the more you become responsible for them.

I was trying to recall Fitzgerald's dedication to George and Sara Murphy in *Tender Is the Night*. It kept becoming confused in my mind with the line in Don Marquis's *Archy & Mehitabel*, something about *toujours gai*. I had resolved that it was something-*fêtes* when the doorbell rang. Automatically, George and I both looked up at the clock on the mantel. It was a quarter to five. The doorbell rang again.

'Some drunk,' George said. 'I'm not going to answer it.'

The doorbell rang a third time and there followed an insistent knocking.

'The doorman or elevator operator wouldn't have let someone come up who was drunk, would they?' I asked. 'It's after two.'

'I guess not,' George said as he stood up. 'I'd better go see who it is.'

I followed George through the living-room and into the hallway to the front door. He opened the door and an hysterical Alice Townsend, her hair dishevelled, her face puffy and streaked with tears, her dress torn, flung herself into George's arms and held on tightly.

Chapter Seven

The afternoon following George's party and Alice's startling and unexpected arrival, I walked to the Central Park Zoo to meet Teddy and found her at the seal tank holding a bright yellow helium balloon. I have seen other girls in their twenties with balloons, but either they were trying too hard to look cute, or they looked affected. Teddy, somehow, looked exactly right. She was wearing a dark brown, bulky-knit turtleneck sweater, snugly tailored bell-bottomed tweed pants of a yellow, blue, green plaid. And when she saw me, she did not pretend indifference, but ran around the seal tank to me, and held me, and kissed me; and I felt self-consciousness, excited, embarrassed, ecstatic and paralysed. We walked aimlessly through the park that chilly afternoon ending up at the boat pond where I bought us cups of cocoa, and Teddy asked me if I had still been at George's apartment when Alice had arrived.

I was looking at her, trying to figure out how in the hell she had known about that. And she was looking at me, savouring my astonishment and then she asked, 'You did know about Alice and Henry Stanley, didn't you?'

'Who's Henry Stanley?'

'He's at Morgan Guaranty. His father was a director there and on the boards of God-knows-how-many-other companies.'

'That's nice,' I said, 'but what does he have to do with Alice?'

'His son, Henry, is the guy Alice has been trying to marry.'

'Alice *Townsend*?'

'Alice Townsend,' Teddy said.

'But what about George?'

'That's what I wanted to ask you,' she said. 'You were at George's when Alice arrived, weren't you?'

I nodded.

'Was her dress torn?'

'Jesus Christ! How did you know that?' I asked. 'She only showed up at five this morning, how could you –'

'Sally Morris called me this morning,' Teddy said. 'Her brother, Fergus, is Henry's best friend and Henry Stanley saw Fergus this morning at Morgan Guaranty and told him, and Fergus told Sally ... So it really did happen ... I didn't know whether to believe Sally or not ... So it really did happen!'

'What happened?'

'Alice tore her dress.'

'I know that, Teddy, but what happened?'

'Alice tore it.'

'Oh for Christ's sake!'

'I love you,' Teddy said.

'Teddy, what happened to Alice last night?'

'Do you love me?'

'Yes, but tell me what happened?'

'Say it, Alfred. Tell me you love me.'

'I love you.'

'Very much? I love you very much,' she said. 'Do you really love me? Tell me again that you love me, that you love me very much.'

'I do, Teddy,' I said. 'I love you very much.'

We sat there by the boat pond smiling as the sparrows bounced along the balustrade near us, and Teddy's balloon swung lazily back and forth over our heads.

'Are you going to move in with George?' Teddy asked me.

'I'm not sure. Why?'

'It would be nice. If you lived there we could go there right now and make love.'

'Yes, that would be nice.'

'It would be,' Teddy said. 'Are you a good lover?'

I smiled and said, 'I would try to be.'

'That's a nice answer,' she said, 'I'm glad you didn't say that you were. I wish we could go to bed right now.'

'Then I guess I'd better move in with George.'

'You and Alice both,' she said and laughed. 'Don't you think after this that Alice is going to move in?'

'I thought you told me she wanted to marry Stanley what's-his-name. Why would she want to move in with George?'

'It's Henry. Henry Stanley.'

'Henry Stanley. Is Alice in love with Henry Stanley?'

'I doubt it, anyway love has very little to do with marriage,' Teddy said. 'Once you've been married you'll find that out. Alice simply wanted Henry's way of life.'

'What's that?'

'What's what? Henry's way of life? It's three million dollars is what it is. That's why Alice put it to Henry last night. She asked him whether he was going to marry her or not, and evidently, he said he was not.'

'Had Stanley given her any reason to believe that he would?'

'I don't know,' Teddy said. 'She must have thought that he was going to because when he said he wouldn't she went to pieces. Sally said that Fergus told her Henry had —'

'Oh for Christ's sake!' I laughed.

'It isn't funny!' Teddy said. 'That's the only way anybody learns anything in New York. Sally said that Alice began hitting Henry and screaming how she was going to tell everybody he had raped her.'

'Raped her?'

'Henry told her to go ahead, no one would believe her. So Alice tore her dress and said "They'll believe me now," and ran out into the hallway. But it was almost four in the morning and no one was there so she just stood around. And then finally the elevator door opened, and a whole bunch of drunks returning from some party got out at that floor. Everyone was milling around like an after-theatre crowd and Henry slipped the elevator man five dollars, told him to put Alice in a cab, and went back into his apartment just leaving her in the hallway.'

'Poor Alice,' I said, 'she really picked herself a bastard.'

'What would you have done?'

'I don't know. I don't think I would have done that.'

'Well, what happened at George's? I'm dying to hear what happened when Alice showed up. What did Alice say?'

'She didn't say much of anything,' I answered. 'At least I didn't hear her say anything. I got out of there right away.'

'You left?' Teddy asked in astonishment. 'You didn't hear a word? Why did you leave?'

'I just didn't think it was a good idea to stay around. Alice showed up and she was crying and George was comforting her or whatever, and she was apologizing and saying that she must look a sight. I didn't hear much more because by that time I had my overcoat on and got out.'

'But what did George say?'

'He said for me to call him.'

'That's all?'

'That's all he said to me, honest,' I said. 'I barely saw Alice. Ask George.'

'"Ask George!" He wouldn't tell me a thing. You know that.' Teddy began pushing crumbs around the table and a sparrow hopped closer to be fed. 'It isn't fair,' Teddy said, 'I told you everything I knew and it isn't fair.'

'But I told you everything I knew, too. I just don't have as good an information source as you.'

'Well, you could at least tell me that you love me.'

'I thought I had,' I said.

'I wish there were some place we could go,' she said. 'Where are you staying?'

'At the Yale Club,' I said. 'But I'm afraid I can't take you back to my room there.'

'We haven't time anyway,' Teddy said. 'I have to get back to pick up some food for Alex's dinner.'

'Speaking of Alex, where does he think you are now?'

'What do you mean?' she asked. 'He thinks I'm at the Central Park Zoo with you. I told him before I left that I was going to meet you here. Why?'

'And he doesn't mind?'

'Why should he? He has his friends and I have mine. I don't object when Alex wants to see his friends,' she said and began to untie the balloon. 'Why should he object when I want to see mine?'

'Beats hell out of me.'

Teddy freed the balloon and wrapped the string around her wrist, then I helped her out of her chair. 'I'm giving a dinner Saturday night,' Teddy said. 'You'll come, won't you?'

'I'd like to very much.'

'It'll be mostly models and their husbands or boy friends.'

'That should be very interesting. I don't know any models.'

'Don't get any ideas about meeting new ones, pal,' she said.

'What kind of girl have you picked out for me? Or do you want me to bring my own.'

'I'm the girl I've picked out for you,' she said.

'You?' I laughed.

'Alex will be in Chicago,' she said. 'That's why I'm giving this party. In fact,' she laughed, 'I only thought of giving it a minute ago. And after the party's over and everyone has gone home we can spend the night together at my place and – what's the matter?'

I laughed at her consternation, 'Nothing's the matter. It's just that you make me feel as though I should flutter my eyelashes.'

There was a note for me from George Dethriffe in the message box back at the club. He had tried to call me and would call back later. I pocketed the note and walked up the worn marble steps of the club, beneath the portraits, to the bar where I ran into an older man who had been in my Uncle Robert's class at Yale and who was a friend of my mother's and father's. I signed for the drink we had together because of his eyes. They were tired and beaten and hurt, and I have seen so many of these men in recent years. They are gentlemen, *gentle* men, and they are locked into some form of business in which they don't belong, because they aren't tough enough or vicious enough or selfish enough or avaricious enough, and they are doomed. This man was wearing all the right clothes, his hair had turned the right tint of grey at the temples, he still had just the right shade of suntan. But, oh God, he was hurting and he was scared. I think about these men often and wonder what becomes of them. I'm not that eager to find out. I think I'll know soon enough. One drink was all I had time for.

I was just getting dressed after my bath when George Dethriffe telephoned and wanted to know when I would be moving into his apartment. 'How's Alice?' I asked.

'She's fine,' he said. 'We stayed up and talked the rest of the night and then we had breakfast I and took her home. She's fine, really. When do you think you'll be moving in?'

'I don't know, George, it seems your life is getting pretty complicated, and I feel I'd just be in the way. I mean, what about Alice?'

'Don't be ridiculous, with you here it would be great! Like I said, we could give the most wonderful parties and Alice could be here all the time and no one would talk.'

'The hell they wouldn't.'

'Why don't you bring your stuff over now? Move in tonight.'

'I can't. I'm going to try to see Walker tonight. But I'll call you tomorrow anyway and organize moving in.'

'Do that. I'll see you tomorrow then. Give my best to Walker, okay? And tell him – well, tell him I think about him a lot. And if there's anything I can do...'

No two brothers look less alike than Walker and myself. He is four years older and four inches shorter. I have a long, thin face; he has a round face with high cheekbones. My hair is light, his is dark. He is muscular and coordinated. I am not. If the two of us were to be put together in a crowded room, I could safely bet any person present that they could not correctly pick out my brother. And yet, despite our physical differences, we are in many ways alike. Our voices, accents, gestures are the same. Our laughter follows the same scales. Our senses of joy and outrage are similar. To a certain extent it is fair to say we think the same way – at least all of this used to be true, and that night as I sat in the taxicab taking me down to the Village to see Walker I wanted to believe that it still was true. He has been a major influence in my life – more important than he would want to be, more than I want him to be, and more than he ought to be. I say this because ultimately we are quite different – no, I am not contradicting myself. Yes, we are very much alike. How could two brothers growing up in the same houses, with the same parents, help but have a considerable amount in common? And yet, just as strongly as we differ physically, we differ mentally. And, therefore, people react to us differently.

There is an aura about Walker that is totally different from mine, I am safe; Walker is exciting, a *fleur du mal*, a corrupt angel, and because there is that suggestion, that hint of depravity about him, others find him irresistible. For the past five years, everyone who had known him, who had loved him enough, had tried to help him. And we had all been hurt – not only hurt, but stunned that we had failed.

For the past five years my brother had been on heroin. And, in order to pay for his habit, he had borrowed from us, he had stolen from us, he had cheated us, he had used us; and God help us, we loved him now just as we had loved him before. The five years had been an emotional bankruptcy from which none of us would totally recover. Walker had hurt us knowing he was hurting us. And we knew *he* knew he was hurting us, but he could not stop.

And with each passing year his eyes had grown colder and colder. His body had shrunk. His face had died – how else can one describe the waxy pallor of a junky? And, oh God, how he lied. How he lied to us! He had forced himself to lie just as hard as we had forced ourselves to believe. For all these years we had desperately wanted to believe him when he told us he had stopped. But he hadn't. He couldn't. And year after year we went on trying to help because behind those cold, dead, furtive eyes we could see the occasional flicker of a frightened little boy, and that boy was my brother, Walker, screaming for help.

For three years I didn't know Walker was on hard drugs, that he had been on heroin all the time he was in Paris and I was in the Navy. It was not until I came home and one of my first jobs was to help our mother clean out his New York apartment that I found out. Walker was then twenty-eight. He had had himself committed to an institution to kick the drugs. It was to take a long time and so my mother and I spent the afternoons up at his apartment packing away his furniture, his clothes, his books, his records, the accessories of his life. And while putting them in cartons and envelopes, I learned how much he had changed. His apartment was dirty, unbelievably filthy. Everything seemed to be decaying.

Walker had always been reasonable about possessions neither becoming overly attached or repulsed with them. Whatever he liked he treated with respect. But his records were all scratched, his books torn and broken spined. His paintings were scarred.

81

The furniture was scratched and stained, the lampshades broken so that they hung like cocked party hats over the bulbs. The rug was covered with burn marks. I could not understand how he had changed this much. But, I had not yet seen him, and I did not then understand hard drugs.

My mother took me up to the institution to see him my second week home. The three of us sat together one Sunday afternoon on wooden benches overlooking the tennis courts and closely-clipped lawns. As we talked to each other Walker would point out one inmate after another: 'That's the friend of Dad's who's in my ceramics class.' 'That's where (a famous actress) stays when she comes back here.' 'That's Andy. He's only sixteen and he's been here four times.' And all around us there were dandelions, their heads feathered away.

The only thing I can remember Walker saying to me was 'Hey, pal, you shouldn't be wearing a black, knit tie up here. Take it off! Black's a bad sign. It means you're really withdrawn, you know? Introverted. You'd maybe better stick with Mom or they might not let you out.' The reason why I can't remember more was because every time I looked at him I was saddened. He had lost over thirty pounds and every few minutes he would shiver as though a chill had overtaken him. When we left him behind us at the institution's iron gates, he pretended he was a prison inmate rattling his tin cup across the prison bars, and my mother burst into tears.

Our mother cried often during these years, and she is not at all the sort of woman who cries. She wept because she could not help her son, because Walker kept going back on heroin. She wept for him because he was killing himself. He was slowly and deliberately and agonizingly killing himself, and it frightened our mother, because she could not understand why. And she was frightened of what Walker might do to pay for his drugs. A junky who has been on heroin for five years has an expensive habit. And when Walker told us that a painting of his had been stolen, or a piece of jewellery lost, or a phonograph out for repairs, we knew that whatever it was, it had been pawned. Each time he returned to the institution, my mother cleaned up his apartment, collected all his pawn tickets, and retrieved what she could. But as the years crept on, the pawn tickets were more and more difficult to find. And eventually, we could find no more paintings, no more books, no more jewellery, and less and less hope for Walker.

It was a few minutes before eight when I got out of the taxi in the Village. Walker's apartment was a six flight walk-up on MacDougal Street just off Washington Square. I waited outside his door for a moment to catch my breath, then knocked. There was no answer although I could hear noises from inside. So I knocked again. 'Walker? Walker?' I said. 'It's me, Alfred.' I waited and still there was no answer although I could hear the floor boards creak as someone walked across them. 'Is Walker in there? I'm his brother,' I said. I knocked on the door again. The green paint had flaked and peeled off the metal door showing rusted brown steel underneath. All around the lock there were scratch marks and the metal was dented near the latch where some one had tried to jimmy the door open. I was about to knock on the door again when I saw the knob turn and the door swing open the width of a chain lock. A young girl looked out at me. She was wearing a grey terrycloth bathrobe.

'Walker's not here,' she said.

'Well would you mind letting me in so that I can wait for him?'

'He's not here,' she said, pulling her robe tight around her.

Beyond her I could see a rumpled bed and old newspapers scattered around the floor. 'When do you expect him back?'

'I don't know,' she said.

'Did he go out recently? Has he been gone long? Did he say where he went?'

'What do you want to know for?'

'Look, I told you I'm his brother. I've just gotten back to New York and I'd like to see him. Now that I've told you who I am why don't you unlock the door, let me in and you can tell me who you are.'

'Walker doesn't like me to let people in. How do I know you're his brother?'

'How do you know I'm not? What do you want? A driver's licence?'

'Oh well,' she said, 'I guess you're all right. Just a minute.' She pushed the door closed, unchained it, then let me in. I walked past her and into the room. I stood looking at the debris on the floor, the cold food stuck on plates that littered the sink, and she looked at me sullenly.

'My name's Alfred,' I said.

'Take a seat,' she said. She walked over to a chair and brushed the clothes off it and on to the floor.

'When did Walker go out?'

'About an hour ago,' she said. 'He said he'd be back soon. He had to see a guy.'

'How is he?'

'Who? Walker? He's fine.'

'Is he really?'

'Sure,' she shrugged. 'Why shouldn't he be?'

'Has he been eating?'

'Yes, Daddy,' she said.

I suddenly wheeled on her, furious. 'Don't give me that shit. I don't need that from you.'

'Hey, man,' she said, 'don't lose your cool. Walker will be back. Sit down . . . sit down . . .'

I sat down boiling mad. I had to keep myself from venting all the rage, the helplessness, the frustration I felt about Walker at that stupid girl. I was just so sick and tired of trying to talk to Walker or his friends and getting the same treatment. Always I was the alien, the outsider, the square, the straight. As the years progressed their smugness was unchanged, only their vocabulary changed. Always I represented the world they had rejected, that they couldn't live with. And when I spoke to them they were so busy shoring up themselves at my expense, they never bothered to listen to me. I was the backboard for their inside jokes and I hated them for it and I hated Walker for letting them do that to me. I wanted to be his brother, not their entertainment.

'You want something to – uh – drink?' the girl asked.

'Does he have anything like beer?'

'I doubt it. I'll go look.'

She was at the refrigerator when Walker came in, a grocery bag in his hand.

'Hey, Alfred,' he said. 'How are you, pal?'

'Fine, Walker. It's good to see you.'

'You met Lisa?' he handed her the groceries. 'Have you had dinner?'

'Not yet,' I said. 'I was hoping we could have dinner together.'

'Sure. I've got enough here.'

'Would you like to go out?' I asked. 'That way you don't have to cook.'

'No, let's eat here. There are some people coming by later.'

'Who?' Lisa asked.

'Annie and Chet and George and some others.'

The girl shrugged. 'Did you see the guy?'

'Sure,' he said. 'We're going to have a fine dinner. It won't be cold turkey after all.'

And the girl laughed.

And so I had dinner with Walker and his girl, and even though we never said anything really, it was good just to be with him. After a while I relaxed and the girl relaxed and Walker relaxed and even when they went separately into the bathroom and shot themselves up, I didn't get upset. There was nothing I could do. And then the others arrived around eleven and I told Walker that I was staying at George's and if he needed anything that he should call me.

'I don't need anything,' he said. 'How about if I call you just because I want to see you?'

'Good. That'll be fine,' I said. 'I hope you will.'

'I will,' Walker said.

But he didn't. I didn't see Walker for another two months. Not until George and Alice's wedding. I went down to the Village a couple of times those first weeks, but he wasn't there. Or if he was there, he wasn't opening the door. Once he called me and asked if I would lend him a hundred dollars. I asked him if he wanted me to bring it down to MacDougal Street for him, and he said he wasn't living there anymore.

'Where are you living?'

'Around,' he said. I could hear party sounds in the background. Indian music. People laughing.

'Well, where do you want me to send the money?'

'Would you just send it to my bank?'

He gave me the account number and address. And I sent it. I honestly didn't know what else I could do. I loved him and I couldn't stand him.

Chapter Eight

The night I went down to the Village to see Walker was the night Alice Townsend moved in with George. Although she still had her own apartment and kept most of her clothes in it, she spent every night with George.

One morning, shortly after I had started to live there I was climbing the wrought-iron circular staircase after shaving in the downstairs bathroom. I was hung over, nauseous, thick tongued, wearing my pyjama bottoms and carrying the tops over my shoulder.

'Must you always use the bathroom with the door open?' Alice asked me.

'I'm not well this morning, Alice,' I warned her.

'And secondly,' she said, 'if you think exposing yourself to me is funny or, or – or exciting, or whatever, let me assure you that it isn't.'

'Alice, please . . .'

'Well?'

'I didn't know you could see into the bathroom from the balcony unless you leaned over the edge.'

'I'm talking about right now!'

I looked down at my pyjamas. The string was tied, but the little button on the fly wasn't buttoned. Still, my pyjamas were closed, and I couldn't see anything. I looked at Alice standing in some ridiculous puff-ball slippers and bathrobe outside George's bedroom door, her hair messed up, and no make-up. And slowly I turned my back on her, pulled my pyjama string and let the pyjamas fall to the floor.

'Gotcha,' I said, and with what little dignity I could muster, shuffled, pyjama pants wrapped about my ankles, into my bedroom and closed the door behind me.

Our paths didn't cross until the next evening when I came

downstairs after showering and dressing and joined Alice and George in the library. George had lit a fire and sat now with his vest unbuttoned, his stockinged feet resting upon the Abercrombie & Fitch pig. Alice was in the opposite leather chair, her long legs tucked under her. 'Hello, Alfred!' she said. 'Come over and give me a kiss. I haven't seen you in ages.'

'Haven't changed a bit,' I said. I leaned forward and we gave each other a sort of cheek-brushing kiss.

'What are you up to tonight?' George asked me.

'I thought I'd try to get in touch with Walker again. Go down to the Village and see if I can find him.'

'Why don't you just call him?' Alice asked.

'His telephone is disconnected,' I said.

'Still?' Alice asked looking at George. 'But I thought you paid his bill. You told me last week that when you saw him, you paid Walker's phone bill.'

'You did?' I asked George. 'Why'd you pay my brother's telephone bill?'

'Well, Walker called me,' George said, obviously embarrassed.

'While I was here?' I asked. 'Where was I?'

'It was the night you went to the movies,' George explained. 'I didn't want to say anything to you about it. I didn't actually pay the bill, I just gave him some money for it.'

'How much was it?' I asked.

'Forget it, Alfred, really,' George said.

'It was a lot of money,' Alice protested. She stood up and pulled George out of his chair and into the living-room. 'C'mon, George, it's time for our backgammon.'

I asked George again how much he had given Walker.

'It was close to a hundred dollars,' Alice said.

'The phone bill was only eighty something,' George said.

'But you gave him a hundred,' Alice said.

I pulled out my cheque-book.

'What are you doing?' George asked me. 'It was my money and I wanted to give it to him.'

'You shouldn't have. He shouldn't have let you.'

'Alfred, stop sounding like such an old fart,' George said. 'Now put your cheque-book away and mix yourself a drink.'

'George,' Alice said impatiently, 'do you want me to roll for you?'

'Did you give him cash?' I asked George.

'I'll roll for you, George,' Alice said. 'You rolled a seven and I rolled – I rolled a nine. So I begin.' She dropped the dice back into the cup and shook again.

'I just happened to have a lot of cash on me,' George said watching Alice's move.

'It's your move, George,' she said.

'There was a girl with him . . .' George said.

'It's your *move*,' Alice repeated.

They played for a few minutes in silence and I wrote out a cheque for one hundred dollars and left it on the gate-leg table.

'Don't Alfred,' George said. 'It was my fault. I shouldn't have given him the money. I just didn't know what else to do.'

'I know,' I said. 'I never know what to do either. But there's no reason for you to get caught up in it. So do me a favour, please? Take my cheque, okay?'

'Family pride?' George asked me.

'I guess so,' I said.

'It's your move again,' Alice said.

'He spent the money you gave him?' I asked George. 'I guess that's not surprising.'

'I must have embarrassed the hell out of him,' George said. 'I mean there I was in my Wall Street six-piece suit and there he was in an old bathing suit getting his back rubbed by some NYU girl. I must have looked like a Martian to them.'

'More like our father,' I said.

'Actually, I think the girl thought I was with the FBI. She couldn't take her eyes off my black shoes.' George laughed. 'Alice, are you sure that's the move you want to make?'

'Positive,' Alice said. 'Your turn.'

'And then he asked you for some money?' I asked him.

'Well, no. As I said he had telephoned me and when I went down to his apartment there was this girl there. I asked him how he was and he said he was broke, that the phone company was hassling him. I said that's the way phone companies are, and I asked him if he needed any money. And, well, you know how

Walker is – and when I gave him the cash that goddam little girl sneered and said, "What's that, his allowance?"'

'And so he felt obligated to spend it, I guess,' I said.

'Right,' George said.

'Well he shouldn't have spent it,' Alice said, 'and you, George, you shouldn't have given it to him.'

'Oh hell, Alice,' George said. 'I had the money. That's what friends are for. Walker is Alfred's brother. He needed the money. He'd have done the same for me. And besides he looked as though he hadn't eaten in several days. He's really terribly thin,' George said to me. 'He's on some sort of herb diet. He won't eat anything unless its brown or something. I don't know what it is, but he really doesn't look well at all.'

'Well, I'll tell you this much,' Alice said. 'It isn't any herb diet that's making him look that way.'

'All right, Alice,' George said.

'Well, it isn't. And you both know it.' Alice said.

'Alice, it's your move,' George said.

One evening, shortly before I moved out, Alice went out to dinner with her mother, and George and I had the apartment to ourselves. We'd had several drinks together and George was talking about the changes he felt would take place once he was married. How much he wanted to have children. That he thought he would like to live in the country. That a few stocks he'd gotten in on were doing so extraordinarily well that he was looking for land to invest in. That it would be so nice to live with Alice and the children in the country and so forth. We were sitting in those leather chairs too lazy to light a fire, and I said, 'George, why in God's name are you marrying her?'

He looked at me over the rim of his drink and didn't say anything.

'Alice isn't the first girl you ever slept with is she?'

'You must be kidding,' he said.

'Then why, in Christ's name, are you marrying her?'

'Because I love her.'

'But can't you just go on sleeping with her? Do you have to marry her?'

'No, I don't have to marry her, of course not,' he said angrily. 'If you mean, as it sounds, "is she pregnant?" The answer is most emphatically, No!'

'Whooey, George, hold on. It's me. Alfred Moulton. Your old friend. You don't have to get stuffy with me.'

'You just don't know her,' he said.

'Maybe. Maybe not. Why don't you, why don't you send her away, just for an experiment. Get her to go back to her own apartment for a while. You're going to get married in a month, why don't you take off? Get her the hell out of here, give yourself a chance to breathe. Listen, I'll take you out. I'll take you to parties, you said you loved parties, and there's always a good one somewhere in town. And if you want to get laid, my God, it couldn't be easier, I know –'

'It isn't just getting laid, Alfred. Anybody can get laid. I'm tired of screwing. To tell you the truth screwing bores my ass off. Making love is different. I love her, and that makes all the difference in the world.'

'Sure, sure,' I said, 'Alice is probably – well, I don't know, obviously, and it's none of my business, obviously, and I should shut up, obviously, but I just know, that something is not right.'

'But you don't know her, Alfred,' George repeated.

'My God, George, how well do you know her? She took over this place like a whirlwind. She's taken you over. She's made all your plans, she's –'

'What you don't understand is that I want her to.'

'But when I see you two, sitting up here playing backgammon, sipping tea – when did you start drinking tea?'

'I've always liked tea.'

'I've never seen you drink it until this past month. You sit up here, you two, with a fire in the fire-place, sipping tea and playing backgammon and –'

'What's so awful about that?' George asked. 'I like tea. I like playing backgammon. I like sitting before a fire. Why is that so awful?'

'I don't know, George,' I said, 'it's just so old. You look like some sort of parody of our parents. You can do that sort of thing for the rest of your life. Why are you in such a hurry to play house? I just don't think – I don't know why, but it just depresses the hell out of me.' I stood up and walked over to the silent butler tray to mix myself a fresh drink. 'Why the rush to reach middle age? What's so hot about getting married and having children? What's so hot about stranding yourself on some farm in the country? Why don't you enjoy yourself while you can?'

'But I do enjoy myself.'

'Well, I know, I know. But why not really go out, get out and have one hell of a good time?'

'Alice doesn't like to go out. She's rath –'

'Oh, the hell with Alice!' I exploded. 'The first thing, one of the very first things you said to me when I came back, when I moved in with you, one of the very first things you said to me was how much you wanted to have parties. To see people. To have a good time. Well, all I'm saying, all I'm trying to tell you is to go ahead. Goddam it, do it. Get rid of Alice. For a month, just a month by yourself. I'm moving out and you'll have the place to yourself and take advantage of it. For God's sake, I'll introduce you to fifty girls who can play backgammon and drink tea and who, in addition, love to go out. To have parties. To have a good time. That's what you said you wanted.'

'But that was because I was lonely,' George said. 'Don't you understand that, Alfred? I was lonely. Lonely. And now I'm not. It's as simple as that. I love Alice. And she loves me. And –'

'Does she?' I interrupted. 'Does she love you, really?'

'Yes,' he said. 'Yes.'

'More than she loves herself? Don't forget, Alice Townsend looks out for herself. And you have every right to be just as selfish as she is.'

'Well, I'm not sure how true that is,' George said. 'But, like I keep trying to tell you, you just don't know Alice!'

'I'm just worried you're going to marry her for all the wrong reasons. I'm worried that you're getting married because you think it's time to get married.' I turned back from the bar and sat down in my leather chair again. 'You feel you're old enough, and you haven't got anything better to do, and so you're going to marry Alice Townsend. All I'm trying to suggest is that you still have time to get out of it if you want to.'

'But I don't want to,' George insisted.

'Alright, here's another idea. Why don't you, instead of getting married next month, why don't you take Alice with you and go off somewhere and live together. Hell, go some place where no one knows you're *not* married. Try it out before you make it legal. I just have this feeling that you're getting married out of some misguided sense of responsibility to – to, I don't know what to. What about your mother? What does your mother think of Alice?'

'She likes her,' George said. 'She hasn't really said anything to me either way. She wouldn't want to interfere and anyway, as you well know, Alice's mother and my mother – your's, too, for that matter, are all friends.'

'Do you think your mother feels at ease with her?'

'What the hell does that mean, Alfred. For God's sake! I suppose she does. It's difficult, or at least awkward for mothers-in-law and daughters-in-law to feel at ease with each other at first. It's only natural.'

'Alright, what about your friends? The IBM guy and his wife, the Trumbulls.'

'Turnbulls, Jim and Nancy Turnbull. Do you mean what do they think of Alice?'

'Or Walt and Missy Carlyle,' I asked. 'What do your friends' wives think of Alice?'

'Alfred, what does it matter? They haven't said anything to me. There's nothing for them to say. They're not marrying Alice, I am.'

'What does Alice think of them?'

'She likes them.'

'What about Alice's friends? Do you like them?'

'Female friends? I haven't met any.'

'Don't you think that's odd?'

'No I don't. In the first place, Alice isn't exactly a "girl's girl", and in the second place, she only has a couple of female friends that I've heard talk about, and they don't live in New York City.'

'Oh well, the hell with it. Let me fix you another drink and we'll toast your marriage. I hope it will be a happy one filled with happy surprises.'

'It will be,' he said.

So, we made ourselves comfortable. George got his new drink and returned to his chair and put his feet up on his pig. And he said he wasn't angry with me, that he appreciated my concern, and that that was what friends are for, et cetera. And then he started to talk to me about Alice, how lonely she was, how beautiful she was, how eager she was to become a really good cook, and that she had majored in art at Vassar and wished she had stayed on to graduate, because now that she had time to paint and really wanted to, she wasn't sure how good she was. And George told me how, as a surprise, he had bought her all the materials, the paints, the easel, she would need. And that they were going to go to Florence on their honeymoon. And that he really loved Alice so much, she made him feel so good, so protective abut her or, not really protective, he said, but gentle and parental, but not really parental, and so on. And he told me about his plans, how because he was doing so well in the market, he could afford to take more time off and travel. Not only to Florence, but all over. He and Alice had talked about trips they wanted to take, where they would go, what they would see, what they would do. And he knew he behaved foolishly at times, but he couldn't help it. Didn't I understand . . . ? Couldn't I see . . . ?

But the only thing I saw, the only thing I understood was that George Dethriffe was inextricably trapped by the enormousness of his illusion. It had surpassed even Alice's, transcended her own image. He had not only accepted the myth, but succumbed to the myth's myth. Jay Gatsby was actually going to get Daisy Buchanan. The little green light he could see at the end of the dock was his own. And who the hell was I to suggest that they were looking across all that water from on board the *Titanic*?

Alice wore the wedding dress both her mother and grandmother had been married in. It was a lovely dress, very old fashioned and nice with a high collar and lots of lace. It smelled of sachets of yesterdays' flowers and spices. Alice was so proud of herself in it, and I liked her for being so proud. She was happy and excited and she became again the Alice of the *Vogue* photograph, but the photograph brought up to date. The indefinable promise had been fulfilled. The anticipation realized. And when George slipped the wedding ring on to her finger, she looked at him with her silver-grey eyes brimming over with love. And even if part of that love was triumph, that was fine, too.

Mrs Dethriffe said an appalling thing to me as I led her out of the church following the ceremony. Half-way back up the aisle, she said, 'Well, there's always divorce.'

The ushers' present to George was a large silver cigarette box with all our signatures engraved on it, George's and Alice's initials and the date of their wedding. There were six bridesmaids, three of whom were married. The Maid of Honour was a particularly beautiful girl, tall, blonde like Alice, with a high bust, good long legs and a marvellous tan which she told me she had acquired in Jamaica. At the reception held afterwards at the Colony Club she confided to me that she didn't really know Alice all that well and that she'd been very surprised when Alice asked her to be in the wedding.

The bridesmaids' present was a Steuben centrepiece and four crystal candlestick holders. While I was in Florence with George and Alice, Alice received a letter saying that one of the bridesmaids had died in Pittsburg following an abortion. George told me her name, but I wasn't certain I remembered which bridesmaid she was. Alice said she was the mousey one.

Chapter Nine

I left Florence, as I had promised Alice I would, the next day; but I did not return to New York. I still had over two thousand dollars left from what the magazine had paid me for the long, short story. And since I could also count on a limited income from my inheritance and trusts, I was confident that even if I didn't earn a penny, I could live in Spain for at least a year on what I had. I was also naïve enough to think that if I really got into a bind, I could just write another short story and sell it. I offer in defence only the incurable optimism of youth. So, I said my good-byes to the Dethriffes and went to Spain to write a book. I did not have any sure idea of what the book would be, but I knew it would have something to do with honour and family and dignity and country and being obsolete. I set a deadline for myself: finish the first draft in six months, the second draft in three more months, and a final, polished draft within a year. I settled into a little town on the southern coast and set to work.

It took me two years to finish the first draft of my book.

During my first six months in Spain I received occasional letters from George or from friends of George's and mine, and the letters suggested that the Dethriffe marriage was in trouble. But all marriages are in trouble unless the couples have had prefrontal lobotomies. And then, about a year and a half after I had left the Dethriffes I ran into Jim and Nancy Turnbull in Barcelona. I did not know the Turnbulls very well, had only seen them a few times at George's parties in New York, but I was so hungry for company I fell upon them like prodigal children. They invited me to join them for a trip up to Valencia, and during the drive I mentioned that I had not heard from George lately and they said that I knew, of course, that George and Alice had bought a converted stable in Winander, Connecticut.

I said I knew they had moved, but little more than that.

Winander is about forty miles out of New York City, almost due north of Greenwich, Connecticut. I went there many years ago for the week-end of their annual débutante ball, the same one at which Alice Dethriffe, née Townsend, was presented. Winander was lovely, with huge, old stone houses overlooking a private lake. Behind the houses were the woods and hills, and on the lake were the boat-houses which I remembered mostly as being dark green with white trim. The dance was held in an enormous old wooden club house which had a plaque commemorating its opening in 1897 with the phrase: 'Upon completion of the sweeping stairway and second storey, the Winander Club, becomes the most sumptuous Club House west of Newport.' It *was* magnificent. The week-end of Alice's début we were all snowed in. There was ice boating and skating on the lake. Skiing down the cut trails in the woods. And it was still open season on grouse and, of course, the débutantes.

The Turnbulls told me they had been seeing the Dethriffes less and less, but not only because they had moved away to Winander. They told me that the last time they had seen the Dethriffes was a few weeks after Thanksgiving. Nancy's parents had come up from Philadelphia to New York for the weekend. And since Nancy's mother was an old friend of George Dethriffe's mother, Nancy thought it might be nice for George and her mother to meet. So Nancy invited George and Alice to join them in town for cocktails and dinner. From the moment Alice arrived she made things difficult. She seemed to resent being there. She wouldn't talk to anyone. She complained of being tired. Alice was, at that time, in her fourth month of pregnancy and had had a miscarriage a year earlier. Nancy asked her if she wouldn't rather have a sandwich and lie down instead of going out to dinner. And Alice said she didn't know they had been invited to go out to dinner, that she thought they had been invited to have dinner there. Jim told her they had decided to go to Luchow's, that it was only five or so blocks from there, and that they could

97

walk it easily; and the fresh air would do everybody a world of good. When it became time to leave for dinner, Alice insisted George get her a taxi. And at Luchow's, when there was a delay while their table was set up, Alice sat by herself in a telephone booth. Evidently George was terribly upset and told Nancy that he knew they were ruining the party and that it would be better if he just took Alice home.

'I told him to relax,' Nancy said to me leaning back over the seat of their rental Volkswagen as we continued along the road to Valencia. 'I told George we'd pour a couple more drinks down her and she'd be all right. I felt so sorry for George because he was so embarrassed by Alice's behaviour.'

'And I told him not to be silly,' Jim said. 'I said, "Don't worry about Alice. We're all used to her acting like this."'

'There was this awful silence,' Nancy said. 'We could both see the hurt, the real pain in George's eyes. We –'

'I wish I could have bitten my tongue out, Alfred,' Jim interrupted.

'I tried to make a joke, but it just got worse. Luckily our table was ready and we could go right in. And we got through dinner and haven't seen them since.'

'Then Alice must have had her baby by now,' I said.

'It was a little boy,' Nancy replied. 'He was born in the middle of April, lucky Alice. Jim and I have been trying to have a baby, but so far . . . How much farther is it to Valencia?'

'Another hour,' I said. 'Why are we all going to Valencia anyway?'

'Why does anybody go to Valencia?' Nancy laughed. 'To look at churches and paintings. Why else?'

'Because we have a reservation there.' Jim said.

The Turnbulls and I separated after that weekend in Valencia, they to look at more churches and paintings and I to return to my town to finish my book.

I was beginning to miss America – not any particular place, except, maybe New York – I was beginning to miss that huge amorphous image of a country that filled me with homesickness whenever I daydreamed about America. Like introductions to old newsreels my reveries would quick-cut from the Rockettes to vast acres of billowing wheat, to the Lincoln Memorial, to racehorses in a white-fenced Kentucky pasture, to Howard Hughes's plywood flying boat, to soldiers and sailors marching through ticker tape, to squirrels and Cardinal Spellman at the zoo, to racing cars coming out of the turn on the Indianapolis-500 brick track, to the inside of Loews' Eighty-sixth Street, to a score of bathing beauties parading with illegible banners. I missed an America I had never seen; an America that I suspected didn't exist outside the *New York Daily News* centrefold. But most of all I missed the excitement. I had begun to sense that Teddy's 'living, breathing, here-today world', had gone network, that all over the country we were beginning to shrug off our middle-age slump. The Walter Brennans were out of the White House, the Kennedys were in. Once more America was a young country. I wanted to go home. But before I could do that there were two things I had to do first: finish my book and go see Walker in Hawaii.

Walker had left New York for Hawaii about the same time Teddy and I departed for Rome. During that year and a half I doubt whether Walker and I exchanged five letters. He wrote me that he had gotten off junk, but I knew the odds were against it, and I had believed him too many times in the past. And as the months and miles separated us even further I found the Walker I thought about was the brother I had grown up with rather than the brother he had become.

During my last six months in Europe, however, I began to hear encouraging news. Friends visiting Hawaii had seen him. 'Walker looked very healthy.' A junky doesn't look healthy. 'He's diving for black coral.' 'He's become one helluva surfer.' I also began to receive letters filled with hope from my mother. And then she sent one with a sizeable cheque and the instruction that I use it for an aeroplane ticket to Hawaii.

That same mail also included the following letter from George:

Dear Alfred:

Jim and Nancy Turnbull came up to Winander for the week-end and spoke of seeing you. Did you know that Nancy is, at last, pregnant? She thinks it happened that night in Valencia – or afternoon, really, since she mentioned having to kill time before anyone could be served dinner. She has made your life there sound most exciting.

The stable is almost finished at long last. The baby has his own room, and we hope you will be coming soon to stay as our house guest. Incidentally, you must see our boathouse. I'm not kidding, we actually have one! And across from it I can see the lights from another boathouse on the lake; it belongs to the Webster Neills. Mr Neill is now in his seventies, and his first wife died thirty years ago in an extraordinary accident at the club. It was the evening of their daughter's coming-out party, a very grand affair with thousands of balloons, Emil Coleman and his orchestra alternating with a jazz band, forests of flowers, etc. Mr and Mrs Neill were waiting with their dinner guests at the club for the other dinner guests to arrive. The limousines were just beginning to pull up when Mrs Neill excused herself to go to the powder room, which in those days was on the second floor at the top of the great, curved staircase. Everyone was very gay and had helped themselves to a great deal of booze. When the other guests were all present, Mrs Neill reappeared at the top of the stairs and said, 'Hey, everybody, look at me!' Whereupon she started to slide down the banister. She never made it to the first curve. Instead, she fell off, dropped two floors to the marble below and died instantly. Naturally the party was cancelled. But, I thought, if you were still thinking of writing like Fitzgerald, it's a scene you might be able to use.

I have thought a great deal about our last meeting in Florence and our conversation about Alice before she and I were married. What good would it have done if I had listened to you? We all marry our Zelda's as someone once said. And I have always believed that we are whatever role we choose to play, and I chose mine a long time ago. Do you remember how you were saying that *The Great Gatsby* was just a series of parties until the last party was over? Well, I've been thinking that marriage is like that, too, with all its settings and props and malice and politeness. Sometimes it's more like a dance where you're stuck with the same girl and hope someone will cut in. But even when they do and the dance is over, you still have to take her home with you. It's funny, Alfred, you know? Alice and

I go to every party we can find. We accept every invitation we receive. Only now the invitations are coming fewer and farther in between. Hurry back so that we can have an excuse to throw a party for you.

Alice joins me in sending love,

George

P.S. I'm enclosing as you requested a photo of our son and heir. The poor son of a bitch.

Chapter Ten

For two weeks I tried to answer George's letter. But there was nothing I could say to him. I did write Walker in Hawaii asking if he would mind if I visited, and he wrote back immediately urging me to come.

Both of us knew I would be going to Hawaii to inspect him.

I stepped off the airplane at Honolulu International wearing light grey flannels, a tweed jacket with elbow patches, a custom-made blue and white striped shirt with a gold collar pin and a yellow silk tie with red polka dots. Walker was wearing faded khakis, a sun-bleached Tahitian shirt – blue with huge white flowers on it – no socks and faded tennis shoes. He had also grown a moustache and beard which the sun and salt water had flecked with gold. As I walked from the plane towards him neither of us knew where to look.

'Aloha, pal,' he said, and draped a flowered lei around my shoulders.

'As we say in New York, "Hello",' I answered. I lifted the flowers to my face and inhaled their fragrance.

'You're beginning to look more and more like Dad – except for the noseful of flowers.'

I laughed, 'You're beginning to look more and more like Mom – except for the beard.'

'Hers a different colour?'

'Fuller,' I said.

We stood there smiling at each other, shifting weight from leg to leg, a little shy, a little embarrassed.

'Well, how are you?' he asked me.

'How are you?'

'Fine. Good. Have you got much luggage?'

'Only one bag,' I said. There was a plastic-grass-skirted Hawaiian hula girl near us posing for photographs with the passengers.

'I don't suppose you'd like your picture taken with her, hey?' Walker asked me.

'Not a bit.'

When the luggage arrived, Walker carried my suitcase out of the airport and across the parking lot to a blue Volkswagen. He apologized for the car being dirty and added, 'But you should have seen the car I had before. It was so awful, hey, that I traded it to a guy for a breakdown pool cue.'

'A pool cue?'

'I've always wanted a good one.'

We drove towards Honolulu past all the automobile and motorcycle showrooms, the tourist boat ride docks advertising trips to Pearl Harbor and sunset excursions, the huge shopping centre, the gas stations and food stands all neon and bubbly. And we talked about his car, that it needed a new muffler, that the Honolulu police were very strict, that he liked the car, that it was the first good thing he had bought, and then he said, 'Hey, I sure am glad you're here.'

'By God, so am I,' I said. 'I've missed you these past two years.'

'I've missed you, too, pal.'

And we talked about Honolulu and how one's first impression of the city was not what one expected of a tropical paradise, and Walker said, 'You keep saying, "By God!"'

'You keep saying, "Hey",' I said.

'Do I, by God?'

'You really do, hey.'

Walker's apartment was on one of the hills overlooking Honolulu. The apartment, tacked precariously onto the back of a three-car garage, consisted of two bedrooms separated by a bathroom, and off the main bedroom there was a kitchen extension. A Hawaiian family lived in the house on one side, a Chinese family in the house on the other, and directly beneath Walker lived Max, a Filipino who had worked at the Royal Hawaiian for the past twenty-five years.

'Max and I are old friends,' Walker said. 'About once a week when I go skin diving I bring him back a fish, and he always gives me fresh fruit. Mangoes, papayas, guava ... He's scared of getting a heart attack so he sleeps with a broom handle next to his bed. We've arranged it so that if he has an attack he can pound on the ceiling and I'll wake up and get him to the hospital.'

He told me this on a small walkway leading to his door. As I waited behind him for him to unlock his front door, our feet were suddenly caught up in a whirlpool of cats. There were seven of them: one mother, her son from her first litter, and five from her most recent of which her son was suspected to have been the father. 'I can't find the switch that turns her off,' Walker said.

'Well, at least it's clear where she gets turned on.'

The front door opened directly on to the foot of Walker's double bed. He entered the apartment then stepped aside so that I could get the full effect.

All I could say was, 'Good God!'

From every beam there hung what appeared to be brightly coloured stained-glass plates. Crimsons, turquoises, golds, emerald greens, deep blues spun lazily at the end of fishing leaders. There must have been twenty-five of them ranging in diameter from five inches to fifteen inches.

'I make them,' Walker said.

They were an astonishing sight. The sun was setting behind them and the plates, hanging at eye level, appeared to be on fire. Each plate, singularly, was quite lovely. Each plate was an experiment in colour: targets whose rings were not black and white but vermilion and ochre, whose rings were not concentric, but off centre like egg yolks in a tilted skillet. Some sparkled like quartz, others seemed almost to throb. But the accumulative vision of so many plates bobbing and spinning from leaders was more bizarre than beautiful.

'They're plastic crystals,' Walker said. 'Different coloured crystals, pieces of lead, glass stripping, nuts, things I find on the beach and like ... You put them in a tray in the oven and it all melts into what looks like stained glass. When it works, it works, when it doesn't then you've got something that looks like electric dog vomit.'

'Electric dog vomit,' I said. 'That's beautiful! The next time someone asks me what you're doing out here I can tell them that you make electric dog vomit. I've never known what to tell those bastards and now I've got the answer.'

'If you'd like we can make some together. You just take one young dog ...'

'Stick your finger down his throat – or do the purists use a feather?' I asked.

'I've found my foot works very well,' he laughed. 'Come on, let me show you the rest.'

There were wood carvings from Papeéte, temple carvings from Thailand, Tahitian cloth, Samoan swords, Japanese glass fishing floats, a net hung like a four poster's canopy over Walker's bed.

'I used to have a girl up here who was terrified that a lizard would drop on her when she was asleep. That's why I put the net up.'

There was one low-backed wooden chair, a long coffee table which held a television set and a stereo. And there were books. Books on shelves. Books in bookcases. Books stacked underneath the chair, on the floor beside the bed, books on top of books next to books bracing other books. And all of them had been treated with respect.

'Let me show you your room,' Walker said.

He led me through the bathroom and into a smaller bedroom, the room in which he wrote. It was a sparse, monastic room with a narrow cot, a chair in front of the wall shelf which held his typewriter, papers, clippings, and pinned to the wall above the typewriter were more notes, papers and clippings. There were more bookcases and next to my bed, on a small table, he had placed a vase of flowers.

I picked up the vase and looked at them. 'They're so pretty,' I said. 'I've always been a little embarrassed I like flowers so much.'

'Don't be,' he said. 'Flowers are beautiful.'

'These certainly are.'

'Welcome to Hawaii, pal.'

Beneath the wall shelf, Walker had tucked his surf board. I put the flowers down and knelt to get a better look at it.

Walker stooped over beside me, 'I'll take you out surfing if you'd like.'

'It looks pretty hard.'

'Well, we'll try it if you like.' He stood up again with his hands in his pockets. 'I didn't know how tired you'd be after the flight,' he said. 'I haven't made any plans. I just thought it would be nice for the first few days if we just relaxed together, caught up with each other, and talked. There's so much I want to talk to you about.'

'Same here.'

'Look, hey, Alfred, if you want to lie down for a while, go ahead. If not, if there's something you'd rather do, or something you'd like, let me know.'

'I think what I'd really like is a drink,' I said.

And so we had a drink. And another drink. And then we just drank.

About three days later we surfaced in a bar called the Crouching Lion. Our plan that morning had been to give me a tour of Oahu; and the Crouching Lion was only a third of the way around the island. We still had all the cane and pineapple fields to go.

'You know,' Walker said, 'I don't really like to drink this much.'

'Christ, I don't either.'

'I honestly don't think I've averaged one drink a month until you came here.'

'Then why have we been drinking so much?' I asked.

'I thought you liked to,' Walker said.

'I do. But not this much. I thought you wanted to.'

'Me?' Walker asked. 'To tell you the truth I don't really drink at all now. The only thing I do is occasionally smoke some dope.'

'What kind of dope?'

Walker saw my look and said, 'Oh, hey pal, don't worry, really. I'm off the hard stuff for good. I just smoke grass – and maybe some hash when it comes in. I want you to try some and then it won't seem like such a big deal. In the first place it's much better for you than alcohol, and in the second place, it makes you feel really good. Don't believe all that crap about if you smoke marijuana you're going to become a heroin addict. It isn't so. That's like saying if you drink chocolate milkshakes you're going to become an alcoholic. You don't think I'd try to turn you into something that I thought would be bad for you, do you?'

'I'm pretty used to drinking . . .'

'There was a time when you used to be pretty scared of jumping from the top rafters of our barn, too,' Walker said, 'but you got over that.'

'Yeah, but to be honest, I never liked it.'

'Shit, I never did either!' Walker laughed. 'I can't remember why I did it.'

'I don't know why *you* did it. I did it because if I didn't, you wouldn't allow me into your elite commando troop.'

'You wouldn't fall for that again, would you? I mean if I told you that unless you smoked a number you couldn't be in my elite commando troop . . .?'

'But why do you need to smoke dope?'

'Come on, Alfred, I don't *need* to smoke it. I smoke grass because I really like it. It makes me feel good. Drinking makes me feel bad. Please, don't make such a big deal out of it. I'll tell you what. Tonight, when we get back to the apartment, I'll roll you a number and you can try it. Don't expect much the first time. If you don't like it, don't smoke it. But in the meantime, why don't we cut down on this drinking, hey?'

'By God, that's a fine idea.'

And so, that night in Walker's apartment, I smoked my first marijuana. I sat on the edge of his bed very studiously, very seriously, and took deep, dark, golden lungfuls of it and held it down and I waited for something to happen. Walker and I shared the first number and when it had burned down to a roach he showed me how to load the roach into the tip of a regular cigarette and very calmly and deliberately I rolled the tobacco out of the tip of my cigarette and with what I knew was a surgeon's precision I tamped the roach down into what was now the empty tube of paper at the top of the cigarette. I looked at Walker and he gave me a light, and I smoked all of the roach, too.

'How do you feel?' Walker asked me.

'Thirsty,' I said.

'What would you like?'

'I'll get it,' I said and stood upright in the middle of Walker's spinning plastic crystal plates and instantly I became wrapped in fishing leaders like Gulliver trapped by the Lilliputians. Walker just looked at me for a long moment and then he said, 'It's very becoming on you, Alfred. Maybe a few alterations here and there, but you ought to consider wearing it right out of the store.'

It took us twenty minutes to get me untangled and during that time Walker and I laughed until our insides ached. I had never felt better, more happy, more relaxed. Walker was wrong that marijuana was no big deal. It was great. I loved it. I don't think Walker and I drank anything but wine again.

When I think back on that first week in Hawaii, I think of all the friends of Walker that I met: the beach boys, the skin divers, the men at the boatyard, the surfers, the girl at the bank who cashed my cheque and was talked into accepting one of Walker's kittens. I think of all the Hawaiians, the Portuguese, the Chinese, the Tahitians, the resident *haoles*, and how much they loved Walker. And I can remember so well how he would introduce me to them: 'This is one of my best friends,' he would say, 'and incidentally, my brother.'

'Yo' bruddah, no kiddin'?' the beach boys would ask.

'My only full brother,' Walker would say.

And they would look at our difference in height and slap Walker on the back and laugh, 'Hey, bruh', wha' hoppen to you, eh?'

And they would all be so *nice* because I was Walker's brother. They would offer to give me free surfing or skin-diving lessons, take me out on the catamarans or outrigger canoes. If Walker were away with someone else and they saw me sitting alone on the beach, they would come down and sit with me and ask me about Spain, about myself, how I liked Hawaii. I couldn't get over how many people knew him, how many friends he had who loved and trusted him. Walker had not had many friends when he had lived in New York, at least not many were left.

Once, waiting in line to buy a soft drink at the beach cafeteria on Waikiki, the Hawaiian woman behind the counter said, 'What would you like, Walker?' calling me by my brother's name. She didn't know mine, but she liked Walker and knew I was Walker's brother. And I was flattered to be called Walker for it meant she counted us as the same. And that was nice.

And then, of course, there were the 'hard-bodies': the twenty-year-old beach bunnies from L.A. with silver-blonde hair and incredible figures. They were all so wholesome looking, so very young, so clean, living in a sort of apprentice hippy world where 'oh wow!' and 'gosh!' and an obscenity were equally favourable synonyms, where sarcasm was still a major defence against a world measured by put downs and put ons and where 'out of sight' was the greatest compliment. They were fascinating to me because I had never seen their type before.

'Oh wow I feel just *awful*!' one of them told me one morning on the beach. 'The party last night was really too much. I mean it was absolutely out of sight.'

'Did you have a good time?' I asked, always the unwitting straight man.

'Like I don't know if I did or not. I don't even know what happened. All I know is that my other two room-mates never made it home.'

'You have two room-mates?'

'I don't know why I drink so much. I must have some sort of compulsion. I can't see why night after night I utterly destroy myself. It's just a totally futile existence.'

'Yes, I suppose it must seem that way,' I said.

'Hey, you're not putting me down, are you?'

'No, I don't think so.'

'Sometimes I really feel like everyone's trying to put me down,' she said. And she rolled over on to her side towards me and my mind boggled at the expanse of young bosom her bikini left exposed. Watching her settle herself more comfortably was like witnessing the surf rolling in.

'I mean it,' she continued, 'all I really want to do is paint. And at college my art class instructor is always trying to put me down by telling me my stuff is terrible. I know it isn't very good, but a person has to learn somewhere, don't I? And I've improved a lot. Everyone says so – except for the art instructor and he's got this thing about technique. And really, it's all such a drag, really. A circus, really. Especially college. Everyone fooling around, taking LSD trips or sleeping around. And it scares me, you know?'

'What does?'

'Taking acid,' she said. 'I mean suppose I dropped and wigged right out of my mind.'

'Then don't do it.'

'But everyone else does,' she said and rolled onto her back. 'It seems so stupid for me not to.'

'Does it seem stupid for you not to take acid because you're scared or because some one else would think you were scared.'

'I am scared! Not by sleeping around, that's a matter of personal choice. But taking acid is something else. Something else entirely. And yet I would hate to miss what could possibly be a major experience in my life.

"You keep reading about kids who drop acid and go out of windows and fifteen floors to the major experience below."

'Sometimes going out of windows seems like a good idea,' she said. She rolled over onto her side again and took off her dark glasses, 'I mean, here I am. I've played around with pot, I've slept with maybe six guys,' she put back her dark glasses, 'exactly six to be honest, I've been drinking a lot lately. And I'm twenty years old and I've done all these things now and I can't help but wonder what I'll be like ten years from now – if there is a ten years from now.'

And on and on she went about identity problems, IBM cards, multi-universities, divorces, California, abortion, drugs, suntan oils, never demanding an answer or even polite interjections until quite seriously she said, 'I guess I've talked about myself long enough. Tell me, what do you think of me?'

'I adore you,' I said.

'You're putting me on.'

'I wish to God I were,' I said.

All the beach bunnies were in love with Walker, who rejoiced in them. He was not in love with them – nor would they have wanted him to be. Instead, he would swoop among them, golden bearded, yellow sun-glassed, tanned and happy, and affectionate and compassionate backboard for their desperate and unrequited love. He always treated them gently, tried not to let them hurt themselves, and no one was burned. And that was nice, too.

And so what we really did, Walker and I, that first week in Hawaii was just get used to each other. From that first day on it was obvious he was not on heroin. He looked extremely well. He had that deep tan, of course, as would anyone after two years in Hawaii, and a tan could be deceptive. But his body was in good condition. His eyes were clear. His hands steady. No sniffles. No hunger for candy. And most important, he seemed at peace – far more at peace than I was. There was that Americans Abroad veneer I still had to lose, that hardness, suspiciousness, defensiveness. A thaw had to set in. And so, during the days I lay on the beach and thawed. And during the nights Walker and I smoked a number and talked. Walker had become a very good cook. So he cooked and I washed up. It worked out fine.

So much had happened during those two years we had not seen each other. We had both changed. And gradually we were able to talk to each other about it. We never laughed about it. How can you laugh about heroin? Talking to each other was difficult and demanding because there was so much to say without there being the proper words to say it. But it would have been so much more difficult had we not been brothers. Clearly, we did still think the same; therefore, we could avoid having to continually stop and explain. We were brothers, and neither asked the other to 'define your terms'. A verbal shorthand sufficed.

And we listened to each other.

We did not take each other for granted, which is what happens too often in families. The brother with whom one grows up is quite different ten years later – or he damn well ought to be! Walker was as interested in learning what I had become, as I was interested in him. There were no attempts to *con* one another. There was no need. For there developed that first week a renewed sense of trust, of respect, of privacy, of camaraderie between us. We could tell each other what we felt confident that the other would try to understand, because the other wanted to understand. We gave each other the benefit of the doubt.

One afternoon in the beginning of my second week in Hawaii, Walker took me for a walk along a beach and seawall to Doris Duke's house. Huge, black lava blocks had been cut to form a wall at least fifteen feet high and the top of the wall was a tangle of barbed wire. The few trees near the wall were studded with barbed wire also. A breakwater and cove had been constructed from these same lava blocks. The house was empty, the cove which provided a relatively safe and calm dock for a motor-launch was unused except for Japanese fishermen who scuttled crab-like up and down the rocks clinging by their big toes to cast their nets or lures. As Walker and I walked along the wall we came to a large black iron door and metal grille, and we stopped.

'When I first came here two years ago,' Walker told me, 'there was an enormous mastiff behind this wall. And I would walk along to just about where we're standing now and the dog would hear me coming, or smell me somehow. And I'd hear it run. I could hear its breath, its feet coming closer and when I'd come to this door it would throw itself against it. Every day for a month I'd hear that dog snarling behind that door. It was terrifying. And then, suddenly, the dog didn't come any more. It wouldn't be there when I came to the door. It had simply disappeared.

'I made myself walk just to pass the time,' Walker continued, 'to keep myself away from drugs. And somewhere along my second month a small white dog would meet me on the beach and walk along with me. I never knew to whom the pup belonged, but I'd find him every day waiting for me on the beach; and we'd keep each other company, walk along the breakwater to the end and back. Then he'd leave me and I'd go home, and I'd made it through another day without heroin.

'Well, one afternoon,' Walker said, 'around the end of the

second month, as the little dog and I were walking along the wall, I heard that mastiff again, just its breath, just about where we're at now. And the mastiff hit that door here so hard I saw the metal give. And the little white dog was so terrified that it jumped into the sea and started swimming out. It didn't get far. The waves are rough here and the undertow sucked the pup down. There wasn't anything I could do to save it, it all happened so fast, and the little dog never came back up. It never came up. And I sat down right where we are now and cried. It was the first time I cried in ten years, pal. The first time I had felt sorry for anyone but myself. I could feel real tears running down my cheeks, not dry heaves or anything else, just honest to God wet tears. And somehow, at some point while I was crying I suddenly realized I had made it. I had kicked it. I could cry.'

When we didn't feel like talking, we would sit on his bed back at the apartment and pick out tunes together on guitars. One of Walker's friends, knowing I liked to play a guitar, left hers with him for the duration of my visit. I'd play 'Georgia On My Mind' trying for the rich chords of a Jimmy Smith, Walker would play 'Samba de Uno Notte' and fill the room with Brazil. Once Max came up with a gift pint of Scotch.

During that second week we were invited to dinner by several of Walker's friends and they would quickly become my friends. We would sit in their living-rooms and talk about the ocean, watch the sunsets, listen to their music. If Walker left the room, they would tell me how much he had looked forward to my visit, how much he had spoken about me. And they'd say, 'It's a beautiful thing to see two brothers as close as you are.' When Walker walked back into the room, we would talk about the ocean again.

One morning Walker heard on the radio that the surf was running high off Diamond Head. It was the biggest swell of the summer with some waves coming in almost fifteen feet high. The sun had just risen when Walker left. And when he returned several hours later his face was flushed, his eyes so alive that I asked him what was the matter. He started to tell me about the surf and why he rides it.

'It's the most exciting – *exhilarating* experience imaginable,' he said. I was sitting on the edge of his bed and he was standing among that galaxy of spinning plates. 'I was alone out there for about two hours. And when you're alone, when the waves are running high you know that if you get badly hurt, or go under, or a shark gets you, there's no one around who can help you. Of course you could choose just to sit out beyond where the waves are breaking, not take off on anything, so really you have no one to blame but yourself if things go wrong. But somehow it doesn't seem that – no, what I mean is that it's the ultimate of being on your own, you know? I mean there's no cheque from home to bail you out.'

Walker was standing now as though he were on a surf board, one foot ahead of the other, knees slightly bent. 'There's a certain moment when you first get up on a wave,' he said and extended his arms and turned his head to one side, 'and you look down the line at something that looks like the Great Wall of China coming at you, and you wonder if you're going to make it or if it's going to snuff you and at that point you suddenly join power with the wave,' he slapped his arms down to his side, 'and honest to God, honest to God it's the most extraordinary Zen moment in all my years of experience. And what's more, hey, it happens on every wave I take off on, every time there's a large swell. This power, this feeling of being one with the wave, becoming part of the ocean – It's extraordinary. It really is.' Walker sat down on his bed next to me. 'I swear Alfred it's as though you were making love to a new woman every time you go out.'

(I never did surf. Men sometimes know in advance how they are to die. I know I will suffocate. Either I will drown or have the air sucked out of my lungs in a fire, or perhaps I will die slowly with emphysema. But I will die because I will not have enough air. And so, I never did surf. With the cowardice which all men are heir to, I force myself to swim, to scuba, to free dive, but surfing? Dealer sticks at eighteen.)

Our days were warm and relaxed. We swam, lay on the beach, talked with whomever stopped by. We went on a tour of Pearl Harbor and Sea Life Park. We went to the zoo and read how carrot juice kept the flamingoes pink. We rode the glass elevator to the top of the Ilikai Hotel for cocktails where Trummy Young played trombone in the hotel dance band. Walker and I had loved him years ago when Jimmy Ryan's and Fifty-second Street were worth going to. And Trummy Young played 'St James Infirmary' just because he remembered, too.

And we watched sunsets. We watched sunsets from all over Oahu. We would drive to the tops of hills, sit in his blue Volkswagen, smoke a number, and talk about buying a house on one of the other islands. We'd talk about buying a Tahiti ketch and sailing it around the world. We talked about how we had always wanted to do something together and how stupid it was for us not to, since at last we were free. And when we became bored with the rinky-dink of Honolulu, we left for the smaller island, Maui, and stayed in three-dollar-a-night rooms over Lahaina bar.

Walker had almost as many friends on Maui: the man who ran the diving equipment shop, the enormous girl who worked the fried chicken stand, the bartender at the Lahaina Broiler, the waitress at the Pioneer Inn, and so many others, all of whom were warm, open and good people who were obviously pleased to see my brother again. At Walker's request, I had brought with us to Maui all of his notebooks and jottings and pages from a book he was trying to write. I read them all one afternoon while he was surfing, and that evening we decided to treat ourselves to a good dinner and another long talk. So, we went to the Broiler, had a bottle of wine at our table while the ocean beat at us below and we watched the setting sun flip colours into the clouds like a man skimming cards into a hat.

'What did you think of it?' Walker asked me.

'I think there's a good book in it. The Tahiti sections seem very strong. I didn't realize you knew Tahiti so well.'

'All of the islands are changing so rapidly now it's hard to know anything well. But I think I knew that part of Tahiti pretty well ... Do you think I could get an advance from a publisher?'

'If you did,' I smiled, 'you'd never finish the book.'

'I know, pal,' Walker said.

'How long have you been working on it now?'

'Off and on, mostly off for about five years. A long time, now.'

'Do you think you'll ever finish it?'

'I'd like to ...'

We were both silent – I, a little embarrassed because my question had embarrassed him; he, a little embarrassed because it was the sort of question a parent would ask. Suddenly Walker said, 'Hey, pal, I'd really like to know what you think of me.'

And we both laughed because I had told him about the 'hard-body' on the beach and her, 'I've talked about myself long enough ...'

'But I really mean it,' Walker said, 'you're my brother and my best friend. You'd be honest.'

I sat there looking out at the ocean. 'What do I think of you? Jesus, Walker, I don't know if I could answer that. I could give you something like a horoscope reading – a bit of good news here, a bit of bad news there ...'

'Try, please.'

I looked at my brother, his eyes so deep and rich now, so different from the death they held for so many years. I looked at the lines in his face that were already tracing the same pattern as the lines on our mother's. I looked at the colour of his skin, not pale and waxy, but red-brown, burnished and taut.

'Try,' he repeated.

'But you're far more than a brother to me. Anything I could tell you, you already know.'

'Like what?'

'Well, to begin with, I think you should get out of Hawaii. We both know its beautiful, that the people love you and that in a sense you love them –'

'I do, I really do.'

'But you should get out of here. You've never been in better shape physically or mentally. For the first time in God knows how many years you're okay now. You don't need any props. And Hawaii is your last prop. It's beautiful, everyone loves you, the sunsets are magnificent, and it's all very nice, but I don't think it's going to be enough for you because there is nothing going on in Hawaii. Nothing! The only thing Hawaii is, is beautiful. But –'

'Nothing's going on anywhere, pal. It all goes on inside your head.'

'Then you should get your head to a place where you don't have so many distractions. If you really want to write this book, then leave Hawaii because you're not going to do it here. There's no reason to. You've got too many excuses not to. A friend is passing through. Your brother is visiting for a month. A girl needs some advice, and she's got a friend who'll need some advice next. A guy wants you to go to another island with him. You see? I mean, look nobody can write this book for you.'

'Do you think it's a good book?'

'You haven't finished it yet, Walker. I think there's a good book in it, but you won't really know until you finish it. And you've got to finish it.'

'I will,' he said.

'When?'

He was silent.

'Don't you see, Walker? It's such a waste, such a goddam shame. Here you've got this wonderful mind – my God! How many people have said that to you? – and you're just letting it idle. You're not doing anything with it. So finish the book. Finish something. It could be a very good book. The worst thing in the world I could do would be to tell you that it might be good when all it is is trash. But it damn well ought to be good. You can write. And after all you've been through, you have enough material for two or three others, but you'll never know until you finish the first. And what you have to do is eliminate every excuse you have for not working on it, then do it. Write the damned thing, not for anyone else but for you.'

Walker laughed, 'I'll be damned if I'll ever ask you for advice when you're drinking wine again.'

'The point is you won't settle for not being the best. You're afraid to commit yourself. You wanted to surf the best and you made it to the semi-finals in the championship, and when it came to competing with the other semi-finalists, you didn't show up.'

'Oh hell, Alfred, the surf was up on the other side of the island. I didn't care about the competition, about winning. I went to the better surf.'

'Come on, you didn't compete because you might have lost, you might have committed yourself to being measured, someone would have found out just how good you are and –'

'Hey, pal, wait a minute,' Walker interrupted. 'Wait a minute now, what's *really* eating you?'

'*You* are! Damn it, you asked me what I thought, and I'm trying to tell you. You're not some little "hard-body" on the beach, you're my brother. If you want, I could just as easily give you a string of compliments. You're one of the nicest, most thoughtful, generous, kind and gentle men I have ever known. You're beautiful, you really are. All of this is true. For every bad thing I could say about you, I could find something equally good. There are an infinite number of bad things you could say about me. Both of us have done more than our share of hurting other people, and neither of us has any reason to be proud of it. But a simple fact of life is that we are both going to hurt plenty more people, no matter how hard we might try not to, because we are two very cold people. And such, my pal, is another fact of life. We can try not to be cold, and we do try not to be, but you and I have a great deal in common. Down deep, down in the innermost Dwarf-soul of our beings, we are *cold*. And we don't let anyone in there.'

'I don't know what you're talking about.'

'The hell you don't Walker. For all our talk of love and warmth and generosity and so forth, we know just exactly to the measured centimetre how much we give and how much we take. We can dazzle people with kindness and thoughtfulness and generosity and warmth, because we were trained to. We were brought up that way. We have no alternative but to be that way and we do it absolutely effortlessly, because it doesn't cost us a thing. I don't know, maybe I'm just talking about myself. But one thing I'm sure of, we both know how to hurt.'

'I haven't hurt anyone in a long time,' Walker said quietly.

'Jesus Christ! Neither have the surviving guards from Auschwitz!'

'Now that's a really stupid thing to say, Alfred. I must admit I'm surprised to hear you say something like that.'

'Ah, Walker,' I said, 'I love you. You're my brother, my only brother. All my life I've envied you, been jealous of you, loved you. If there is such a thing as a Younger Brother Complex I've got it. I've always wanted to be like you, to be as smart as you, as clever, as great looking, as successful with women. But I'm not going to be. We're two different people. I'm twenty-seven going on forty-five. You're thirty-one saying you're twenty-six. Both of us want to make up for lost time, time we've wasted trying to be what we think others would want us to be. So don't be angry with me. What did you want me to say? You asked me and I really wanted to tell you what I thought so that we really could be as close as we keep telling everybody we are.'

'But we really are close,' Walker said. 'You're my best friend, and I'd like you to know we're close without having to pick it apart to find out why.'

'I'm not trying to find out why, Walker, I'm trying to find out how close is *"close"*. I don't mean to take measurements, I'm not asking you to prove it or anything stupid like that. But when we say that we're close I want to know who we think "we" are, that's all. And if I know who "we" are then I – oh, the hell with it. I think all I'm trying to say, to go back to the very beginning, when I told you I thought you ought to leave Hawaii – The problem here is that everybody here in Hawaii thinks you're great. They all love you and think you're great. But I *know* you're great, and what gets me so goddam mad is that you won't take a chance on proving it. Not to anyone else, the hell with them, I'm talking about you convincing yourself. I want this book of yours to be so good, that you can get out from under it forever. All your life you've said that you were a writer, but you've never believed it. You've been around Lahaina, you've been around Honolulu and you've seen all those people who call themselves writers and you don't believe they're writers any more than I do. You don't become a writer by filling up little spiral notebooks with great ideas for stories or bits of dialogue or suggested scenes, that's a cop out, it really is. All you're doing is fooling yourself. I want you to do this book, and I want it to be

119

so good that all the people you've known will be proud of you, too. So that they'll be able to go around saying, "I knew him when..." Do you see what I mean? I want them to be proud of you, too. God knows I am. I've been so filled with pride in you on these damn islands that I've wanted to burst. But I've been proud not because all the people love you, or because you've got parts of a very good book written, or because you've got a great mind and can surf so well. I'm proud of you because you kicked your habit. You kicked it, Walker, and that takes more guts than anything I can imagine. If there were a Congressional Medal of Honour which I were able to award you, I'd do it. Because you've given me something better than anything you can imagine. You've given me the chance to tell our mother that it's all over. It's all over. "Walker's all right." And by God ... by God, that's nice!'

'But it's not enough ...'

'It's one hell of a start.'

'I wish you could stay here, pal,' Walker said. 'We could buy that Tahiti ketch and just sail anywhere we wanted. There are so many places I'd like to show you. I want you to see Papeéte before it's ruined. We could go to India. We could go to Kyoto. You've always wanted to go there.'

'I can't. I got an appointment with a publisher in New York.'

'I know you do.'

'Look, why don't you come back to New York for Christmas? Stay with me. See the family. I'd like you to do that, it could be fun.'

'I'd really like to,' he said.

'Then why don't you? Why don't we plan on it?'

'I don't know – New York's so cold. You forget I've been out here for two years. I don't know if I could stand that cold.'

'But New York's so pretty at Christmas. The big department store windows. Rockefeller Center and the old men skating with their hands behind their backs. The Christmas trees on Park Avenue –'

At that moment, the man who rented motor scooters to tourists came over to our table and said quietly, 'It's okay, Walker, I got the acid, enough for your brother and the rest of us. Two cubes and a cap and I think the cap's as strong as the one you have, so you and your brother take those. They're better.'

And there it was.

Walker and I had talked about LSD, he had taken it a few times, and I had said that I would like to try it. Why? I suppose for much the same reason as the young girl on the beach – 'the great experience'. I had not had many *great* experiences during the past years. I knew, of course, that the experience could be a bad one. And taking LSD scared me far more than surfing, because even if I fell off a surfboard the ocean was a danger with which I believed I could cope. But if I lost my balance on LSD, who knew into what ocean I might fall? Still, I wanted to try. Perhaps it was just to take a chance, any chance. Perhaps it was because I had such contempt for my mind. Perhaps because I was still the little boy on the top rafter of the barn whose brother, far below, was yelling, 'Don't be so chicken! I did it, you have to do it, too!' And even though I knew I was no longer a little boy, that I did not have to do anything I did not wish to, I suppose there must have been that sense of *proof-nécessaire*.

I looked across the table at my brother, and I wondered whether I could trust him. It was drugs all over again. The only difference was that this time I was being asked to join. Why? If we really were so close, would he be deliberately asking me to risk my head? Was this closeness all a myth? Or was Walker asking me to do this for myself, as he wanted me to believe.

There had been a lot of trouble getting the acid in Hawaii. And I suppose I had hoped that we would be unable to find any. And yet, when I heard Walker's friend say that he had gotten some I was happy. I told Walker that it frightened me; and he said that it was natural to be nervous, but that I shouldn't worry, because no one was more stable than me, that it was going to be a beautiful experience, a *profound* experience, one I would never forget. Still – why do it?

Maybe I was tired of being told no one was more stable than I was. Maybe I was tired of being such a bore to myself. All my life, it seemed to me, I had done those things which I ought to have done – without ever really considering the alternatives, or asking myself why. I knew that if I did not accept this risk, take this chance, I would never forgive myself. And Walker wanted us to do it together.

We were to drop the acid on top of Haleakala, the extinct volcano crater on Maui which the Hawaiians called 'The Birthplace of the Sun'. It was a deliberately staged trip. The sunrise from Haleakala is spectacular to begin with, but under the influence of LSD it was supposed to be incredible. Walker and his friends wanted my first trip to be a good one; and, if on the slight chance that it turned bad, that I went on a bummer, they would all be there to help me out — they would all be on acid, too. And could Walker help me out? That was the question which none of us would be able to answer until I had made the commitment, until I dropped the acid and was into the trip.

In essence, Walker was asking me to trust him. He was asking me to trust him with my mind. I looked across the table at my brother, that *fleur de mal*, that corrupt angel. What would happen between Walker and myself if I said I would not do it? The implications were obvious. But still, I could not understand why, if he had kicked heroin, he was now taking LSD?

Ultimately, however, all the questions I had raised were meaningless, because I did trust Walker. And when he told me that he wanted us to do it together, I knew it was because he wanted to share something he thought lovely with me.

'It's going to be a good, a beautiful trip, pal,' Walker said.

And I smiled uncertainly. 'I hope so.'

'It will be. You'll be fine.'

At two o'clock that morning, the bartender from the Broiler, the man who rented motor scooters, Walker and myself drove in a borrowed Volkswagen bus to the top of the Haleakala volcano crater. It was a long drive from Lahaina taking just under three hours. At eight thousand feet we crested the clouds and above us and all around us was three thousand feet more of extinct volcano, the moon, and the sky. The road curled back and forth and we alternately found ourselves tilting towards the white full moon, or skimming over the silver clouds. The higher we climbed the more beautiful and isolated it became, until upon reaching the top of Haleakala and the darkened observatory, we had the eerie sensation that there was nothing else in the world but the four of us, the Volkswagen bus, and Heaven.

We took the LSD, held the capsules or cubes under our tongues and waited for it to dissolve. We got out of the car and stamped our feet, and waved our arms to start the circulation and keep warm, then we moved away from the truck to the darkened lip of the volcano, and waited. The LSD would take effect in about thirty minutes.

As Walker and I stood overlooking the dark crater, he said, 'You know? It's strange, but all the time I've been in Hawaii, I've felt myself being drawn towards this place. But I've always saved it, held off coming here until I had a special reason. Now I know why I didn't come here before. I'm glad I waited until we were here together, pal.'

The moon was just now beginning to fade over our shoulders and into the clouds behind us. We sat down near the edge of the huge crater and ten minutes later the moon had disappeared entirely, and across the crater from us we could begin to perceive the first light of the sun as the blackness gave way to deep purples and then more gentle blues.

'How do you feel?' Walker asked me.

'Still a little nervous.'

'Don't be, pal. You're okay.'

I could feel a slight chalkiness in my mouth, a metallic taste on my tongue. It was cold on top of the volcano, and I turned up my coat collar to keep warm. The distant rim was the colour of flame now, with pink licking all around it. Below us I could see that the rim we sat on dropped down to more rims. The huge crater cupped lesser craters which contained cones cupping lesser cones like intricate Chinese boxes within boxes. Suddenly, the distant ridge exploded into white light as the sun's edge rose above the far side of Haleakala and then slowly, ever so slowly the browns and greens and yellows poured off the tops of hills and drifted like smoke into the valley below. A cone began to throb. I watched it fascinated. It seemed to be alive; the lava, stretched like a membrane, rose and fell as though it covered lungs beneath. I looked around and saw that all the cones had begun to pulse. There was a warm, alive, gentle, uninhibited friendly rhythm like a huge heartbeat all around me, a soft hush of air being inhaled and exhaled by the crater, a soothing, caressing, comforting, murmuring aliveness all about us; and timidly, cautiously, I extended my hands towards it, stretching my fingers over the edge of the crater until my fingertips were within it and I could see them pulse as the vibrations whooshed soundlessly past them. I was not afraid. I had never felt more safe, for this was the Beginning. This was before pain, before violence, before evil, before time itself began. The sun was above the distant ridge now and the whole world was lighted. The crater lay before us in its cushion of clouds, a giant goblet waiting to be filled. On a rock beside me I found a fragment of brown glass, and I picked it up and held it to the sun. The brown melted and poured down my thumb and into my palm. I passed the fragment to my brother, 'Look what it does, Walker. Look what the glass does.'

He smiled and took the sharp glass away from me.

There was a valley far away, all the way across the crater. It was greener than any of the other valleys. More friendly, too. That was where I wanted to go, but there was no hurry, because I had all the time in the world, and all that there was of the world was what we could see. The crater was our universe, and this was its dawn.

'I never knew there were so many greens before!' I said.

'Don't get hung up on colours, pal,' Walker told me. 'Tell me, what do you see?'

'The world,' I said. 'The creation of the world.'

'And we're guests!' the bartender laughed happily.

We were all smiling now, my head bobbing up and down with happiness, 'Yes, yes, yes,' I was saying, 'we are all guests!'

'And it's nice?' Walker asked me.

'Sure it's nice,' I said. 'And you know? ... You know?'

'Know what, pal?' Walker asked me.

I raised my arms to encompass, to enfold, no really to hug, to hug the entire creation, 'He's doing it exactly right! He's doing it exactly right!'

'You wouldn't change it?' Walker asked me.

I looked at my brother. He was smiling at me – no, *with* me. 'No, I wouldn't change it,' I said. 'Even if He asked me, I wouldn't. For a moment, for a little while I thought that the valley over there might do with a little more green, but it's okay now. It's just exactly right.'

'Good,' Walker said, 'I'm glad that it's the way you wanted it. That's nice.'

'Yes, it is nice,' I said.

I felt so much joy sitting there on the edge of the world that I had to cross my arms over my stomach, hold myself in so that I would not explode. I was glad, too, that the others were there with Walker and myself, it was too beautiful not to share, and I loved the joy they felt, too.

The bartender stood up and walked behind us to a flat rock. 'I would like to perform a little dance to the sun,' he announced.

'That would be very nice,' my brother said.

And very slowly, the bartender began to dance. He stood with his arms outstretched waiting until he was certain of the rhythm, then, having caught it, kept time with his fingers. Snap – snap – snap – *Snap!* – *Snap!* – *SNAP!* – *SNAP!* His foot began to move. SNAP!-tap-shuffle, shuffle – SNAP!-tap-shuffle, shuffle, SNAP!-tap-shuffle, shuffle, faster he danced, faster and faster, round and round, lightly he danced, never missing a step, never off the beat, round and round and we smiled and laughed watching him, clapped hands to his rhythm. And it was so lovely, so moving that I had to turn away, for I wished I could dance, too, to somehow show my appreciation. And I still could not. I turned back to look at my valley, my friendly valley far off in the distance. I wondered whether the people who lived there would be happy, too. I hoped so.

Somebody tugged my arm. 'Hey,' a man said, and he tugged my arm again. 'Hey, buddy, excuse me. Do you have change for the cigarette machine?'

The cigarette machine?

I wondered how there came to be a cigarette machine at the top of the world during Creation. And then I smiled, because of course there would be. And probably a coke machine, too. I looked up at the man, and he looked nice, so I gave him all my cigarettes.

'No, no,' he laughed, 'all I need is change for a quarter.'

I gave him all my change, about seventy cents. 'Take what you need,' I said. 'What you don't want, you can return to me, if you'd like.'

The man went away and I looked back at the valley. I saw that Walker had taken his shoes off and had buried his toes in the soft ash, and I did the same. The ash felt warm, and I wriggled my toes into it and liked the earth colours the ash turned my feet. I curled my toes down and dug into the ash and the vibrations came up through my feet and entered me as if somehow I had plugged myself into life-energy itself. I simply sat there feeling the heartbeat of God, and I knew that if I had a choice of that precise moment in my life into which I would want to be frozen and fixed eternally, that moment was now. For now was pure joy. I was watching God create the Heaven and the Earth and I was His guest, His *guest*! I didn't know how it had come about, did not even dare ask why. I merely sat there and accepted it, feeling unabashedly joyous and humble and so entirely happy that tears came to my eyes.

'You all right, pal?'

I looked up at my brother who was leaning, concerned, over me.

I could not speak. All I could do was nod, and a tear jarred loose and ran down my cheek. I looked back up at him to talk to him, to ask him why we had been chosen, and he was gone. In his place more people had appeared. There was a little boy who squatted toad-like on a rock above us who kept repeating over and over again, 'Are-you-hippies-Are-you-hippies-Are-you-hippies?'

And a woman's voice behind me was filled with venom and scorn, 'I told my husband, Mr Harris, be sure we have enough gas. But did he pay any attention to me? No, of course, he didn't and so we ran out of gas half-way up the mountain and missed the sunrise entirely.'

A flash of silver beside me, 'Here's your change back, thanks.'

Didn't they know what was going on?

Walker reappeared again and touched my shoulder, 'Let's get out of here.'

The four of us followed a path down into the crater. I told them about my valley and that I thought it would be nice if we all went there, and they agreed. The path down the lip of the crater was narrow so we had to walk single file. The bartender and the man who rented motor-scooters gradually pulled ahead of Walker and myself because I kept stopping to pick up rocks. Each rock was more beautiful than the last. Each rock was a universe within itself, a cornucopia of colours and textures, and I gave them all to Walker. I followed him down into the crater and watched the wind blowing through his hair, his beard dancing away from his cheeks, his elbows sticking out as he bounced down the path.

And I loved him because I knew for generations and generations back in all our other lives we had always been brothers, as we would be brothers in future lives as well.

Another rock caught my eye, and I picked it up and hurried to catch up with him.

'You know, pal,' he said, as I handed him the rock, 'all these years I've been the older brother. I've always led and you've always followed. Well, I've just been thinking that I'd like to follow you for a while. You're my best friend and I want to be your best friend. I'd like you to lead.'

'I know,' I said, 'but I like following you. I like you to lead. It's okay. And besides, farther on where the path gets wider, we can walk side by side.'

'I'd really like that,' he said.

George
Dethriffe's
Book

After making love to his wife, the peasant suddenly struck her full in the face, knocking her from the bed on to the floor.

'Why did you do that?' his wife asked.

'If I knew why,' he said, 'I would have killed you.'

– Russian joke.

Chapter Eleven

The present younger generation whom I see on weekends at the Winander Club describe me as being up-tight since I fall into that category of persons who neither lose their self-control nor their inhibitions. These same young men and women tell me that I should relax, be more natural and in a tone that occasionally seems to me to be patronizing, they have urged me 'to do my own thing'. But when I explain to them that I am naturally up-tight and that my thing is to have self-control, they look upon me with the same calculating eye that I associate with those African game wardens who spray paint on certain old and useless animals so that hunters will recognize these beasts as selected for extinction.

I have never had many friends – acquaintances, yes, those men with whom I stand at the Winander Club bar or with whom I sit on the commuter train and share solutions to the *Times* crossword puzzle and the *Daily News* 'jumble' – close friends escape me. With other contemporaries I have passed through varying stages of closeness; but with Alfred Moulton I have always felt a comforting constancy. He is, perhaps, my best and only friend.

During my Groton and Harvard days I used to envy those men to whom the others in my class naturally gravitated. I don't mean those ones who in other schools might have been voted most popular, there was always something a little fishy about them; I mean, rather, those men whom others described as being by nature open and friendly. As the younger generation has pointed out, I am not an open person and as for being friendly – well, I'm not even sure what that means.

I do not intend to examine too closely why Alfred and I are friends. I am grateful that we are. I think, simply, our different interests contribute to it. I am incapable (or perhaps unwilling) to become too close to someone with whom I share business interests. It isn't only that old chestnut about business and friendship not mixing. It's also that I am so entirely involved in business during the working day (or was, until this difficulty between Alice and myself became so all-consuming) that I don't care much for discussing business in the evening. It's a little like playing poker for chips and not money: what's the point? And since Alfred never talks about business beyond a polite question or two we get along just fine. I don't believe I've ever met an individual with less business sense than Alfred. Alfred used to be so flattered that anyone wanted to publish something he had written that he would practically give it away. Fortunately his literary agent put an end to that. His novel, *Heirs to the Myth* which was published in 1964, made the best-seller list, it was a book club selection and I think Alfred probably made quite a large amount of money for a first novel. I read it and liked it. But because I know Alfred so well and because the main character, it seemed to me, resembled Alfred rather closely, it was difficult for me to determine how much was factual and how much was fiction. However, I find making the same sort of judgements about stock market reports just as difficult.

At any rate, Alfred seems to be doing all right. I keep seeing his articles on civil rights and ban-the-bomb protests in various magazines. I thought his *Esquire* piece on the California drug culture was fascinating. And the one he did a couple of years ago on turning thirty was nice, a bit light of weight, perhaps, but probably what the *Times* wanted. Alfred seems to have developed his own style of reporting: a bit less frenzied than Tom Wolfe's and less ego-oriented than Mailer's and unfortunately nowhere near as good. If I have a criticism of his articles it is that Alfred seems incapable of taking anything very seriously. He seems as awed by the discovery that feeding flamingoes carrots will keep them pink as he was that chromosome damage occured among those who use aspirin and coffee in the same proportion as those who took LSD. But maybe I am not being entirely fair. Even though some of the pieces have seemed facile, particularly the one on Pope Paul's *Humane Vitae*, the ones he did on the last August's Democratic National Convention in Chicago and the one on the murder of Robert Kennedy were very touching. Good and angry and sad.

Well, I have missed Alfred. And that is why when his letter arrived a few days ago asking me to meet him for lunch at the Yale Club I so eagerly complied.

I left my office at 48 Wall Street at noon and walked enjoying the chill in the air, the crispness of a relatively pollution-free early December morning in New York City. I started across Broadway by Trinity Church and was almost run down by a middle-aged banker driving a dented and dirty Lincoln Continental. I could see his mouth moving, his hands chopping angrily at the steering wheel. No one else was in the car. As I continued across I, too, had to prevent my lips from moving. I have caught myself lately talking more and more to myself — something I have not done since I was a child. I walked down into the Wall Street Uptown IRT subway station and waited among the candy and chewing-gum machines and 'I Got My Job Through *The New York Times*' posters for the train to come in. A group of leather-jacketed teenage boys in tight pants came crashing down the steps and bullied noisily through the turnstiles. The people on the platform with me watched nervously as the boys darted from machine to machine, ducking down to look at themselves in the mirrors above the stacks of Chiclets. Black rubber combs whipped like switchblades out of their back pockets, and they combed their long hair and snapped their chewing-gum and shouted obscenities at each other until the subway pulled in and they boarded along with the rest of us.

Across from my seat there was a poster of an ecstatic telephone operator Miss Subways whose hobbies were dancing and literature. On one side of her was a poster advertising Preparation H, and on the other an advertisement that read, 'f u cn rd ths thn u cn wr 250 wpm n en mo pa'. There were no seats left at the stop where the pretty young girl boarded and as soon as she stood holding on to the metal pole by the door, the teenage boys surrounded her. When she pushed through them to a strap not far from me, the boys moved with her, packed around her until all that was visible was her face. One of the boys began to nudge her with his thigh, another pressed himself against her back, and her eyes turned white and rolled back as though she were a tethered cow among a pack of wolves. The boys were making clicking sounds, curious almost insect noises and when the train slammed into a curve and the girl was flung back against them, one of the boys grabbed her across her breasts and I got up and wedged between her and the boys and told her to take my place. However as soon as I had gotten to my feet one of the boys took my seat, and the girl and I were left standing.

'Thanks anyway,' she said.

'How far are you going?' I asked her. At my shoulder stood one of the teenagers, his lips and jaw constantly working over the juicy fruit gum.

'I'm getting off at Fourteenth Street,' she said.

'Hey, Meester, you like my seester?' the pimply face kid said.

'I thought there were supposed to be policemen on these cars,' the girl said.

'Only at night,' I said.

'I geeve her to you. Only five dollars. You like her?'

I shifted so that my back was between him and the girl, and we rode that way in silence until the subway began to slow. The girl got off at Fourteenth Street, seats were available again, and the teenage boys wandered off to the other end of the car.

I left at Grand Central and made my way up to the main lobby. The Christmas shoppers and early week-end departure crowd were hurrying through, their faces white and tense, their lips moving, their eyes glazed. I stopped at a Union News stand to pick up a New York Post and, because my stomach was acting up, I asked the dealer for a package of Tums.

'Get them yourself,' he said.

'Where are they?'

'Yuh nuts?' he said. 'Right in front of you.'

When I handed the newsdealer a dollar, he said, 'The moon.'

'The moon?' I said.

And then, behind me, this voice said, 'The moon. The celestial body next in conspicuousness to the sun. Right? The lone satellite of the earth, orbiting around the latter from west to east, right? – in little less than a calendar month, accompanying the earth in its annual and celestially glorious revolution about the sun. Right?'

'Right,' the news man said. And it was this elderly Negro, very distinguished looking, with a quiet voice who was just standing there watching the newsdealer. The newsdealer winked at me as he handed me my change and as I turned away the dealer said, 'Jupiter.'

'Right, Jupiter,' the old Negro said. 'The fifth and largest of the planets, right? Having a mean diameter of eighty-seven thousand miles. Shining with a clear, white light; Jupiter ranks second only to Venus in planetary brightness, right?' And as I walked on, I assumed the man was discussing Jupiter's density, its orbit, its moons, and I was thinking the whole city has gone crackers. I made my way across the terminal, people knocked into me mumbling to themselves sore as hell about something, and I felt those waves of violence, of psychosis as though the city were on the edge of a nervous breakdown. When I walked out on Vanderbilt Avenue I had the feeling that suddenly every siren in New York was going off; I hurried across the street, through the Yale Club's revolving door and up the marble stairs beneath the portrait of Nathan Hale or King George III or whoever and found Alfred standing at the bar, a Martini in hand.

'Sanctuary. Sanctuary,' I said.

'Breakfast of Champions,' he said, tipping the glass towards me slightly, 'How are you? You look a bit rattled.'

'It's been a helluva ride up here,' I smiled. 'How are you?'

'Awful,' Alfred laughed.

Later, at lunch, Alfred asked his polite questions about business and I told him about having been made a partner the year before and that I was making too much money, that by the end of the year I expected to make close to seventy thousand dollars in commissions alone, that I couldn't afford to work harder because of the income tax bracket it would put me into, that I had bought Alice an emerald the size of a lima bean for her birthday and that I was handling more and more of my family's money, had been made a trustee of the Dethriffe Corporation which was my grandfather's fund, and that I had to spend a lot of time soothing great-aunts who wanted to take a chance on some hot tips they'd picked up over tea.

'Well, it sounds as though you're keeping busy,' Alfred said. 'How's my beautiful God-daughter? How old is she now?'

'Sydney? She's three. She's fine. They're both fine. Ashbel finished second in his first-grade class at the last report. They're both great. Beautiful.'

'And Winander?'

'It's not all that bad. Some of the people are nice. And the land is so beautiful, the lake, the mountain, if you could call it that, those old stone houses – they still call them "cottages" you know, fourteen bedrooms, eight servants' rooms –'

'– And the big stone wall and the big stone police gate at the entrance,' Alfred said.

'Okay, sure, but it's a beautiful place and that's why we moved there. It's a marvellous place for the children.'

'It's the worst place in the world for children!' Alfred said. 'You'll raise your children to be so out of touch with reality it's frightening. They'll be eleven before they find out there are children who have brown skin and black skin and yellow skin, too.'

'That's somewhat of an exaggeration, Alfred.'

'You mean there are black families who live in Winander?'

'Of course,' I said.

'Are they somebody's servants?'

'Yes, but there isn't any reason why any Negro family couldn't live in Winander if they wanted to. For Chrissake, Alfred, we went to school with Negroes. It's not a new thing for us.'

'Sure we did. All of us went to school with them. Until our schools ran out of Ralph Bunche's sons. I sure as hell never met any uptown blacks. I never saw any of those blacks in any of my schools.'

'"Blacks!" ... "Blacks" ... Do you remember when there used to be Negroes?'

'There still are,' Alfred said. 'They're those servants up in Winander.'

'Touché,' I laughed.

'Well, I don't mean to be fencing with you, George. It's just that I think this is really important. I think that one of the big problems we have is that all our upbringing has been shaped towards an appreciation of the past –'

'But that's perfectly natural,' I said. 'That is what is called an education. If one can understand the past then one can provide continuity with the future. One can prepare, plan –'

'And you think your children are being prepared for the future by bringing them up in Winander?'

'It's certainly better than bringing them up in a ghetto,' I said. 'At least in Winander they stand a good chance of surviving until their future. They're not going to die of an overdose of heroin in the fifth grade.'

'Don't be too sure,' Alfred said. 'Winander doesn't protect them from that.'

'What does?'

'You do,' Alfred said. 'But most of all they, themselves, do. I've seen an awful lot of children from so-called good families who are heavy into drugs. And I think one of the reasons this happens is that their drug world has more relevancy to them than the world they escaped from. What I'm trying to say is I don't think we can any longer afford this reverence for the past. There's not enough time. Our days on this planet are so limited – I'm not talking about a nuclear holocaust, George, I'm simply talking in terms of a person's life span – our days are so limited that it is all we can do to properly appreciate and participate in what is still alive and warm all around us without getting ourselves trapped in ritual behaviour that is cold and dead. My God, when I think of the damage done to my head under the guise of teaching me manners, when I think of the inhibitions I've had to shed, the meaningless behaviour patterns I've had to break, just the nonsense I've had to forget – what I mean, George, is that by living in Winander you're preserving an order that has ceased to have any meaning, that has ceased to contribute.'

'Alfred,' I said, 'you're full of shit.'

He looked at me for a moment then burst out laughing. And then I laughed too, and in a matter of minutes Alfred and I were best of friends again. We were once more boys who had grown

139

up together, instead of men who had grown apart. He sat across from me in the dining-room on the twentieth floor of the Yale Club smiling at me and I was smiling at him, and everything was fine. 'Would you like some coffee?' he asked me. 'Do you have enough time?'

'I've got plenty of time,' I said. 'How about you?'

'I've got to meet an editor at *Esquire* at three and one at *The New York Times* at four. It's only two so we've got plenty of time.'

'Well, good,' I said. 'I've really been looking forward to seeing you.'

'Me, too. How are you?'

'Me? Fine,' I said.

'How are you really?' he asked. 'How's Alice? I had a letter from someone saying that they'd seen the two of you and that you didn't seem very happy.'

'Well I don't know how much happiness has to do with anything,' I said. 'But I'm seeing a psychiatrist about the marriage.'

'Is Alice going, too?'

'Not yet,' I said. 'She'll probably go later.'

'Then it's pretty serious?'

'It's pretty awful,' I said. 'I mean, everything would be great, if only I were happily married. But I'm not. And so I see a psychiatrist and it's all so obvious that I feel as though I were passing through the stations on my way to some plastic glow-in-the-dark Jesus Christ on the cross.'

'What is the trouble between you and Alice? Is it something you can talk about?'

'Not very easily,' I said. 'Every time I go to the psychiatrist I have to attempt to articulate the pain that Alice and I cause each other, I'm left with words like *despair* and *loneliness* and – and feelings which have no words but which just tear at me. I don't know what it is that we do to each other, I only know that there hasn't been any joy ... or love ... or sharing ... and I know, I know I do the same to Alice. And that's so sad. So awful. And we make each other feel so terribly lonely. I never knew – another cliché, Alfred – I never knew how lonely it could be living with someone else. And I never knew what it would be like to feel so guilty all the time.'

'Why do you feel guilty? Is there any reason why you should?'

'Well, sure, Alfred, there have been things I've been guilty of. I've had two affairs in the eight years we've been married and Alice knows about them both. She found out because she went through some papers of mine and found letters written by the girls to me, or carbons of the letters I had written them and –'

'Why?' Alfred asked.

'"Why?" what? Why did Alice look for them? Or why was I silly enough to have saved them?'

'Why'd you keep carbons?'

'. . . I kept the carbons because they provided continuity between the letters. Questions I asked in one letter, she answered in another, that's why. Oh hell, I always save letters. Particularly letters from people who mean a lot to me. I have all the letters you've ever written me. I save letters the way other people save photographs. And I saved those letters because I was proud that these women loved me. The letters were a sort of – well, not proof, evidence maybe. A token? I don't know what the word is. The letters were a contact with them. I used to take the boat out into the middle of the lake and read those letters over and over again. I've done so many idiotic things in my life I feel virtually no embarrassment in telling you about that. I used to take the old Chris-Craft out into the middle of the lake, cut the engines and just drift alone and read the letters. And by reading those letters I could re-create, if only for a moment, the joy, all the love, the happiness that the girl and I had shared. I never kept them to flaunt in front of Alice, or to show to anybody else, I kept them because it meant there was still a part of me Alice hadn't absorbed. Devoured. I kept them for reassurance, you know? So that I could tell myself that at least there was someone, some woman who didn't think I was so awful, such an ogre or whatever. And as for repressed or subconscious desires to get caught, I can assure you, getting caught by Alice was no great treat.'

'How did she catch you?' Alfred asked.

'Well, that's what I don't understand. I don't understand what made Alice look for those letters when she did. I mean we'd had a damn pleasant evening in the city, dinner, at the Maison-

141

ette – that we went to a friend's opening at a gallery. He did very well, sold four big canvases and several pen and ink drawings. And then Alice and I and the friend and his wife went off to Arthur's, and then we went back to their place for a nightcap, and finally Alice and I drove back down to the apartment I keep these days in the city. We left reasonably early for the sole reason of making love. I'd gotten a nurse to stay with the children, and Alice and I were to have the weekend in New York by ourselves, to have a good time, to try to recapture whatever we'd lost. Anyway, I dropped her off at the apartment building and went off to park the car. It took maybe fifteen minutes at the most, and by the time I'd returned to the apartment and let myself in, she'd found the letters. Well, if I'd been stupid enough to leave them up in Winander, or to have left them around the apartment in the open, on top of my desk, or tucked under the blotter, or even under the handkerchiefs in the bureau drawer, then maybe I'd understand how she might have accidentally come upon them. But, I was gone as I said maybe fifteen minutes at the most, and Alice found them closed up in an empty typewriter case which was inside my closet. And the closet was closed, the case was between a tape recorder and the wall, underneath a briefcase. And I don't have the faintest idea how she found them so quickly. I don't know how she did it! All I know is that when I opened the door to that apartment and walked inside, I found Alice standing in the centre of the room with the letters in her hand and she was shaking, literally shaking all over like one of those goddam Walt Disney volcanoes in *Fantasia*. As soon as she saw me she started screaming, "YOU SON –" sorry "you son – You sonuvabitch, you fucked her right here!" And she'd read aloud parts of the letters – not just read them, she'd scream them at me: "'My darling George, I love the feel of you –' The Feel Of You you sonuvabitch!" and she kept on screaming – this is no exaggeration, Alfred, for about fifteen minutes. Fifteen minutes at the top of her lungs. Now, maybe that doesn't sound like a long time to you, but you just try being screamed at for fifteen minutes and you'll see how long it is! And the neighbours – there was this old Jewish couple in the apartment next to ours, and the old lady called and Alice answered the phone and in this absolutely dead calm voice said that she wasn't being murdered, or raped or whatever and hung up, WHAP! No, wait, "I'm not in danger," is what she said, and all the time I'm trying to quiet her. And the superintendent came up with two doormen because the other neighbours were complaining. It's one of those apartment buildings with paper-thin walls. And they knocked on the front door, and Alice ran into the bathroom and locked the bathroom door. And she kept reading aloud, screaming those letters. And I had to tell the super that it was all just a misunderstanding. Christ, I don't know what I told him. It was one of those scenes that only a Marcello Mastroiani could have handled. And throughout my explanation to them Alice was reading from those letters. Finally, the super went away, and Alice stayed in the bathroom. She wasn't screaming now, just being loud. And I was thinking about how all the neighbours were clustered around the air vent that went from the bathroom into the hall, clustered in a circle as though the vent were a TV screen. And it went on for six hours. Six hours! All about how I'd taken advantage of her, how I'd wronged her by having an affair with that bitch so-and-so – And, hell, you can understand why, can't you, Alfred? I mean you can see why I'd want to go to bed, to be with, to love someone else, can't you?'

Alfred didn't say a word.

'I mean adultery to me is – adultery's peanuts compared to the sort of emotional harassment she puts me through. Her constant despair, her moodiness. The sulks. The being told over and over again that I don't love her. "You don't love me, do you?" she'll say. Or, "You really hate me, don't you," never a question. Just those goddam sulks which I never seem to get her out of no matter how hard I try. And I do try, honest. Look, maybe if I can give you a typical day it would help you understand what it's like, okay?'

'Sure,' Alfred said.

'I get home from work usually around seven and Alice is in the kitchen and I come in and say, "Hi, darling, how're you," and I kiss her and she just sort of looks at me with this tight expression as though she's been sipping alum. And I ask her what kind of day she had, knowing she's had to spend the day with the children, that she'd had to clean the house, but goddam it that's what being a wife is all about. I mean what's the point of getting married if you think having children and keeping house is degrading?'

'Does Alice think it's degrading?'

'Christ, I've had that argument a thousand times with Alice. All these goddam women who complain that their husbands don't treat them like they should, that their husbands aren't men. What makes these wives think they're such big women? A woman is supposed to want to take care of a child, to raise it, nurse it, take care of it. She's supposed to want to look after her husband, to keep his house, to take pride in being a woman. But now, it's gotten so that wives think being a woman is degrading! Why is it that every wife seems to complain that her husband doesn't want a wife, he wants a maid? A man can fire a maid! I didn't want a maid, I wanted a wife. A woman. A companion. And instead I've ended up with some sort of goddam receptacle of depression. She just mopes around the house, shouts at the children, sulks when I come home and wonders why the hell I'm not happy with her. The truth is she's a goddam drone. A – an – I don't know what, but not what I wanted when I married her. You know, I can't think of a single friend's wife who can really cook a meal worth a goddam. Cooking must be degrading too. The ones who can cook, all learned from their husbands.

'Anyway, I've offered to get her help. Every maid I hire quits after two weeks because Alice just lies in bed expecting to get waited on hand and foot. And Alice doesn't know how to treat servants. She's so overbearing and rude that they quit. I would too. She treats them as though they weren't human beings at all, but pieces of property she owns. And so, we don't have any servants.

'Anyway, I know Alice doesn't have much news. But even when I just ask her what her day was like, I don't get any answer.

'"What happened today?" I'll ask her. "How was your day? Anybody call?"

'"No," she'll say.

'"Alice, please ... What's the matter?"

'Again, no answer.

'But of course something is the matter. You don't need to live with someone for eight years before you know their moods pretty well. But there isn't anything I can do either, so I go on upstairs and take a look at the children who're in bed. If they're still awake, I'll talk to them for a while, or just sit with them until they sleep. And then I'll take my bath. If we're not going out anywhere I'll probably just put on pyjamas and a bathrobe, and while I'm doing that Alice will come up and take her bath. Ignoring me. She'll walk back and forth without looking at me, deliberately avoiding me. And when we meet back down in the kitchen and I ask Alice what's for dinner, she says, "Liver. Why?" with this goddam chip on her shoulder as though I'd accused her of deliberately cooking something I hate. The truth is, I like liver. Calves' liver is one of my favourites. Or maybe she thinks what I really meant by my question is why isn't dinner ready. All I was trying to do was to make some conversation, to get some response. To reach her somehow ...

'Anyway, there we are in the kitchen. If there's something on television, we usually carry our dinner up on trays to the bedroom where the TV set is. So, I set up the trays, get out the mats, the silver, the napkins, salt and pepper, glasses. Alice plunks the liver into the skillet. Drops a couple of packages of frozen vegetables that have flavour pellets into the boiling water, still not speaking.

'"Alice, what would you like to drink with dinner? Would you like some wine? A glass of beer ? Milk? Ice water?"

'"I don't care," she says.

'"Well, make a choice."

'"It doesn't matter," she says.

'The other night I got so goddam fed up with her, I told her to bark once if she wanted wine, twice for milk. She was not amused. And, okay, I admit it. I know what my attitude was there, but I must admit it's an attitude bred from despair. Of trying to get to her. Finally, she'll say, "Milk," or something, and I'll get it for her. But still I'll keep trying. "Alice, look,

145

please tell me. What is it? What's the matter? Were the children bad or what?"

'"Nothing's the matter."

'"Then why are you behaving like this?"

'"Like what?" she'd ask.

'And so the hell with it. We have dinner on trays in front of the TV, and during the commercials Alice gets up and starts walking around the room – stalking, really. Like some bear in the zoo, you know? Seven paces east, shift turn, seven paces west, shift turn, seven paces east and so on, never saying a word. And I'll ask her if she would like some coffee, and she'll say, "I didn't make any. Do you want some?"

'Well, Alfred, maybe I'm making too much of a minor thing. But I really love coffee. I order it all the way from McNulty's down on Christopher Street in the Village. French style continental coffee. We grind our own beans, make the coffee in a Chemex. I doubt if there have been four nights in the eight years we've been married that I haven't wanted a cup of coffee after dinner, and the coffee in the Chemex is the same I made for breakfast when I left for the office before Alice got up. She never gets up for breakfast any more. I have to leave the house around seven to make the train. She and the children get up after I leave. She puts Sydney to bed before I get home. I've asked Alice to keep her up a little longer so I can see her at night but she just tells me to get home earlier. There aren't any trains and so I rarely even seem to see my daughter. And I think she does this deliberately, you know? As though she were trying to punish me, keep her for herself somehow.

'Anyway she won't make the effort of making coffee, so I go down to the kitchen, I take the trays and dishes downstairs, rinse the dishes, put them in the dishwasher. Heat water for coffee. And sure, I know it's her job, but I do it just because it isn't worth the scene. I'd rather do it myself than suffer through the sort of crap Alice would cause. Besides, it puts some physical distance between us – the other kind of distance we have enough of already. For fifteen minutes or so, the time it takes for me to make fresh coffee, smoke a cigarette, gives me a chance to be myself, by myself. I can unwind a little. Smoke. And dread having to go back upstairs because I know, I just know that she's still up there, pacing back and forth, radiating this fury, this despair. So I make fresh coffee, take the coffee up, give her a cup and ask her for God knows what time, the tenth, ''Alice, what is it?''

'''Nothing.''

'''Would you like to talk? Do you want me to turn off the television?''

'''Do whatever you want.''

'Well, what I'd really like to do Alfred is kick her in the ass. But what does that accomplish? I'm just so tired of arguments, of always having to fight with her to get her to do anything or say anything. Arguments end up nowhere, and I've been through so damned many with her, that now I just figure, what the hell, it's going to come, put it off after the news. And that's exactly what I do. I watch the eleven o'clock news, then turn off the television, brush my teeth and get into bed. The minute my head hits the pillow Alice sits up and lights a cigarette. That's a sign, too. She doesn't smoke unless she's upset. Another sign is rearranging the hangers in the closets. She'll get up and move all the hangers around; push the wire ones to one side, or collect them to be thrown away, and shift the wooden ones back and forth. And so there I am trying to get to sleep and she's rearranging, rattling these goddam wire hangers around in the closet. So I sit up and ask her if it could wait until morning, and that gets her sore, but it at least gets her talking. And finally, it turns out after all this time that she found a copy of *Playboy* in my bathroom and Alice is upset because I've been looking at the girls in it with their big knockers – bigger than her's, anyway, and that means that I've been – just because there's a copy of *Playboy* in the bathroom Alice thinks I was – well, . . .'

'Taking the situation in hand?' Alfred asked, smiling.

'Well, damn it, so what if I was? The point is, I need to get some release. Some relief from all the tensions she builds up in me. I've even tried to explain it to her.'

'And she wanted to know why you didn't make love more often?'

'That's exactly what Alice said. "Why don't you relieve them with me?'' And how do you explain? I mean, My God, I've tried, I've tried to many times. How can a man want to make love to someone who's been sulking all day long, all evening, who's made no effort to be nice at all, for whom you've felt no closeness, no affection, only this increasing despair? How can I be expected to want to make love?

'And so Alice says, "You don't love me."

'And you know? You know? Alfred she's right! How can you love someone who behaves that way? Who won't talk or share or love, who never laughs? I can talk to just about anyone in the world better than I can talk to Alice, now. And they respond, you know? It may be the most dinky sort of conversation, but they respond – accept, reject, yawn, laugh or something, anything, and I feel I've made some contact. And I can't get this from Alice at all, I don't even – am I talking too much?'

'No, Jesus,' Alfred said. 'I was wondering about those letters. When did she find them? How long ago was this?'

'That was three weeks ago tomorrow. She screamed at me all night long, and the next morning, Saturday morning, we drove back to Winander. There wasn't much point in staying in New York. I mean, so much for romance, right? We went back up to Winander and I paid the nurse for the full week-end, and for the next nine or so days, Alice really gave it to me. She never let up. She's a real pro. Better than any goddam Frenchman in Algeria. No marks, no electrodes, just internal damage. Every day I went into town and tried to work, and every night I came back to it. Until the ninth day, I guess it was, it was a Sunday night and I told Alice that I'd had it. I wasn't going to put up with it any more and was going to live in the apartment in New York until she cooled down.

'And she said, "The hell you are! If anyone is taking off for New York it's going to be me."

'So I said, "Fine. I'll help you pack."

'She left that night. Threw her suitcase into the back of her Chrysler and took off. She wouldn't stay in the apartment, she wanted to stay with friends in New York; and I just cannot tell you how relieved I was! My God, it was wonderful! I got the nurse back to take care of the children while I worked and every morning we'd have breakfast together, and I'd drive Ashbel to school before going to work and the nurse would let them stay up for an extra hour when I got home. We had one hell of a good time!

'And Alice kept calling from New York to tell me that she wanted to come back. And I kept telling her that we needed the time away from each other, that it was good for us. And I told her that the children were fine, that the house was fine, that the nurse was taking care of everything – which was exactly the wrong thing to say since every woman likes to believe the moment she leaves the house that it falls into shambles. But, I must admit, the house never ran more smoothly. The children never seemed more happy and relaxed. And we'd play together for that hour or so in the evening, and if it went a little late, so what? The nurse would put Sydney down for her nap earlier the next day. And it was terribly exciting for me. You know? I mean, I was getting a chance to know my own children. Before that I was only really seeing them on weekends, but now here I was seeing them twice a day. As soon as I'd get home there would be all this excitement – on my part and the children's. And the nurse, too, would feel it. She'd have a whisky with me, and we'd all smile and laugh and crawl around on the floor and play with whatever three and six year olds play with. And my children were even getting to know me. I'd see them respond to me! And it was so – it was so – well, it was just so damn nice! So I kept telling Alice to stay away, that the time apart seemed to be doing us all some good. And what the hell, it seemed to be all right with her.

'And then on Friday, last Friday, I met Alice for lunch in town. And after lunch Alice said she wanted to go to Saks – hold it, the night before, Thursday night when Alice called, I had suggested she come back to Winander with me on Friday, and spend the night since Saturday was the dance at the club, and she could have Friday with the children. But she said that she didn't want to, it wasn't worth it since she had to be back in New York the next morning for her appointment with Kenneth ... It wasn't worth it . . . Jesus! How about all the husbands who come home on trains at seven-thirty in the evening, then get up at seven the next morning to go back into town. What makes wives think they're worth it? Anyway, Alice felt she might not be able to make it back into town on time, and a hairdressing appointment with Kenneth is evidently not something a woman can break. And so I felt well, all right, maybe that is permissible piece of personal vanity. She could have made it back if she drove in early Saturday morning. She could even have taken the train but, what the hell. So, after lunch, Alice went off to Saks and I went back downtown to the apartment to finish the prospectus I was working on. And when I completed that, I met Alice for drinks at the King Cole Bar. And that was pleasant. I've always liked that bar. The King Cole had been in a sense "our " bar – an identification Alice felt more strongly than I did – but with our marriage in the shambles it is, anything that creates an atmosphere or illusion of *sharing* is something worth clinging to. It somehow seems important to feel that some so-and-so is *our* so-and-so. And we stayed there and had a drink. It was obvious Alice was still very upset with me, but she wanted me to see the dress she had bought at Saks and it was ready for her to pick up. So we went to look at it.

'It was a lovely dress. Is a lovely dress. And she put it on and looked very pretty in it, and was so excited about it. And it was very odd. I don't know whether Alice was aware of it or not, but it was almost identical to the dress she had around the time of the Irving Penn *Vogue* photograph. A grey strapless very tightly fitted evening dress. It was uncanny how much that dress looked like the other dress but I didn't dare say anything because she was so excited, and you can guess how much it meant to me to have her feel excited about something.

'Alice modelled the dress for me, paraded back and forth in it, showed me the shoes she bought to go with it, and as I looked at her I became aware for the first time how much she had changed. Here she was twenty-nine, and the *Vogue* photograph had been taken when she was sixteen. Thirteen years difference right before my eyes. And it wasn't that Alice looked old, or even older – she just didn't look young any more, you know? It was there in her eyes. Not the little lines that were beginning to appear. Lines like that I love. No, it was something else. The brightness was missing. There was a disappointment, a sadness, a resentment that I hadn't noticed before. And it made me so sad because I suppose in a way I knew I had done it to her, certainly I had done it to her as much as she had done it to herself. She had lost something and I had never seen it steal away. And I felt so damned sorry for her, and I asked her if she'd like me to spend the night in town with her. Not at the apartment, but we could stay at some place like the St Regis, have dinner with some friends or by ourselves, and she thought that would be fine, but that it would be silly to stay at the St Regis when we had the apartment. So I called up the nurse and told her we would be home the next morning, and little Sydney wanted to speak to me, and of course I couldn't understand what the hell she was talking about, but it was nice anyway.

'And after Saks we went to F.A.O. Schwartz and bought the children a couple of toys, and we ran into the Turnbulls, and, as it turned out, we had dinner with them. And during dinner Alice began to slip back into one of her moods, and it was so damned depressing! Because these friends of ours have had to go through it so many times before, and they were so nice to us, and it just got worse and worse until dinner was over and I took Alice back to the apartment.

'As soon as we were inside, Jesus, there they were again. All the old tensions, the despair, the – the grittiness. And I know, I know she expects to make love. It isn't that she even wants to, it's just that she goddam well expects to. And it kills me. When the time comes, I just can't. I can't because of all the despair, her moodiness, the memories of the last time we were in the apartment, her screaming. And we're in bed together and I'm trying to get excited, trying to blot all this out, but I can't. And finally, I just tell her that. I say, "Alice, I'm sorry. I just can't. Not tonight – It just seems too planned."

'"What do you mean, 'too planned'?" She asks me.

'"As though it were too obvious," I tell her. "As though it weren't making love at all, but some sort of ritual."

'"You don't love me at all, do you?" she says.

151

'And, well, I told her I loved her. And I do, you know. It's funny, I must be some sort of masochist, but I do love her – I just don't like her very much.

'And so I tried to explain to Alice what I meant about "proof", about how it made me feel like a performing seal. And that it wasn't making love at all. It was screwing. And I wouldn't be able to get – she'd tell me I was soft. Soft . . . That I didn't get aroused the way she did. And she'd say, "What's the matter?" And what could I say? What can I say? That I don't want her? Alice is a very attractive woman. A beautiful woman. She has a marvellous body. If I could just disassociate her body from her mind, everything would be fine. But, of course, I can't. So there we were in bed down at the apartment, and I rolled away, and I was thinking about the girl I'd had there and how nice it had been, how marvellously warm and loving and fine it was to have made love with her, how giving she had been and all of a sudden Alice said, "You're thinking about that girl you fucked down here aren't you!"

'And, of course, I told her I wasn't, that I was just ashamed and sorry I wasn't able to make love to her, and Alice just said, "Forget it!" Jesus, if only I could! So Alice got up and started stalking up and down the apartment again, and I could see her getting angrier and angrier. "You didn't have any difficulty fucking her, I bet," Alice was saying, "You weren't soft with her, I'll bet."

'And, oh God, the way she would say "soft" as though it were the filthiest four-letter word in the language. And there wasn't anything I could say. I'd try to get excited. Close my eyes, try to think of something, someone to get myself aroused, and even that didn't work. Or as soon as I began to think it might work, Alice would say something else. And she went on for three hours. And I was so tired, so goddam desperately tired. I'd been up since seven, and I'd had all those Bloody Marys at lunch and the drinks at the King Cole Bar and more drinks with the Turnbulls and it was about three in the morning and I guess I must have fallen asleep because the next thing I knew it was morning. Saturday morning . . .

'You know, it's curious, somehow some sort of miracle rejuvenation always occurs in the morning a revitalization somehow of us. As though the morning, as though having had some sleep makes the awfulness of the night before seem somehow less awful.

'Well, Alice went off to have her hair done and I cleaned up the apartment and tried to get back to work, but I couldn't concentrate. I mean, what the hell's the point of trying to determine the growth potential of a new company over the next five years when you can't determine your own? I have a five-year plan for my customers and a six-month plan for myself. And that depresses the hell out of me, too. So, I got out of the apartment and just walked around for a while, then went up to meet Alice.

'Well, her hair had been done in a way which, one must suppose, was very *chic* but it just didn't seem all that flattering. And even though I told her that I liked it very much, it was clear that I wasn't overwhelmed by it. So, we drove back out to Winander, and the entire way there was this blah moodiness, the sulking. We were in the Cord and it was cold, and the heater isn't too good. And there had been a light snow in the night before and it had stuck to the trees and on the sides of the parkway, and I said to Alice, "Aren't the trees pretty?"

'No answer.

'And after another couple of miles I said, "Aren't you excited about seeing the children?"

'And she goes, "Ummm."

'And I say, "Well, you are excited, aren't you?"

'"I'm looking forward to seeing them again, yes."

'And that's all she said the entire trip! And so I drive on gripping the steering wheel too hard, and all the time I'm thinking, "God, get me out of this," and I'm wondering whether it would be possible to skid off the road in such a way as to make it look like an accident so that Alice is killed and I'm not hurt too badly – And I do think of things like that, I really do. And yet, I'd never do it. I'd never do it because the children love her and I'd sure as hell get caught. I guess I'm not the sort of man who kills his wife, I don't like killing anything. And anyway, the police are so smart nowadays they'd be out there measuring skid marks...

'We made it back, through the gates and up the long road to the lake and our house. And our children were all bundled up in their snowsuits playing on a neighbour's lawn, and I slowed down and asked Alice if she wanted to see the children, to stop, and she said, "No."'

'She said "No?"' Alfred asked.

'And of course the children recognized the car, and little Ashbel started to wave – and we just drove right on past them, and I felt awful, as though we were hitting them in the face. I don't see why she wouldn't want to stop ... Maybe it was the wind, maybe the wind would have mussed her hair, but I don't remember any wind. In fact, for some reason it was almost balmy that day. The snow had already melted around our place, and it was warm enough to be outside to wash the car – and that's another thing! I'd forgotten about that!

'After I'd carried our luggage up to our room, I started back outside and Alice asked me where I was going. I said I was going to see the children and that afterwards I was going to wash my car so she wouldn't get her evening dress dirty. And she said, "You'll do anything to get away from me, won't you."

'I mean, *Jesus*! I don't deny that I wanted to get the hell away from her, but I still really wanted to see the children. And as for the car, well, the dinner was white tie and tails, and maybe I'm stuffy or pompous or maybe I'm just absurd, but I didn't want to go to a white tie dinner in a dirty car. So, I left Alice in the kitchen, then went out to speak to the children. Ashbel had a new scratch to show me and little Sydney just wanted to show me herself.

'And we played for a while and talked, and when it was time for their baths, I washed the car, and then Alice and I dressed. I don't think she ever said hello to the nurse.

'We drove over to the Boyds in the Cord, and that pissed Alice off, but I love that little car, I love to drive it. And that road to the Boyds is great for driving. Hills, valleys, curves and – I can see you're smiling, I never said I was mature, did I?

'And during the drive Alice and I were still trying to make

some sort of contact with each other. Touch antennas or whatever it is that insects do with each other to determine whether or not their intentions are friendly. And I'm saying to Alice. "Look, please, you've got to at least make the effort, you've got to try –" And she says, "Why?"

'And at the dinner there was some very pretty young eighteen-year-old friend of the Boyds' daughter who especially asked to sit next to me; and, of course, I was terribly flattered, but it made Alice sore as hell. And there was some problem as to where Alice would be sitting – she wasn't seated at the main table. But neither was I. I was sitting at a table with four other men, the eighteen-year-old, and a nice lady who writes an investment advice column. But Alice thought she was being snubbed. She wasn't being snubbed at all! After all, it was the débutantes' party and Alice should try to understand that she simply isn't a débutante any more.

'And in the Cord on the way back to the Winander Club Alice bitched the entire trip – about the dinner, about the Boyds, the débutantes' dresses, the girl who had sat next to me. It turned out the girl knew that I had invested several times in various plays and musicals and she was "simply dying to break into the theatre." And Alice started mimicking the eighteen-year-old's voice; I hate to admit it, but Alice was terribly funny.

'Once back at the Club, Alice and I danced for a while and then drifted back to a table to have a drink with some friends. I excused myself at one point to take care of a few duty-dances: our hostess, the Boyds' daughter, and the little girl at the table, and then I came back. It took maybe twenty minutes. And when I returned Alice was sulking. She wouldn't say anything to anyone at the table. I could tell she was just waiting to let me have it. But, for Christ's sake, there are certain things one has to do at that sort of function, certain expected patterns of behaviour, Man the Social Animal, et cetera ... And so I danced with Alice again and we danced and we danced and hell, Alice is a beautiful dancer. And the whole time I kept hoping someone would cut in. And the whole time Alice was going after me: "Why'd you spend so much time with so-and-so? – Why do you always like to have little girls around?" – and so on.

155

'So, by now, in this continual atmosphere of accusations and guilt and despair and frustration I just can't get any work done. I can't think about anything except how much I want to be *free*! To get out from under. And I know, I *know* if that's the way I feel, then why don't I get a divorce?'

'Why don't you?' Alfred asked.

'I don't know why I don't. I just don't know. I suppose it's because I love the children so much. And maybe it's because I love Alice, too. As I said, I do love her. You don't have to like someone to love them. But then I think if I get a divorce I won't be able to live with the children. And I'll have to get rid of the cat and the dog. And you can't help but wonder, but worry about these things. You wonder whether you'll have to put your pets to sleep. You wonder whether – You wonder whether it wouldn't be best just to put the children to sleep, too. Whether it wouldn't be easier for them. And, oh God ... It's all so sad ... So terribly, heart-rendingly, overwhelmingly sad and ... and ... oh hell, Alfred, you should never have asked me about Alice. You should never have let me go on for so long. But I've just had to tell somebody. You see, I just love my children, and I love that old house and the lake and the boat-house, and I wish to God I were married to someone else – anyone else who could be happy. If she could be happy, then I could be happy too.'

'What are you going to do?'

'I've got to go back to Winander tonight. And Alice is sore at me again. She called me at the office this morning just before I came up here just to tell me that she'd found out about this friend of ours, a divorcée in Winander who had me to dinner while Alice was in New York – well, we're friends this girl and I, and she's a damn good friend of Alice's or was. And Alice is going to throw that friendship away because the girl felt sorry for me and had me to dinner. "No friend of mine would have had dinner with you alone," is what Alice said. Isn't that stupid? Isn't that ridiculous?'

'It depends on the girl,' Alfred said.

'Well, I just think that unless things change radically, I've got to get out of this. I just don't see any other way – I can't work. I can't laugh. Listen, let me tell you about my first affair, can you stand a little more?'

'Sure.'

'It was a girl I'd known for years before, someone I'd grown up with almost. And we met by accident in the city and I took her to lunch, and then to lunch several more times and then one night when Alice was away somewhere, we spent a night together. And I loved her more than I thought was possible. And the reason why I loved her so much is because she made me smile ... That's all, really. She made me smile.'

'That's nice,' Alfred said.

'And now, now I've got to go back to work, drive my car back to Winander and go home to Alice who is already mad at me. I have to go home to ... to what?'

'To Alice,' Alfred said. 'What else can you do?'

'Nothing. I think I'll just try some more. I think I honestly do try, but I don't know how much good it does to try when one senses it's doomed.'

'Would it have any, would it help if I talked to her? I mean maybe I can help her understand that if you don't get away from each other for a little while then you'll break up for good. Would it help if I spoke to her?'

'She won't have forgotten that you weren't any too eager for me to marry her in the first place.'

'That was a long time ago,' Alfred said. 'Don't you think it might do some good if I tried?'

'Hell, yes, Alfred,' I said. 'I'd be willing to have you try anything. You could even come up and try tonight if you'd like and spend the weekend with us. There's a dance at the club tomorrow night, that might be fun for you. In fact, the more I think about it, the better the idea seems. I have got to go off to a Governors' meeting at the club tonight at around nine which will last an hour or so, and it would be a perfect chance for you to talk to Alice alone. What sort of plans do you have for tonight? Do you think you could come?'

'I can't stay for the weekend,' Alfred said, 'but maybe I could come up tonight. I told a girl I'd meet her at Elaine's tonight around midnight, but she wouldn't mind if I didn't show up. How would we get there? Is your car in town?'

'I hope so,' I laughed. 'It was this morning. I'll give Alice a call and tell her you're coming up for dinner. Why don't I swing by the club at quarter after six and pick you up?'

'Good,' Alfred said. 'And now, let's change the subject and talk about something pleasant.'

'Do you remember the night when you were living in the Adler with me and you said we had spent an evening right out of F. Scott Fitzgerald?'

'Sure I do,' Alfred said. 'We were in the library after your party. It was just before Alice showed up. I said it because of a lot of things, but the one thing in particular that touched it off was – do you remember the scene in *The Great Gatsby* where Nick Carraway and Jordan Baker, the girl who supposedly cheated in a golf match, went looking for Gatsby at his party and they wandered into the library and found the owl-eyed man who'd been drunk for a week who was so astonished that Gatsby's books were real? He said, "Knew when to stop, too, – didn't cut the pages." You remember?'

'Sure. That's why I showed you the Wordsworth which had been hollowed out and hey, did I ever thank you for the pistol? Where'd you get it anyway?'

'Where else? I got it in Hollywood,' Alfred laughed. 'I thought it'd be a perfect fit.'

'What were you doing in Hollywood?'

'Rubber-necking, gawking,' he said.

'Have you ever seen whats-her-name, that nice model?'

'Teddy? Teddy Baldwin?' Alfred said. 'No, not after Rome. I keep looking for her and hope I'll run into her, but I haven't. Jesus, she was a marvellous girl. She really was. Much too good for me, I'm afraid. I mean, her head was right there, right on it and my head – well, I'm still working on it.'

'Are you still using drugs?' I asked him.

'Isn't everybody?' Alfred laughed. 'Aspirin. Coffee. Seconal. Nicotine – but I'm not going to get into a drug discussion with you, because I've got to run. Listen, George. I'll be here at a quarter past six and we'll talk the whole drive out to Winander.' He pushed back his chair and stood up. 'I'll ride part down on the elevator with you. I have to pick up some papers from my room.'

Chapter Twelve

When I stepped out of the elevator on the ground floor, I spotted Missy Carlyle in the Ladies' Waiting Room. She was sitting on the sofa beneath the mirror and her skirt had ridden part way up her thighs, and I was surprised at how fine her legs were. Why had I never noticed them before?

Missy saw me and waved and I walked over and said hello and asked what brought her to the Yale Club?

'I had lunch with Sandy Stoddard on the roof,' she said. 'And now I'm trying to gather up enough strength to do my last Christmas shopping. How are you? What are you doing here?'

'I'm fine. I had lunch with Alfred Moulton. You know him, don't you? I think you met him at one of those parties in the Adler.'

'Wasn't he the best man at your wedding?'

'That's right.'

'He's the writer, isn't he?' Missy asked.

'Well he got a full story today. I'm afraid I just spent the entire lunch whining.'

'I did that this morning,' Missy said. 'But I don't subject my friends to it. I get it all out of my system with a shrink.'

'A psychiatrist? You?' I asked dumbfounded.

'Dr Devereaux,' Missy said. 'Don't tell a soul.'

'But he's *my* doctor!' I said.

'You see him, too?' Missy laughed.

'Do you think it helps at all?' I asked. I sat down in the easy chair next to her.

'I think it helps having someone to talk to,' she said.

'But how do you talk about it?' I asked her. 'If I could just pin it down on three-by-five cards, all tabbed and cross-indexed for easy reference, "Anger", "Anguish", "Angst", dot, dot, dot, see "Inability to Communicate". How the hell can someone talk about an inability to communicate? I mean I'm just so sure he's heard the same sort of complaint so many, many times before –'

'That's what he's paid for,' Missy said. 'For fifty dollars an hour I think I could even listen to someone read the Manhattan telephone directory.' She lay her hand on top of mine. 'If it's any consolation,' she smiled, 'you're the last person I'd expect to meet coming out of a psychiatrist's office.'

We were both silent for a moment, and then I asked, 'Are you and Walter getting a divorce?'

Her hand jerked as though I had stung her.

'I'm sorry,' I said, 'It's none of my business.'

'It isn't that,' Missy said. 'I just didn't know it was so obvious.'

'It isn't obvious. I just wondered why else you'd see a psychiatrist. You don't have to answer.'

'I don't know if I can. The closest I can come is a tentative probably. I suppose statistics show that the majority of people who see psychiatrists because of their marriages end up in divorce and, I suppose, I'm – we're, Walter and I, we're not going to be any exceptions to that rule . . .'

'Well, I'm terribly sorry,' I said, 'but at least you don't have any children.'

'That isn't *my* fault!' she said angrily.

'I didn't think you wanted children.'

'I don't. Not now. Certainly not now . . . What I really want now is a drink. Are you doing anything? Would you mind terribly if we just went somewhere for a drink?'

'Anywhere you like.'

'Mother's meeting me at our apartment at three so some place near home.'

'How about Allen's?' I suggested.

At Allen's Missy ordered a bull-shot and I had a Bloody Mary. We made small talk for a few minutes and then Missy said, 'George, you remember that part in Alfred's book where the wife went to the marriage counsellor and was told to lipstick her nipples and –'

161

'That came from *The Chinese Room*,' I said.

'But it was in Alfred's book.'

'I know, but Alfred told me he got the idea from *The Chinese Room*.'

'Well, it doesn't matter. The point is there was that part and the part about the black silk stockings – and, well, I even thought of trying that, but of course I didn't. Walter would have hated me for it. It would have embarrassed him and I would have been mortified – I really did consider trying it, but I just knew it would have been awful because I just couldn't have done it with Walter. He would have thought – I don't know what he would have thought, that I was making fun of him, or I'd gone insane, or, or I don't know what. But I was willing to try anything because – well, listen, George, the point is, the only reason why I'm telling you any of this is because of what Alice said to me Walter hasn't made love to me in over four months, not since – isn't it awful? I can remember the exact weekend! It was the Labour Day weekend dance at the Club. And he was drunk. And it was only because he was drunk and took so long that I reached an orgasm.' Missy was looking down at her hands which she had folded in her lap. She did not look up at me. 'Please, George, don't be shocked if I talk to you like this. I would never have the nerve to talk to anyone about it except Dr Devereaux and you. And the only reason why I can talk to you is because of what Alice told me. She said you didn't make love to her either.'

'She said *what*?'

'She didn't tell me anything explicit,' Missy said, still not looking up at me. 'She only said that before the two of you were married, when you had that penthouse in the Adler that you and she –'

She was interrupted by the waiter who brought two fresh drinks. While he was straightening up the table, putting down cocktail napkins, our drinks, figuring up the cheque, I was thinking that if Alice had told Missy, then no doubt Alice had also spoken to Mary Fielding about us. And Mary Fielding would have told Ann Baker by now. And Ann and Wendy Thayer were inseparable, and Wendy is Winander's biggest gossip. So God only knew how many people up at Winander were getting their

jollies out of my inadequacy in bed. And I was angry and mortified and frustrated because I knew that before this I had rarely
gone three nights without making love to Alice unless she was
pregnant, or was having a particularly tough period, or that we
were fighting so horribly neither of us wanted to be near each
other. I was also willing to admit that a great many of those
times Alice and I had made love, it had been initiated on my part
not so much out of desire as it was self-preservation. And so I
had been performing regularly for what? To be condemned *in
absentia*, expelled from the Sexual Grace of Suburbia, excom-
municated for *ennui*, for Paradise Ignored.

The waiter had left and Missy was again saying, 'Before you
two were married, when you and Alice were living together, the
two of you used to make love all the time. But now, according to
Alice, you never make love to her.'

'Did Alice ever bother to say why?' I asked.

'Why she was telling me this, you mean?'

'Oh Christ, Missy, you know Alice well enough to know she'll
say anything if it'll get her some sympathy, get people to feel
sorry for her. And there's just enough vicious truth in what
she's said to guarantee circulation.'

'But is it true?'

'What do you think?'

'The only reason why I'm asking you is because of what I've
already told you. That Walter hasn't made love to me in such a
long time and maybe it's for the same reason. Alice told me that
sex doesn't interest you.'

'With Alice it doesn't,' I said angrily. 'Goddam her, really!
The reason why I'm seeing Devereaux is because for the last
month or so I haven't been able to do it anymore, I just can't get
myself interested – at least, not in Alice.'

'But why not?' Missy asked. 'Alice is so pretty. She has such a
beautiful figure. Why wouldn't a man want to make love to
someone as lovely as Alice?'

'Some man would. Some stranger looking at Alice would want
to make love to her,' I said. 'But we've been married eight years
and we're not strangers to each other any more. I'm not just
"some man" wanting to put pretty Alice into the sack. I also

163

have to get Alice out of the sack. I have to come home to her when she's angry or upset or in one of her moods, which is what coming home has been like for as many nights back as I can remember. That's why I – oh hell, Missy, the only point I'm trying to make is that I *love* making love. I just don't like what it can turn into when a wife makes it become a proof, when all sorts of unrelated pressures are imposed upon it so that it becomes not making love but sexual intercourse, something as dried and as limp as it's name.'

Missy said nothing. She was swirling her swizzle stick around and around in her drink.

I took a sip of my drink and became angry all over again. 'Goddam Alice, really! What *is* the matter with her? It's not just Alice, even. I've sat next to too many of you wives at dinners to know it isn't just Alice. Where do you wives get these ideas from, this insecurity, which causes you to behave this way? You complain that the romance has gone out of your marriages. Jesus Christ when was there ever romance in your marriages? When a husband works his head off all day, comes home on a train that's stuffy or been delayed or filled with smoke or too hot or too cold and he's had to duck rocks thrown at the train by kids, and he's had to stand for the first thirty minutes because he gave his seat to some grotesque women laden down with shopping bags so that he's exhausted by the time he gets home. And he walks into a house where his wife is depressed or angry or whatever, to a house that's a goddam pigsty and then is given some dinner that's a bore – some precooked, frozen, floating cellophane bag of something – when the husband comes home and he knows his wife hasn't made the slightest bit of effort for him, when he knows that all she's done is waited for him to get back so that she can unload her troubles, empty her venom sacks into him, then how the hell does a wife expect her husband to want to romance her, to want to make love to her?'

'Wives work hard, too, George,' Missy said. 'It works both ways.'

'Oh, Missy, I know wives work hard, that some wives work hard. And the rest think they're working hard which amounts to the same degree of exhaustion. But since that's so why don't they, why aren't they a little more understanding, instead of taking it out on their husbands?'

'Is Alice like that?'

'Fifty per cent of wives I know are like that. The minute the man walks through the door the wives start complaining. The children this, the plumbing that. Mrs So-and-so snubbed her in the supermarket. The druggist was rude. The car's transmission this, the dishwasher that. What the hell do I know about an automobile transmission? I was a history major at college not a mechanical engineer. If I'm lucky I can fix a leaky toilet, but you tell me where it says that because I have a complete set of male genitals that I'm supposed to know how to fix a transmission?'

Missy was laughing and I was scowling across the table at her.

'I think you're very sexy,' she said.

'You think what?' I growled, and then I began laughing, too, 'You really didn't listen to a word I said, did you?'

'Of course I did,' Missy replied. 'You said you were seeing Dr Devereaux because, and I think I can quote you exactly, you said, "because I can't get myself interested – at least not in Alice," and I was wondering who you were interested in, who you were having an affair with.'

'I'm not having an affair with anybody,' I said.

'Maybe you should,' Missy smiled. 'I think maybe you probably are. I wish Walter were. I wish there were some little girl down at his office that Walter was having an affair with. I think it would be marvellous for him.'

'Why?'

'Because maybe it would make him feel more like a man,' she said. She was looking at me solemnly. 'Maybe it's my fault. That's what makes it so awful. Sometimes I feel as though I castrated him.'

'It seems to me that the one who really needs to have an affair isn't Walt, it's you.'

'Who would want to have any affair with "Good-Old Missy"?' she asked. There was no bitterness, no 'fishing for compliments' in her voice, only an immeasurable poignancy and resignation.

'I would,' I said.

She looked up at me and held my eyes for a moment and then looked down at her hands folded in her lap.

'I wasn't just being polite, Missy,' I said.

She fumbled through her purse then pushed a quarter across the red and white checked table cloth at me. 'Put something in the jukebox,' she said, 'it's too quiet in here.'

When I returned to our table from the jukebox there was a third round of drinks waiting. As I sat down Missy leaned forward and took my hand in her own, 'George, help me, please?'

'How, Missy? I'll do anything I can.'

'You can tell me how I can get Walter to want to make love to me. You're a man. What should I do?'

'Ohh, Missy,' I said shaking my head, 'I can't answer that. You know Walter better than I do. How long have you been married?'

'Ten years,' she said. 'We got married just after college.'

'That's a long time. You can't expect him to behave like a newly-wed.'

'Be serious,' she pleaded.

'I am being serious,' I said. 'I simply don't know what to tell you. After all, you've heard what Alice has said.'

'But that's why you're in the best position to tell me,' Missy said. 'Maybe it's the same reason. What would you want Alice to do?'

I didn't answer.

Missy squeezed my hand, 'Please, George, please?'

'But it's not the same. You're not the same as Alice. Our problems aren't the same as your problems. Alice is a sulker, you're not.'

'But you were saying there was pressure, maybe I'm putting too much pressure on Walter. What does "pressure" mean?'

'It means simply that I don't have the initiative any more.'

'You mean you're not the aggressive partner?' She saw my look and shrugged. 'I've been reading books about it. *Harmony In Marriage, Love Without Fear,*' she smiled, 'that sort of thing. Except I can't understand half the words.'

'Just look at the pictures,' I laughed.

'I did. They're little wooden dolls. It makes everything so awful. Like "insert Tab A in Flap B".'

'Well, all I mean, Missy, is that you should let him make the first move. If it's "romance" you want, let him seduce you instead of you seducing him.'

'But what if he doesn't?'

'Give him time,' I said.

'Time!' she said bitterly. 'I've given him since last Labour Day week-end!'

'But do you just lie there waiting for him?'

She nodded.

'Then don't,' I said. 'Just go to sleep. Don't set up any goddam candlelight dinner from McCall's a husband can smell a set-up for miles. Just let him come home, unwind, and go to sleep. Don't expect him to make a pass at you the first night.'

'But he never does,' Missy said.

'Well, then, hell, Missy – I don't know what to tell you.'

'Help me, George, please?'

'I wish I could, Missy,' I said. 'But I don't know how. I'm not a marriage counsellor.'

'You're a friend,' she said. 'How can I excite him? Please tell me. I don't mean just *hint*, I mean use the words because I simply don't know *any*thing. I mean don't use the medical words because I never know what they mean. There was one which I don't know how to pronounce that began with "f" that I had to look up and it said it was "oral stimulation of the penis",' Missy ducked her head to see if anyone was around. Her cocktail napkin was already in nervous shreds in her hands. 'And that was a big help, you can imagine, I mean really! Why can't they just say "cock sucking"? I mean there's this whole *world*, I don't understand!'

'You understand it well enough,' I laughed, 'you're just a little short on vocabulary.'

'And there's the one I can never pronounce which is doing it to a woman.'

'Did Walter ever do it to you?'

She nodded, twisting and tearing at the napkin.

'Did you like it?'

167

'I loved it!' she said and a twitch sent the shredded napkin into the air like confetti around us. 'Whoopee!' she laughed. 'Listen, George, look, does this embarrass you to talk about this? I mean, I'm practically in tears myself.'

'Well, did you ever try doing it to Walter?'

'He wouldn't let me,' she said. 'I tried, but it embarrassed him.'

'Why? I mean, didn't he think you wanted to?'

'Yes, but he felt it was ... I don't know.'

'Disgusting?'

'No, not that at all. I think he just felt maybe I was doing it to him because he was doing it to me, or had done it to me. And he didn't want me to feel I had to, well, return the favour. Maybe it did embarrass him. I don't know. Do you do it to Alice?'

'I used to,' I said.

'But you haven't since you stopped making love? Because Alice doesn't interest you? Please tell me, please!' Missy pleaded. 'You just don't understand, I've never ever talked to anyone about any of this before and if it weren't for these drinks, I'd probably never have the nerve to even – I mean, George, I keep telling you, you just don't understand what a neat little world I come from. I mean, I can't help it. How can I ever find out anything? I never had an older sister or even a brother to ask. And as for my mother – she probably hated to uncross her legs long enough to give birth to me. So please, please talk to me about this. I certainly can't talk to Walter about it. If I could, I wouldn't be seeing Devereaux. And I can't even really talk to him about it. I mean, he's such a nice old man, so who else is there? Everyone thinks I'm just Good-Old Missy, and what I need is a *friend*.'

'But you have a hundred friends,' I said. 'There must be someone's wife you could talk to.'

'I wouldn't want my married friends to know about this. So please, tell me, why didn't you want to do it to Alice?'

'I simply couldn't enjoy it any more. It was something personal, something between Alice and myself, and I don't really think it's fair to talk to you about it. I just didn't enjoy it any more. But in the beginning, I liked it very much. I thought it was very exciting. Now I am getting embarrassed,' I said. 'I'm getting embarrassed at myself.'

'Why?'

'Because I sound so stuffy and I don't mean to be.'

'You're not stuffy,' Missy said, 'it's just not the sort of idle conversation you and I generally involve ourselves in. And I'm sorry to keep on like this. You must think I'm the most frustrated woman in the world – I guess I am! – Is "frustrated" the same as being "horny"?'

'It can be,' I laughed.

'See? That's what I mean about that neat little world? I feel like Sessuie Hayakawa saying, "You'rre surrrprrized I speak yourr ranguage!"'

'How's your drink?' I asked.

'Fine. Deadly. Yours?'

'Fine . . .'

'George . . . ?'

'Yes?'

'Did you really mean it when you said you'd have an affair with me? You weren't just being –' Missy stopped in mid-sentence and pushed herself away from the table and hurried over to the jukebox. She was reading over the selections when I approached her. 'I shouldn't have asked you that,' she said. 'Forget I asked you. What shall we play next?'

I looked at her and her expression was so alive, her face so flushed, her eyes so excited. What shall we play next, indeed.

Missy was looking at her watch. 'I guess we don't really have time to play anything. Dear mother is always prompt, damn her!'

On the walk back to her apartment building, Missy linked her arm through mine and I could feel her practically skipping as she told me over and over again that she had had such a good time, that she had loved talking to me, that it had been very exciting, and I halted her in mid-block, backed her into a recessed doorway and kissed her. It was a very gentle kiss a sweet kiss, nothing more and she didn't pull away, but held me for a moment and then, when we seperated, she said in a voice so tight and quiet that I barely heard her, 'I haven't kissed a man since Walter and I were married.' And I was shocked for the first time all morning.

Just before we reached Missy's apartment building she said, 'You've done me more good than Devereaux ever could. I should give you the fifty dollars.'

'Wait 'til you see my couch.'

'I'm looking forw*hoops*! Here comes Mother! G'bye, G'bye,' she said, 'I'll call you.'

I left Missy at the corner then I hailed a cab and went downtown. The telephone was ringing when I entered my apartment. It was Alice: 'Where have you been? I've been trying to reach you all afternoon.'

'Why?'

'Where were you?'

'I was with Alfred. We had lunch at the Yale Club.'

'All afternoon?'

'Jesus, Alice, it's only 3.30. What does it matter? I spent about an hour after lunch just walking around, looking in windows. I tried to do some Christmas shopping. There wasn't any point in going back to the office so I stopped off here. Incidentally, Alfred's coming up for dinner tonight.'

'Tonight?'

'I'm driving him up. We should get there around seven, maybe a little later. It depends on the traffic.'

'What's Alfred coming for?'

'Because I asked him.'

'Well, thanks for asking me,' Alice said.

'Come on, Alice, I don't do that very often. He's an old friend of ours, just back in town for a little while. And we had a pleasant lunch and I thought he'd like to come out to the country, so I asked him.'

'Is he coming for the week-end?'

'Just dinner tonight.'

Silence.

'So, we'll be there a little after seven, okay?'

'What should I have for dinner?'

'Anything,' I said. 'You decide.'

'But what?'

'What do we have in the house?' I asked. 'What's in the freezer?'

'Nothing that'll thaw in time – oh George, I just wish you'd given me some warning.'

'I didn't know about it myself until I asked him,' I said. 'It's just three-thirty or so now, and we won't be eating much before seven or eight. Eight-thirty. Things would thaw, wouldn't they? Pull out a steak.'

'We had a steak the other night.'

'Well, then something else,' I said, 'really, Alice, anything would be fine.'

'But what should we have?' Alice asked helplessly.

'Alice, look, anything you decide will be fine. I'd like you to decide.'

'But what about the Governor's meeting? You didn't forget about that, did you? Are you going to skip it? It's at nine.'

'It won't start on time, and anyway, it won't take more than an hour. I'll go and come right back.'

'And what am I supposed to do with Alfred while you're gone?'

'Talk to him,' I said.

'About what?' Alice asked. 'What did you two talk about at lunch? Why's he coming up tonight?'

'He's coming because I asked him. We talked mostly about what we've been doing.'

'Me and you?'

'Alfred and me,' I said.

'And did you tell him about us? Did you talk to him about us?'

'He already knows about us. Evidently everyone knows about us.'

'What does that mean?'

'It means simply that too many people know too damned much about our private life. And anyway, anyone looking at us can tell our relationship hasn't been exactly rosebuds in spring.'

'What did you say to Alfred about me?'

'I said you'd be delighted to see him.'

'I'll bet,' she said.

'. . . Isn't there a roast in the freezer?'

'It's not very large.'

'Well, anyway, let's have that. Put in a couple of bottles of the rosé to cool, fix a big salad, maybe some – do we have any of those little red potatoes?'

'I think so,' Alice said.

'Okay then, we can have the roast, lots of little potatoes since the roast is small – some baby peas? – wine – a salad –'

'What about dessert?'

'Anything. Fruit.'

'With a salad?'

'Jesus, Alice, I don't care! Anything. Just make some fresh coffee, would you?'

'What time will you be home?'

'A little after seven – and oh, listen, Alfred drinks Martinis, so you'd better check the gin supply. If we're low, give me a call here and I'll pick some up before I get my car.'

'We've plenty,' Alice said. 'I've already looked. Nancy came by and we had a gin and tonic together to make us think it was summer. It's been so grey lately . . .'

'How was Nancy?'

'Fine.'

'What'd she have to say?'

'Nothing, you know. Nothing. Really.'

'Well, I'll see you a little after seven,' I said.

There was a pause, and Alice said, 'I love you.'

'I love you,' I said. 'See you around seven.'

A moment after Alice and I hung up, the telephone rang again. It was Missy Carlyle, her mother had left early. 'George,' she said gaily, 'Mother wanted to know if I was having an affair, can you believe it!'

'Sure,' I said. 'Are you?'

'Of course not. Mother said she thought I looked different and of course she wanted to know who you were, and I told her we had had a couple of drinks before meeting her, but isn't that incredible?'

'Astonishing,' I laughed. 'How was lunch otherwise?'

'Delicious. For an appetizer I had, "When are you going to become pregnant?" During the main course it was, "When is Walter going to get a larger apartment?" And for dessert it was, "Isn't it about time for him to get a raise?"'

'That's a shame,' I said.

'No, that's mother.'

'It was nice seeing you this morning.'

'It was nice seeing you – oh listen! Are you going to the dance at the club on Saturday?'

'Probably,' I answered. 'Why?'

'Walter was saying last night that he thought he might like to go.'

'Would you like to stay with us?'

'I don't think we can. The Fieldings asked us already. So if we go, we'll have to stay there. But you and Alice are going definitely?'

'I think so,' I said. 'Maybe we could get a table together.'

'Sure, that would be fun,' Missy said. 'Will you dance with me?'

'I'd be delighted,' I said.

'Oh, George, I had such a nice time with you today. Will you always talk to me the way you did this morning?'

'You mean dirty?' I laughed.

'It wasn't dirty at all!' Missy protested. 'You were terribly nice – a little embarrassed at times, I think, but still very nice.'

'Missy, you're the one who's nice. Just stop thinking of yourself as "Good-Old Missy", you're a very attractive woman.'

'Do you think so really?'

'Of course I do.'

'That's nice, George. That's very nice to hear.'

'Well, I mean it.'

'... George? Can I say something very private to you?'

'Sure, what?'

'You won't be scared or angry?'

'Good God, what is it?'

'It'll wait, it's not that serious, I'll tell you about it at that club, okay? And you promise to dance with me?'

'We'll dance all the dances,' I laughed.

'Can I come down to your apartment some afternoon?'

'Is that the private thing you wanted to say to me?'

'It might just as well have been,' Missy said.

'I think that would be very nice.'

'You want to get off the phone, I can tell,' Missy said. 'It's funny, but at times I feel I know you better than I know Walter. I can always tell when you're getting noodgy and –'

'Getting what?'

'"Noodgy", nervous and edgy. G'bye, g'bye, I'm hanging up. I love you. G'bye.'

Chapter Thirteen

At a little after six I picked up Alfred at the Yale Club and we bullied our way through the heavy traffic to the East River Drive and from there to the Triborough Bridge and the expressway up to Connecticut. On the way we talked about mutual acquantances and what they were doing. And Alfred told me how three years ago *Life* magazine had commissioned him to do an article on ten of his Yale classmates who had been members of the Pundits, a group which theoretically consisted of the ten funniest men at Yale. The idea behind the piece was that these ten men had been out of college long enough to have completed all their graduate school and military training and were at last doing what they meant to for a living. Alfred had hoped they would provide a very upbeat, funny, perceptive look at the world around them. But the first six that Alfred interviewed were each so disillusioned and depressed and unfunny that Alfred went back to *Life* and told them he couldn't do the piece.

'But I would have thought their disillusionment plus your own disillusionment with them might have made an even better piece,' I said.

'It might have,' Alfred said, 'but it would have cost me their friendship. And I liked them all, I really did – It wouldn't have been so bad if they'd just been disillusioned, but they were all being so damned cautious! They were so frightened of having what they said quoted that I couldn't get them to give their opinions on anything. It was "don't quote me", the whole time. That and "don't make waves". And it was all right there – the generation gap. The silent generation talking about the younger generation and not willing to be quoted.'

'Well you talk about being concerned with what's going on,' I said. 'I've been living up in Winander for how long – seven? – almost eight years now. And I read *The New York Times* and each week I read *Time* or *Newsweek* or both, and I read a lot of business magazines; and I watch Walter Cronkite on the news, and I watch the television specials and I try to read at least one new novel a month and I try to see at least one new play a month – in other words I'm trying like hell to keep up with what's going on, but I'm beginning to think that all I'm really doing is keeping up with what New York thinks is going on. And I also think New York is getting more and more out of touch with what's really going on, that it's gotten itself wired into a pattern of fads and irrelevancies and violence and is going under, just through the weight of its own verbal and visual garbage. I mean, I've honest to God tried to read the *New York Review of Books* but now that it's become more and more "New York Review" and less and less "of books", I've suddenly realized it just isn't worth the effort. I just don't care what these people think about the war and civil rights and each other – in fact, I'm beginning to think that *they* don't even care what they think about these things just so long as they can be terribly urbane and liberal and witty. I just wish they'd stick to reviewing books instead of national policies.'

'Why?' Alfred asked.

'Why what?'

'Why do you wish they reviewed books instead of national policies?'

'Because it isn't their job,' I said.

'Whose is it?' Alfred asked. 'You sound as though you think there ought to be restrictions placed on the membership of those permitted to review national policy. It seems to me every barber, cab driver and cop has been doing it for as long as I can remember and what's more they're the first to want to ship out all the kids who disagree with them.'

'You were in Chicago, Alfred,' I said, 'what happened there? What were those people really like?'

'Which people? Chicago had just about every type of "people" that could be assembled in one place.'

'Well I meant those kids, they –'

'They may have been "kids" before they came to Chicago, but they weren't when they left.'

'Well then these young people or whatever. What were they looking for in Chicago? Why'd they start those terrible riots?'

'They didn't start those riots,' Alfred said. 'The Chicago police started those riots.'

'So I've heard, so I've heard, but I can't say I entirely blame them. I think of some bearded fuzzy-headed kid stood in front of me calling me the most awful names I'd want to clobber him, too. It seemed to me those kids – young people – wanted the police to riot. I don't understand what they hoped to accomplish by calling the police "pigs". I mean I may not like police much either but it doesn't mean I have a right to shout "Pigs" at them. I can remember when the Nazis used to shout *schweinhünde* at the Jews. Another word those kids flung around: fascist. Jesus, Alfred, I remember the Fascists. And those kids don't know what they're yelling about. If this country was as fascist as they say they wouldn't have just been clubbed they would have been put in front of a firing squad.'

'That may come next.'

'Oh horse shit, Alfred,' I said. 'Our country would never do that.'

'I wish I were as confident as you. A government that revokes a young man's draft deferment because he protests its war and then in reprisal sends him to that war where he stands a good chance of getting killed is only setting up a very roundabout bureaucratic sort of firing squad. The thing that the majority of these flag-waving Americans don't understand is that these young people are the real patriots. They love this country – or at least they love their idea of what this country stood for and what it yet could be. Sweet land of liberty, remember? We used to be a democracy –'

'We were never a democracy,' I said 'If you'll take the time to reread your history books you'll find that –'

'Oh fuck the history books, George! I'm talking about what's happening today and –'

'– and today would be meaningless if it weren't for all the yesterdays that got us here. If there is any hope for our future it lies in our building upon the foundations of our past.'

'What past? The exploitation of the Indians? The Mexican

War? Slavery? The United Fruit Company? Hiroshima? Assassinations?'

'Oh for Christ's sake, Alfred! Why don't you include the fixing of the 1919 World Series? Compare this country's standard of living against any other. For everything you can find to be ashamed of in this country with a little effort you could find two or three more to be proud of.'

'That's the point!' Alfred said. 'These young people know this country could be great again. And if they don't get disillusioned and if they don't "cop out" they might just be able to do it.'

'I don't see how the rioting contributes to making a country great.'

'And you probably wouldn't have helped dump tea bags into Boston Harbor,' Alfred said.

'I don't think they used tea bags then,' I laughed.

We were both silent as I slowed approaching the toll booth; and then after I'd put my quarter into the machine, called it a pig, and got back to normal turnpike speeds again, I asked Alfred what he really thought those young people wanted.

'I don't know that it can be defined. There's a lot more to it than peace and flower-power and love-love-love, and I'm not sure I really understand it all that well. It reflects the decay of the Protestant Ethic and adaptation of the pleasure now principle. We're both over-thirty. They *are* different from you and me. You and I have been out in the world too long. We know what is practical and what isn't. We call it being realistic; they call it copping out. They're a very moral group of people. They are unwarlike. They think it is immoral for a nation to intervene in another nation's domestic affairs. They think it's immoral for a nation to spend more on war than on health and education combined. They think it's immoral that a nation spends billions trying to put what amounts to two animated robots on the moon when in cities in our own country on our own planet, babies are being bitten by rats, children suffer from malnutrition; where a vast percentage of our urban population live in slums unable to escape, without decent educations or decent jobs. You see, these young people have been educated too well. They've heard their professors talk about principles such as liberty and justice and

178

integrity and these young people believe in them. And yet when they turn on television – and this is our first generation to have been raised on television and all the broadest instant communication that implies – and they see anti-war protesters being beaten, when they see civil rights leaders assassinated and their murderers go free and when they go up to Chicago and the stench of political corruption surpasses even the stench of the slaughterhouses, they question our practicality and realism and ask just why this is permitted to go on.'

'No one permits this sort of thing to go on. It just goes on by itself. It has always gone on,' I said. 'And we're trying to improve all the time, but if I may be realistic and practical, it's not going to change in our lifetime.'

'Well, that's where these young people differ,' Alfred said. 'They realize they must change it because you and I won't. They know we've given up. They also know that our lifetime is going to be a lot shorter than we think if something isn't done fast.'

'Well, Alfred,' I said, 'We'll see.'

'I keep trying to tell you that they're different, these young people. They won't give up as easily. You asked me what's happening now and I'll tell you what I think is going on. I think we're in the opening stages of a world revolution. It isn't limited to the blacks and whites in this country, it's going on all over the world. Look what the young people have done already. The ones who went up to New Hampshire with Eugene McCarthy – and, incidentally, don't think they'll be taken in by that phoney bastard again ! – but they're the ones who got rid of L.B.J. The old men are going or are gone all over the world: De Gaulle, Adenauer, Franco, Salazar, Syngman Rhee, Sato – it's happening in Hungary and Czechoslovakia, the Soviet Union, both Chinas – can you imagine what would happen in Red China if the Red Guard ever got hip to what's really going on? The young people in these countries aren't going to put up with it forever. They don't have to. Old men die. But even before that happens they'll be out. Too many people – over and under thirty – in America and other countries are looking around at the endless crap they've been putting up with because of their governments; and they're saying, "Enough!" There's been enough war! Enough violence! Enough poverty! Enough pollution! Enough lies!'

'Nobody likes these things, Alfred. There's been enough cancer, too. And they can picket and denounce cancer all they want but until they find a cure it won't change.'

'Well then, why don't the drug companies satisfy themselves with a mere one hundred per cent profit and donate the rest to research. It would be a tax deduction and to their surprise they might discover the joy of helping people. Or we could pull out of Vietnam and put a portion of the money we're spending there back into health. Medical research.'

'Money can't buy cures, Alfred. And we can't and won't pull out of Vietnam until it's over.'

'That war will *never* be over until the United States learns that wars aren't scored like football games. These body counts. Jesus, don't you think that if President Nixon could get the Vietcong to publicly state that the United States had won the war that he'd goddam well give them Vietnam? Do you think the Vietnamese people are really grateful for the lives Americans have lost in Vietnam? The only thing they are grateful for is the money and the black-market goods they can skim off. Do you think democracy means anything more to them than communism? They – the majority of the people, the Vietnamese people that are getting killed in this war – don't even know what Vietnam means. They don't even know what being a country means. It doesn't matter to them whose side anyone's on – they're getting hurt by both sides. Nobody wins wars. It took us until the Depression to learn what it cost us to win the First World War. The Korean War taught us how we'd lost the Second World War. And the only reason there hasn't been a Third World War is the realization that whoever starts it loses it. And my point, old George, is that there are a great many people who think it might just be possible to put an end to the mess we've made of this planet. And if it means getting a few cracks on the head in the process, still it's worth it.'

'And there'll be a church and a school, Martha. It'll be a decent town where decent people can raise their children decently, I saw the movie,' I said. 'Gary Cooper and –'

'It's no laughing matter,' Alfred said.

'Well it won't be much of a New World if there's no room for laughter. The one trouble with all these kids is that they don't have a sense of humour.'

'I think what you see them doing they take pretty seriously,' Alfred said.

'As they should,' I said. We were silent for a few moments and then I asked, 'Are you planning to stay in New York for good?'

'For a few months.'

'It'll be nice to have you back in town,' I said. 'Where will you be staying?'

'A friend is sub-letting me his apartment. He's in Europe until next April and so it works out fine.'

'Well, I'd offer you mine, but I'm glad you already have one.'

'It sounds like you'll be needing your apartment yourself,' Alfred said. 'Particularly if we can get Alice to agree that a trial separation is a good idea.'

'She won't think it's a good idea,' I said, 'but I hope she'll accept it as necessary.'

Alfred and I drove up through the gates of Winander and along the winding road through the woods past the lake to our house. I parked in the back then we walked around the house to the front door and let ourselves in.

My heart went out to Alice as she knew it would. She was standing just inside the front hallway with our two tow-headed children who, clearly dazzled by Alfred's presence, swirled and eddied at Alice's side. She was wearing the deep blue velvet, high-collared, medieval looking robe I had found for her and which she knew I loved. She had washed and brushed and fixed her hair in such a way that it had the texture and highlights of Rumple-stiltskin's spun gold. The house had been cleaned and the tables waxed; I could smell the roast cooking in the oven from where we stood, and I knew that Alice had made all this effort because she sensed she was on trial. And it was so sad, so awful that I made her feel that way – and even more awful since what she sensed was true.

We had cocktails by the fire in the living-room and Alfred was as entertaining as always, his light conversation and literary gossip buoyantly carrying us through cocktails and into dinner. Alice was charming and gracious and I began to feel the way I always feel when I have to bring the automobile into the garage and say, 'Well, it was making that "ping-ping-ping" all the way down here . . .' Unfortunately I had to leave for the Governors' meeting before dessert and coffee.

The tension was so great upon my return, walking to my former chair between Alfred and Alice was like stepping through hot cobwebs. Alfred was leaning forward being articulate and firm and Alice, sitting back, sore as hell, was having none of it.

'I see you Governors had a few drinks,' she said as I sank heavily into the cushions.

'It's the only way to govern,' I said. 'Whitman tried to sell me his boat again.'

'Did you buy it?'

'No. How's it going with the two of you?'

'Fine,' Alfred said and looked at Alice.

Alice said nothing, merely frowned. She was angry because I had brought somebody, an outsider in to solve our own problems. And she was right; I shouldn't have. But I just didn't know what else I could do. 'I'm sorry the meeting took so long.'

'It gave us a chance to talk,' Alfred said. 'I was telling Alice, that a slight separation, a chance to get away from one another might do some good.'

'And I was telling Alfred,' said Alice, 'that if you go away for six months I don't want you to come back.'

'Which,' I said, 'is pretty much what I told Alfred you'd say.' But with all the booze I had poured down myself I found I was mellowing. The discussion had obviously gone on so long, it had been so tedious, and I knew that Alice, too, shared a desire to end it. And because we even shared that, shared our anger, our resentment, our frustration and pain, a certain closeness emerged. And I stood up and walked over to Alice and sat down on the arm of her chair and put my arm around her and Alfred said he thought he ought to be getting back to New York.

'Spend the night here why don't you?' I said.

'No, thanks George, I've really got to leave. If you can give me a lift down to the village I can catch the ten-thirty bus. I sort of said I'd meet that girl at Elaine's.'

'Are you sure you wouldn't prefer to skip her and get an early start in the morning?'

'The guest bed is already made up,' Alice added.

Fifteen minutes later Alfred was gone and Alice and I drove back from the bus stop alone with each other, for better or for worse.

'Would you like a nightcap, Alice?' I asked her when we were back in the house. 'What were you drinking? Would you like a brandy?'

'You know I can't sleep when I drink brandy.'

'Then how about something else?'

'What are you having?' Alice asked.

'Milk.'

'Milk?'

'Milk,' I said. 'I've had enough.'

'Maybe I'll have a brandy and soda,' Alice said. 'That won't keep me awake will it?'

'Probably, but what the hell. Maybe I'll have one with you.'

'Instead of milk?' she asked and, I began laughing, and Alice, sore again, wanted to know what was so funny.

'I'm not making fun of you,' I said, still laughing. 'It's just that I can remember worrying what married couples talked about after a couple of years. I had no idea it was possible to talk for thirty minutes about milk.'

'It's been only a minute.'

'I know, but it seemed longer.'

'That's because you hate to talk to me.'

'Ohhh, Alice, please,' I said. 'Don't start anything now, not now, please.'

'I wasn't starting anything,' she said. 'I was only stating a simple fact.'

'... You wanted a brandy and soda?'

'Please.'

When I returned with the drinks and handed Alice hers she said, 'The dog's whining. He wants to be let in.'

'Maybe he'll just go away.'

'Are you going to let him in?'

'Alice, come on now, please?' I opened the French doors and said, 'Come on, pup, in you go,' and in came the dog all hip wiggles and tail wags, eyes rolling with pleasure.

'The dog is your responsibility,' Alice said.

'The dog and the garbage and the kitty litter. I'd like to know who drew up the duty roster for this chicken outfit.'

'What is that supposed to mean?'

'It's just an Army joke, my dear,' I said.

'What are your plans for tomorrow?' Alice asked me.

'Nothing exactly. I thought I might do some work in the morning. Why?'

'There're at least a dozen things that need to be done around the house.'

'Can't I do them in the afternoon?'

'We have to be at the art show and book fair at the club. I'm serving tea from three to five.'

'Why do we have to be there?' I asked. 'Who's going to look after the children?'

'They've been invited to a birthday party. Mary Fielding's daughter's. Ann's coming by to pick Ashbel and Syd up with her children.'

'But why do I have to go to this thing at the club?'

'Because you're a Governor,' she said. 'I should think you'd want to go.'

'That shows how much you know about Governors. I'll bet I'll be the only man there.'

'Maybe it would be good for you.'

'Why, because it would boost my sensitive little ego as you once so beautifully put it?'

'I shouldn't have said that,' Alice said. 'I'm sorry.'

'For what?'

'I said, George, I'm sorry,' Alice said and crossed her legs. 'So will you be able to do some work around the house?'

'What needs to be done?'

'You said you'd paint the children's bedroom, and if you did that in the morning then it could dry during the day. And the garage needs to be cleaned out. I can barely fit my car in. The leaves have stopped up the gutter and –'

'– That's plenty. You've given me enough for a week. How am I supposed to get the leaves out of the gutter? We don't have a ladder that tall, do we?'

'Can't you climb out the window onto the roof?'

'Yes, and I can also fall down and go "boom" as Sydney says.'

'Syd has the sniffles. She may be getting a cold.'

'Then I'll go up and take a look at her. She seemed fine when I came in, but I'll check her.'

'Would you give me a hand with the dishes, first?'

'I'll be back in a minute,' I told her.

Dear God, what happens to two people who marry each other out of love? Where does it all go? What turns us into cell mates?

I stood in the children's bedroom looking down at their small bodies. Ashbel lay curled up tightly, his mouth open, one delicate hand beneath his cheek. Syd, in her bed, lay arms and legs outstretched like a free-fall parachutist.

What do they dream about I wonder? Once, when Ashbel was a little over two, I heard him speak just one word in his sleep. He said, 'Truck!' and, oh God, I hoped he was dreaming of the most glorious truck there ever was. Ten huge wheels with chromium rims on either side, a high crimson cab with air horns sprouting like rococo angels' trumpets from its peak, a trailer of silver with bright lights for its trim, lights along that trailer like a midnight passing train.

'Truck!' said my son and the wind rushed out of his throat like tumbleweed across a darkened interstate.

I have never heard Sydney speak in her dreams. She, like her mother, holds it in.

I cover both my children with their blankets, place the stuffed animals at the side of Syd's crib, then go back down to help Alice with the dishes.

'How was she?' Alice asked handing me a dishtowel. 'You only need to dry the wine glasses. The rest can go in the washer.'

'She was fine. No rattles. Have you ever heard her talk in her sleep?'

'No, I don't think so. Why?'

'I was just thinking about it up in their rooms. I was wondering what Syd dreams about.'

'She dreams about Ashbel's toys,' Alice laughed. 'That's all she's really interested in.'

'Well, she was sleeping so soundly I'm sure she'll be fine in the morning.'

'I hope so,' Alice said. 'It would be a shame if she had to miss the birthday party.'

'Are those glasses washed?'

'All you need to do is dry them and put them away.'

I began drying the glasses. 'You really looked so lovely tonight, Alice.'

'Why, thank you, George.'

'I mean it. You were just lovely. Almost like a new person – and I don't mean that in any unkind way. You're always lovely, it's just that tonight there was something special about the way you looked that was extra.'

'You've always loved this robe.'

'I know. I do love it. I never was really sure though that you liked it.'

'Of course I do,' Alice said.

'I'm glad. It looks so well on you. Perhaps you should have been a Renaissance princess – except that I can't picture a blonde Renaissance princess. Somehow I've always sort of imagined them to have dark, rich hair, or possibly very bright red hair. But either way their hair was long and shiny; and they always had the palest, porcelain complexions; and they held roses to their cheeks and the roses turned their eyes violet or very green – I think one of the first things I ever noticed about you were your eyes. Did you know that?'

'My eyes? Really? Why?'

'Because they seemed so out of place – not wrong, but just an unnecessary luxury. I mean you were lovely enough looking already so that you could have been given just plain old blue or green eyes, but your eyes are almost silver ... You know? When

I was growing up I used to read all the pulps, things like *Wings* and one, I think, called *Flying Aces*. And I always wanted to have eyes like the fighter pilots. The writers always described them as being the palest of blues flecked with silver and implied they got that way because they had looked at so much sky. Silver eyed pilots – unless, of course, the pilot was sighting down the nose of a P-39, Aircobra, at some Messerschmidt or Folke-Wolfe 190 – actually I don't think the P-39 was used much in Europe. It would have been the P-47 or the Lightning and –'

'Can you reach me the salad bowl?'

'Sure, here. But I bet they were used in North Africa.'

'What were?'

'P-39's. The point I was trying to make was that the pilots' eyes were silver-blue unless they were shooting down the filthy Krauts or dirty Japs! Then their eyes were tinged with red.'

'My eyes are probably tinged with red right now,' Alice said.

'Even so you have fighter pilots' eyes. They're so pale! I hope Syd has them too. Ashbel, I'm afraid, has eyes more like mine.'

'Yours are hazel.'

I laughed, 'Well, that's very sweet of you, but they're just plain brown. Brown and becoming myopic.'

'You're very handsome. Why do you pretend you're not?'

'I'm not pretending anything,' I said. 'But – maybe I will become handsome. We Dethriffes age very slowly and gracefully. Like rare burgundies, and, probably like burgandies we don't travel well. Did you know my maternal grandfather had silver hair? He had the most beautiful hair of any man I've ever seen. I wish I thought I'd have hair like that.'

'You're too dark.'

'And my paternal grandfather was bald. Isn't – I mean, aren't things like hair and eye colour supposed to skip generations? The heredity factors? Maybe I'm wrong, but I'm almost sure I learned that in some biology class. Do you look like any of your grandparents?'

'They're all dead now, but I suppose you meant before?'

'For Christ's sake! Of course I meant before, what did you think?'

'I think you're feeling very chatty tonight,' Alice said and handed me another wine glass to dry.

'Am I talking too much? Do you mind? My father always used to say to me, "Babble on little brook, babble on." Only, for years I thought he was saying, "Babylon", B,A,B,Y,L,O,N, the tower of Babel and so forth – Are we finished?'

'You could make one last tour of the living-room to see if we've got everything.'

I returned a moment later with an ashtray which I handed to Alice. 'Alfred certainly seemed in good form tonight didn't you think?'

'I suppose so,' Alice said. 'Although I can't really think of any circumstances when he hasn't been entertaining – I think we're all finished here. Why don't you drop another ice cube in my brandy and soda and I'll carry it upstairs with me. Where's yours?'

'I poured it out. I got about half-way through and knew I didn't want to finish it, or if I did I'd –'

'– But it was good Brandy!' Alice protested.

'I know, but so what? I couldn't pour it back in the bottle and I didn't want to finish it. Are you planning on taking a bath or watching TV or anything?'

'Why?'

'Well, I just felt like staying up, maybe taking a walk or doing some reading.'

'Is there anything on television?'

'What time is it? "the Late Show" or Johnny Carson or something.'

'I'm pretty tired, actually. Stay up if you want. Come to bed when you feel like it.'

'Okay,' I said, and felt this enormous relief wash over me. I walked Alice to the foot of the stairs and she went up one step then paused by the Currier and Ives print of 'The Fall of Richmond, Va., on the Night of April Second 1865'.

'Good night, George,' she said, I thought a trifle sadly. I leaned forward and kissed her gently on the cheek, the flames over the city of Richmond leaping about us. 'Don't leave me, George,' she said, holding me tightly to her for a moment, 'what would I do if you left me?'

'You'd be perfectly all right, Alice, so don't worry. Besides, I'm not going to leave you.'

'But what about the trial separation? I wouldn't know what to do if you left me for six months.'

'Alice, I'm not going anywhere except maybe for a walk down to the dock for a few minutes and then I'll come up to bed, too. So you go on up and get some sleep. I'll be up soon. And tomorrow after a good night's sleep, I'll work on whatever you want, the garage, the children's bedroom. And then we'll go off to the book fair and you'll serve tea and I'll talk to the ladies, and then we'll go to the club dance and have a good time there, okay? We'll have a nice day tomorrow.'

'You're talking to me as though I were a child.'

'I don't mean to, Alice,' I said. 'You go on up to bed, I'll be up in a half hour or so, and maybe you'll be asleep by then. Sweet dreams,' I said, and moved away from the stairs before she could speak. I could hear her continuing up the steps behind me and I went through the living-room and out the front door. I walked down the lawn to the edge of the lake then to our boat-house and dock. The moon backlighted the pines upon the crumbling mountain's peak and a gust of wind brushed the treetops like a mother's hand upon a small boy's cowlick, then the wind swept down the bald rock slope, vaulted the shadowy bank and skimmed on to the lake, dimpling the dark, silver water. Crystal fragments flashed upon the shattered mirror as the wind doubled and redoubled back upon itself in a flurry of indecision, then skated across the deep lake caressing the stillness with its smooth breath until its coolness enveloped me in my solitude, scattered by cigarette ash in a starshell of sparks against the boat-house door, and was gone. The moon began to fade behind a cloud, blending the worn and aged crown of the mountain into the horizon. The lake, smooth once more, reflected the silence. Something splashed far out in the lake. In the diminishing light the familiar landmarks became blurred and threatening. The cove in which our boat-house lay closed in about me. The water deepened

189

and opened. The horizon blackened and met the vaulted sky. Across the lake, an automobile leaving Webster Neill's entered the road beneath the mountain, chased its headlights along the shore, then, picking up speed, swiftly zippered shut the darkness and was gone. One by one the lights in the Neill house were extinguished until the sole light left was the bulb at the end of their dock twinkling dimly green in the distance.

How I envied Webster Neill to have loved and have been loved by two women for so long! How is it possible? Where does anyone find a woman he can be happy with for twenty-six years?

I turned back and looked up at the house. The light was still on in our bedroom. The house looked so warm and inviting. The children were asleep in the room next to ours. The dog was sleeping in the living-room. The cat on top of a book-shelf somewhere. But I did not want to go back inside. A shadow crossed the bedroom window. Alice was pacing and I turned back to the lake with a desperate animal sense of being hunted.

Each night when I slip into bed and lie like some log long fallen into primaeval ooze, she rolls towards me, throws her arm and leg across my trunk like tendrils and, pushing herself against me, I feel myself drained.

I wear pyjamas now. I never used to. I wear them like armour. To keep my skin intact. There are times when I feel I am being eaten alive. Her 'Coming to bed, dear?' makes me feel like the Western lawman in the desert who dares not fall asleep lest his prisoner rise up and kill him.

Nights, in our bed, her foot scuttles across the sheet towards me, piling up little linen ripples until her foot touches mine, one uncut toenail stabs my instep and my foot, in an involuntary spasm, leaps away.

'George . . . ?'

I turn. She has opened the bedroom window and is standing there calling me.

'Yes, dear?'

'Are you coming to bed soon?'

Tonight is the third night since we have made love. And tomorrow the dance is at the club and it would be nice if she were in a good mood for that.

'I'll be there in a minute,' I tell her.

The light blinks off on the Neill's dock.

Chapter Fourteen

When I came upstairs I found only the light on my bedside table was lit, and Alice was back in bed, the covers pulled up to the tops of her breasts, her shoulders bare.

'You aren't going to put pyjamas on, are you?'

I smiled at her and shook my head, 'No, but I thought it might be nice if I brushed my teeth.' I passed through to the bathroom, undressed and stood toothbrush in hand looking at myself in the mirror. My eyes returned my gaze, neither bored nor interested, merely guarded. I looked at myself and a stranger looked back at me. I brushed my teeth and walked nude back to our bed.

'Are you tired?' Alice asked me.

'A little.' I stretched out beneath the covers and immediately she rolled towards me and I felt her breasts full and separate against my chest and farther down her thigh which pushed now between mine. I touched her hip softly, following the curve of her pelvis to the indentation of her waist, then up the hollow of her spine to the back of her neck.

'Ummm,' she murmured and pressed her forehead into my throat.

I massaged her neck muscles gently. I closed my eyes but nothing happened. I could not conjure up any satisfactory pictures, and I grew increasingly aware of myself, still soft, against Alice's thigh. For a few minutes we lay there holding each other.

'Nancy asked me to go antiquing with her,' Alice said.

'Oh? – When?'

'Monday or Tuesday. Do you know what she told me?'

'What?' I asked. My hand moved down her back to her buttocks.

'She told me she thought you were very sexy.'

I waited for Alice's laugh, but none came. 'How did the subject come up?'

'Well, as I told you on the telephone, Nancy came over this afternoon and we were having a drink and were talking about the different couples and – oh! Charlie and Ann Baker are getting a divorce, did you know that?'

'No I didn't. When did they decide that?'

'After the last dance at the club – the most recent dance.'

'How did you find out?'

'Nancy told me,' Alice said. 'You remember how the Fieldings asked everyone back to their place for a nightcap? Well, Ann didn't want to go, but Charlie did. So Charlie left with Wendy Thayer and Paul Thayer took Ann home.'

'That's not what anyone would call a new switch,' I laughed, 'they were the scandal of Winander when we first moved up here. Did Nancy go to the Fieldings?'

'Of course! Nancy wouldn't have missed it for the world. She said that Charlie and Wendy made quite a couple.'

'What is that supposed to mean?'

'Nothing. Only they seemed very affectionate.'

'Overly so? Was that the evening the Fieldings showed the skin flicks?'

'Nancy said they were awful.'

'The movies? The Fieldings? Or Charlie and Wendy?'

'All three.' She rolled over on to her back and the covers slid down baring her breasts. 'Have you ever seen any dirty movies?'

'Not since college,' I said. 'I had a friend who was kicked out of Harvard for projecting one out of his window on to the building across the street. It was incredible ... Of course it didn't show up very well because it was so far away, but still there was no doubt what was going on. Quite a crowd collected before the cops got him.'

'Well, I've never seen one,' Alice said.

'Would you like to?'

'Sure, I don't know, what are they like?'

'The next time the Fieldings ask us, I'll take you and you can see for yourself.'

'But what are they like?'

'Depressing. I remember the first time I ever saw one. For the first few minutes I was astonished that the people were letting themselves be filmed; and then they were so businesslike about it, so matter-of-fact that in a way it became pretty erotic. But, unfortunately, the film ran about ten minutes more and it just became a couple of pieces of meat.'

'What did they do?'

'Everything.'

'It showed them doing everything? ... What did they look like?'

'It differs. Some of them aren't so bad looking. I mean the girls are surprisingly attractive. Not raving beauties, God knows, but they're not pigs either. In fact I thought the girls always seemed more attractive than the men.'

'I should hope so!' Alice laughed.

'Well, you know what I mean. I mean the girls, I felt, didn't need to be in those films. I was surprised by them. The men – or boys, in some cases, looked like the sort of acne crowd who hang around amusement arcades, and they were so sad in a funny way. I mean I can remember one film in which the guy could never –'

'Never what?' Alice asked. 'You mean he never got a hard on?'

'The entire film. He just stood by the others and watched ... How did Nancy like them?'

'Oh you know Nancy,' Alice laughed. 'She said she spent the entire time with her hands over her eyes.'

'And peeping through her fingers.'

'That's right.'

'I'll bet she didn't miss a thing.'

'She didn't. She said Charlie Baker had his hand up Wendy's dress the entire time.'

'Ahh, Suburbia,' I sighed.

'I think it's awful,' Alice said. 'Nancy told me that in one of the films there was a white girl and a Negro.'

'Negro man or woman?'

'A man!' Alice said. 'Nancy said that the girl even took him into her mouth.'

'Is that so?' I said smiling. I rolled over on to my side and looked down at Alice's body. Her nipples were hard and I wondered whether it was because of the cold. As I moved my hand down to her stomach Alice said, 'I think that's awful don't you?' I felt her thighs open wide; as my hand moved lower she drew in her breath and closed her eyes. She was sopping wet.

Oh, Alice, the hypocrisy of you wives!

I fucked her with a vengeance. No gentle love making this, nor was I soft this time. Instead, it was as though all my rage, my frustration, all my scorn and humiliation had swollen inside me and I lifted my hand away, moved on top of her and cut into her as though I were using a knife, as though I were goring her with a rhino's horn. I felt her body shake each time I drove into her, and I raised myself so that our only connection was our lust. With each jolt the violet flush spread farther and deeper beneath her throat and down her breasts. With each plunge her breasts bounced, their tops filled, then slackened. Again and again I pushed into her as deeply as I could. Her lips pulled back baring her teeth. Little groans escaped marking our rhythm. I went at her absolutely cold-bloodedly and brutally, skewering her and all the Mary Fieldings and Wendy Thayers and Ann Bakers of Winander. It was a slamming, bruising, murderous fuck; and when her 'oh yes's' came closer and closer together, when her head was rolling from side to side on the pillow, when her eyes – which had been so tightly shut – opened but did not focus, I let myself back down on her body, reached beneath her buttocks to the junction of her thighs and so savagely wretched her legs apart that she groaned with pain and I knew that in hurting her I had pushed her to the brink. She clutched me to her, lifted her knees high and locked her ankles over my back and flung herself back up at me, bucking, clawing and imploring me not to stop.

I had no intention of stopping. Again and again I stabbed her until her second orgasm came and with her I came too in an orgasm so painful, so stinging, so convulsive, so filled with rage that I was sure my ejaculation would burn her, sear closed the entrance to her womb. And not even then did I leave, would I leave her. Not until she begged me to stop. Only then did I roll away from her and only then did I think of her again as my wife.

For a long time we lay on our backs not looking at each other, not speaking. The covers lay twisted like snakes at our feet. I could hear my heart pounding, the blood pulsing in my ears. I heard Alice move and then felt her roll towards me, her foot brush against mine, her hand slid across the covers to my stomach. And when I turned my head to look at her, her eyes met mine, and they were full and shining. She had loved it. She had absolutely loved it.

She had not even understood my rage or my reason. And I understood that I had sentenced myself to performing in kind.

Alice went to sleep almost immediately. Not I. I sat up in bed looking at the crack that ran along the wall above my bureau, and I thought of how many times on how many evenings of tension and anger had I sat looking at that same crack. I got up, put on my bathrobe and went in to look at the children. They were both sleeping soundly. I adjusted their covers and went back to bed. Still, it took me a long time to fall asleep, and still later to relax.

Chapter Fifteen

Four inches of snow turned Winander white overnight. Alice and I awoke Saturday morning to the grating of snowplough blades clearing the lake road and the soft, deep *chrummrum* of passing automobiles' tyre chains. It snowed off and on all morning and I busied myself shovelling out the drive and clearing paths to the front and back door while the dog tracked back and forth playing connect-the-dots from shrub to shrub.

When I came back inside for breakfast the children were pink with excitement and I promised them the first thing we would do would be to buy a sled. Which we did. Ashbel could barely contain his impatience with me while I Brillo'd the paint off the bottom of the runners and soaped the blades. Sydney, of course, had no real interest in what was going on; she only knew that the sled was a toy and limited her concern to whether or not she would have to share it with her brother. When I finished I took the children outside, sat them on the sled, and told Ashbel to hold on to Syd and towed them around and around until we had packed enough snow on the gentle hill behind the house for Ashbel to steer the sled himself.

And so, while they played and the dog chased them, I shook the snow off the young pines we had planted the previous spring, rearranged the garage so Alice's Chrysler would fit, and wondered what the hell anyone really wanted a Chrysler station-wagon for.

And then, after lunch, and after the children had gone off to their birthday party we drove to the club where Alice served tea to the ladies of the art and book show; Mrs Gorwell spiked hers with vodka. Jim Whitman whisked me away to the men's bar to be the sixth player in the Saturday afternoon poker game. Chauncey Halpert, the polo player, was there. And during one hand of seven card stud he embarrassedly interrupted the dealer after his fifth card, turned up all his cards, and apologized for having received a Royal Straight Flush in clubs.

'What the hell'd you do that for?' Whitman asked.

'I couldn't help it. They were just dealt to me,' Chauncey said. 'It would have been unfair to play out the hand.'

'Jesus Christ!' Whitman said. 'I've waited thirty years for a hand like that. And it's dealt straight to the man one seat on my left and what does he do with it? He doesn't want to play it. Jesus Christ.'

'What was the point?' Chauncey asked. 'I only would have won more of your money.'

'Jesus Christ!' Whitman said.

And old Mr Mapes said, 'Gentlemen, we are playing poker.'

I lost seventy-five dollars. All I was ever dealt were mediocre hands. Good enough to stay for the few raises necessary to buy enough cards to see that it was hopeless. The only hand I won was with a staight against Mr Mapes's poor eyesight which had led him to believe he had a flush when all he really had were four hearts and a diamond. The game ended when the staff came in at five to begin spreading evergreen boughs, pinecones, berries and other winter decorations for the dance. I picked up Alice and we swung by the Fieldings to scoop up the children. The Carlyles had not yet arrived and Mary Fielding made us promise not to be too late for cocktails since the dinner was to be seated at 8.30. 'Are you going to the Hamlins' cocktail party first?' Mary asked Alice.

'I don't know,' Alice said. 'I've got the invitation lists at home.'

'Everyone was invited to the Hamlins,' Mary said. 'I do hope some nice people decide to come.'

'I like the Hamlins,' I said. 'I'm glad they moved here. I had a long talk with him on the train the other morning. He has something to do with automobiles.'

'Auto parts,' Mary said. 'He sells accessories. But they're terribly nice, really. And she's simply adorable. And they so want to make friends.'

'Who doesn't?' Alice said.

In Winander, one's social position was measured by one's inclusion on or exclusion from cocktail party and dinner invitation lists. Winander wives with social aspirations studied the invitation lists as intently as their husbands studied the market reports.

One of the cocktail parties we attended was given by the Hamlins. We arrived (Alice glorious in a dark green Mainbocher, blonde hair hanging down, and me dinner jacketed, waistcoated with the gold watch chain and patent leather pumps) in time to see Chauncey Halpert settling his bet with Charlie Baker that he could jump the Hamlins' shetland pony over their living-room couch. The pony refused and Chauncey was thrown over the couch, and into a plate glass sliding door which miraculously didn't break. Chauncey was urged not to try again.

'Nonsense, that was just first refusal,' Chauncey said. 'One must get right back on.'

And Betty Hamlin burst into tears.

I led Chauncey and the pony outside and asked him what he had wanted to do a silly-ass thing like that for.

'Nobody hurt, old boy,' he said.

'Except Betty Hamlin.'

'Why was she crying?' Chauncey asked. 'I thought it would liven up her party. Give her something to talk about, to show how she was included in our fun. You'll see, George, I really did her a favour.'

We stabled the pony and walked back inside. Betty Hamlin met us at the door. 'Oh, Chauncey,' she said, 'are you alright?'

'Never felt better,' he said, 'I hope I haven't upset you?'

'Me? Why should I be upset? I was so relieved that the glass didn't break. It might have killed you! Are you sure you're not injured?'

'Only my pride,' Chauncey said, and taking Betty's arm, led her back into her party.

We went directly from the Hamlins' to the Fieldings' and the moment we arrived Toby Fielding made a beeline for Alice which was fine, since it gave me an opportunity to speak with Missy Carlyle who approached me with such shining eyes and so wondrous a smile that I felt my stomach churn.

'I've missed you,' she said.

'I've missed *you*. How are you?'

'Fine. Walter's talking to Mary Fielding. There's the strangest thing going on here.'

'You mean the Couples Game?'

'If that means what I think it means,' Missy said and laughed. 'It's vocabulary class again!'

'Don't worry, it's too early in the evening for it to get beyond the game stage. There are enough different people here to keep our host and hostess distracted – speaking of which, here comes Mary.'

'What are you two talking about all by yourselves in a corner, as if I didn't know?' Mary Fielding asked us.

'Nothing much,' I said.

'Just standing here laughing and scratching,' Missy said.

'Ah well, if you've got an itch –' Mary waved her hand, said, 'Ta-ta' and was off again.

'I positively feel as though all the women around here were in heat,' Missy said. 'It's incredible! I feel safer in New York where they're just simple muggers and rapists and junkies. I can cope with them, but these women! Do you know what Mary asked me while we were dressing? No, of course you don't, but she almost came right out and asked me if I had been unfaithful to Walt. I mean as if I'd *tell* her.'

'What did you say to her?' I asked.

'I said why would I ever want to do a thing like that since as everyone knows Walt and I are so divinely happy together. That's what I told her, although there are moments when I get tired of putting up a brave front and – and don't think I don't know what you're thinking, George Dethriffe, so you can just raise your eyes from my padded bra this instant.'

'Ah, Missy,' I laughed, 'you're a wonder.'

'Have you ever seen anything so beautiful as Winander in all this snow? Makes it almost seem clean. And tomorrow being Sunday, Central Park's Mt Seventy-second Street will be overflowing with little mothers in Pucci parkas towing their little trust funds to the tops of the hills. Does Ashbel have a sled?'

'Got him one this morning. A Flexible Flyer.'

'And did you soap the runners?'

'Scraped the paint off first,' I laughed.

'Darling,' Alice said to me as she approached. 'Oh, hi, Missy – Darling, would you get me a drink?'

'Sure,' I said. 'Missy, can I get you something? What're you drinking?'

'A Martini,' Missy said, then shrugged. 'Why not? It's the quickest.'

'One Martini,' I said. 'And you, Alice? What will you have?'

'I don't know,' Alice said. 'Scotch, I suppose. Make it a weak scotch and soda.'

'One Martini and a scotch and soda,' I said.

At dinner I sat between Ann Prodell Baker and Wendy Thayer. Wendy's C-cups were, as usual, running over, but she was directing them across the table at Charlie Baker – which made Charlie undisguisedly happy, and Ann not so. Therefore, I spent most of the dinner talking to Ann, who told one story that fascinated me. It seems that one of Ann's mother's closest friends had recently died and the lady's former male secretary telephoned Mrs Prodell and asked if he might be able to meet her for lunch in the city. The only reason he gave was that it concerned Mrs Prodell's late friend. Mrs Prodell neither liked nor approved of her friend's relationship with the male secretary, but she nevertheless agreed to meet him and made a reservation for lunch at 21.

Mrs Prodell arrived at 21 and was promptly shown to her table by one of the Krindlers where the former male secretary was already seated. Until their cocktails were brought Mrs Prodell and the young man exchanged polite comments and then the secretary said, 'Mrs Prodell, I know how much you loved Mrs T—, and what good friends the two of you were. I also know how much Mrs T— would have wanted for you to have something of hers as a keepsake, a memento. Several times I heard you mention how much you admired the alligator purse I had given her and I thought, perhaps, you might like to have it. I'd be willing to give it to you for exactly what it cost me –'

According to Ann her mother stood up, said, 'I'm very sorry, but I've suddenly recalled I have a previous appointment,' and left.

'That's not all,' Ann said. 'The man stayed on at 21, had lunch, and had the bill sent to Mother.'

'She paid it?' I asked.

'Certainly she did, and feels she got off cheap.'

Dinner ended and brandies followed, the gentlemen and ladies retiring not so much to separate rooms as separate corners. But the whole time I stood listening to Charlie Baker extolling the virtue of some petroleum stock I was watching Missy Carlyle and my wife having an animated conversation. And when, during the drive from the Fieldings to the Winander Club I asked Alice what she and Missy had been talking about, Alice said, 'Oh, nothing, really.'

'Well, you seemed to be having a good time,' I said.

'We were,' Alice said. 'I like Missy. I think she has a crush on you.'

'On me!' I laughed.

'Toby Fielding wants us all to come back to their house after the dance.'

'To show his films?'

'He didn't say.'

'Who's "us"? Who's coming?'

'The Bakers, the Thayers, the Carlyles and us.'

'All the beautiful people,' I said. 'I didn't think the Fieldings' house had that many bedrooms.'

'Now just what the hell does that mean?'

'Nothing, except that it sounds like the starting line-up for one of the Fieldings' games. Does he choose up sides, or do we just all throw our keys in the hat?'

'Really, George, I don't think that's what he has in mind at all.'

'The hell it isn't.'

'Well, I said we'd just stop in. If it gets rough we can leave.'

'In other words, you'd like to stay for the movies.'

'Would that be so awful?' Alice asked. 'I've never seen one.'

'No, it's not so awful. If you feel like going, we'll go. Listen, there probably won't be any place to park near the club so I'll let you out at the front and go park.'

'You won't be upset if we go back to the Fieldings?' Alice asked.

'It depends on what you're going back there looking for.'

'You sound as though you think I'm going back there to swap partners. Is that what you're thinking?'

'What *do* you want, Alice?'

'Oh Christ, sometimes you're such a drag, George, really you are.'

'I have that feeling myself,' I said.

'And you're a hypocrite.'

'No doubt.'

'You think that because you and Missy Carlyle have kidded yourselves into believing that you've got a crush on each other, that you love each other, then you two can climb into bed and everything's hunky-dory. It's all clean and cotton baby-bunting. You think that because she spreads her legs and calls it "love" that it's all right. But if I were to spread my legs and admit it's sex then it's cheap. It's dirty. Would it make it all right if I called it love? Would you still mind?'

'You're goddam right I would.'

'Double standard?'

'Absolutely.'

'And you don't think that's hypocritical?'

'I think it's honest.'

'Well then, let me be honest with you, George. You hurt me more than I knew I could be hurt. I think I could have forgiven you that girl you had at your apartment if only you hadn't told her you loved her. As soon as you told her that, you gave her something which you took from me. I could have forgiven you if it were just a one-night stand, but that wasn't enough for you or for her. You weren't satisfied until you had also given her my pride. Do you understand what I mean? How can I have any pride when I know you don't love me, when you make love to another woman and tell her you love *her*? When you want to make love to her and not to me? Just what exactly do you want me around for? What are you keeping me for?'

'You're my wife, Alice.'

'Shit. What's a wife?' she asked. 'I don't want to be just your wife, George. Can't I mean something more to you than that? Before we were married, when you and I were living together you used to make me feel as though I were something special, as though I were some sort of princess. You made me feel as though I was beautiful. And I wanted to be beautiful. For you. For you, George. And, and I was!'

'You still are,' I said.

'Somehow I felt beautiful because you told me I was. But now – now I see you look at Missy Carlyle the way I want you to look at me and I don't want you to go to bed with her, George. I really don't. Please don't George? Promise me that you won't.'

'Alice, there's nothing going on between Missy Carlyle and me. We're just friends.'

'Ohhhh, George . . . ,' Alice said dejectedly.

And we drove in silence the rest of the way to the club.

Chapter Sixteen

It was snowing again; big, wet, heavy white flakes that gathered in soundless clumps along the arc of my windshield-wiper blades. I pulled into the entrance of the club and told Alice that I'd see her inside and she said, 'Don't worry about me, George.'

'What does that mean?'

'What I said. You go park the car. I can take care of myself.'

'Of course you can,' I said, 'but where do you want me to meet you?'

'Don't bother,' Alice said. 'You just go see your friend, Missy.' She got out of the car and slammed the door and I rejoined the line of automobiles patiently orbiting about the drive in search of parking places.

It did not look as though this snowstorm was going to end before morning so, to avoid getting stuck, I parked on the level ground down by the tennis courts and stepped out into the cold, night air.

A slight wind was pushing the snowflakes like winter moths against the ornamental standing lights whose electric globes, like a string of grandmother's pearls, had become so pockmarked by age that one could now only dimly see by their muted lustre the snowdrifted path that began at the tennis pavilion and rose beyond the drained and boarded summer swimming pools, up the gentle slope upon whose crest had been built the Winander Club. The club's fogged windows were lit from within by so many Christmas coloured lights that from where I stood, part way up the path, the building had less the air of a stately club house than that of some midwestern hog and corn baron's isolated, overcarved and ornamented, Tiffany lamp filled mansion. The orchestra was playing 'Lady Is A Tramp' the chorus ghostly thin and chilled by gusts of wind which blew the music and the snowflakes down to me and beyond to where a young girl picked it up and sang, in mock temper, 'Hey, California, it's *cold* and it's *damp*!' And when I looked back I saw the most startlingly beautiful girl with the most extraordinarily rich mane of red hair. She was leaning on her date's arm for support as she daintily placed each foot in my footprints on the path behind me. Her fur coat came no lower than her mini-dress and she was showing a lot of very, very long and very, very pretty leg underneath.

'Hey!' she called up to me, 'would you mind taking shorter steps?'

Her date waved and I waved back and it wasn't until they were closer that I recognized the young man as Lollie Edmund's son, Tom, who was, I think, a junior at Princeton.

'Hi, Mr Dethriffe,' he said when they caught up. 'Excuse Jennifer for shouting at you.' We were introduced to each other and Tom wanted to know if that was my Cord he had parked next to.

'Yes,' I said. 'Do you like it?'

'I sure do,' Tom said.

'I'll let you drive it sometime when the roads are clear.'

'Oh, I know how to drive in the snow,' Tom said. And I smiled and said I was sure he could, but that I only meant he would have more fun driving it when the roads were clear.

We continued up the path and far ahead of us a young man in a long, dark overcoat and white silk scarf scooped up his evening-gowned companion and carried her through the snow in a short-cut to the front door.

Alice was not in the lobby and I searched for her in one of the smaller rooms where buffet tables had been set up with little Christmas tree centrepieces and hors d'oeuvre in the shapes of holly wreaths. Because of the party, the men's bar was open to the ladies and it was there that I found the Fieldings with row upon row of whisky, gin and vodka bottles stacked like votive candles over their shoulders.

'Have you seen Alice?' I called to the Fieldings across several shoulders. But my voice was lost in the busyness of the bartenders and guests. Ice cubes crashed about me. Charm-braceleted arms jingled past me reaching for drinks. Glasses clinked together, laughter bubbled between them. I wedged my way through to the Fieldings and asked again if they had seen Alice.

'I think she's dancing,' Mary Fielding said. 'Come have a drink with us.'

During the next thirty minutes I met a dozen people whose names I immediately forgot and then Missy Carlyle strode in with her long loping walk that made any evening gown she wore seem like sports clothes.

'I am getting absolutely blitzed!' she laughed. 'I've never seen so many people! Who are they? I've just spent the most awful time dancing with the most awful man who couldn't keep his hands off my rear and the whole time he was mumbling into my hair. I couldn't understand a *word* he was saying. It all sounded like, "Pant, pant, pant, bed, pant, pant, pant, you pant, pant, pant, me." I finally left him twirling alone in the middle of the dance floor. Where've you been? I've been looking all over for you.'

'I was looking for Alice,' I said. 'I got this far. What're you drinking?'

'A Martini.'

'Still?'

'Forever,' Missy said. 'You promised to dance with me. Alice is dancing with Walter now. Let's have a drink later. I want to dance with you now. I love dancing and I never get a chance to. Don't you love to dance? It's a divine orchestra – really. They're from New Haven of all places, but they're really very, very good. Don't you love parties this huge? I adore them like this. They're so intimate. You can talk to anybody you want, or sneak off, or whatever. They're so much more intimate than little parties. Don't you think so, really?'

Missy swept us into the ballroom where we joined the dancers. There were the older couples who still could do a foxtrot or a discreet two-step around the perimeter of the dance floor. In the middle were the younger members abandoning themselves to the pleasure of the chase. There were still the Long Island boys who danced with their elbows bouncing, their girls playfully swooning backwards into their arms. There were still the débutantes and their escorts locked into steamy box steps, eyes heavy-lidded, brows damp. There was still the momentary applause as a débutante danced by with her father, the orchestra struggling to keep their waltz in time with his unsteadiness. There was still Wendy Thayer casting her ample body around and the assurance that later in the evening, when she had had enough to drink, she would dance in front of the orchestra alone. And pathetic little pigeon-breasted Leslie Cotter danced by pressing her thighs around her partner's leg. And the music which had grown steadily louder as the guests grew steadily higher, went on. There was Charlie and Ann Baker dancing a stiff and tightly controlled embroidery in one corner. In another corner a group of young Greeks were being entertained by the chairman of the Racquets Committee and at another table sat Mr and Mrs Mapes, their faces full of the excesses of wealth.

'You haven't said a word to me,' Missy protested.

'I know,' I said. 'I'm sorry.'

'Are you tired? Would you like to sit down?'

'Whatever you like, Missy,' I said. 'I'm sorry I just don't feel very gay tonight. Would you like that Martini?'

'Sure,' Missy said. Her hand dropped from my shoulder to my wrist and she led me off the dance floor and into the bar.

'I still haven't seen Alice,' I said. 'Where do you suppose she is?'

'I haven't seen Walter either,' Missy said. 'They were dancing together. You don't suppose —?'

'Divine retribution?' I laughed.

We pushed through the crowd around the bar. Chauncey Halpert and Toby Fielding were at the backgammon table. Chauncey had doubled and Toby had taken it thinking he was in position for a good back game. Off to our right two young couples were playing eight-ball in the billiard room. And all around us were the sounds of ice cubes rattling, glasses clinking and the rustle of smoky laughter.

I picked up our drinks and led Missy out of the bar to the staircase near the back entrance to the club. 'We can sit here,' I said. We could still see into the bar and beyond the bar to a corner of the dance floor. Just as we were lowering ourselves on to the steps the back entrance opened and a trio of party-goers swirled in with the cold.

'God I wish I were in Florida,' Missy shivered. 'I have a terrible longing to go somewhere warm. Some semitropic beach where I can wallow about in the shallow water like a brontosaurus, ferns dripping from my lips. Last winter Walt and I went down to Barney Langlund's vast plantation in North Carolina. Do you know Barney?'

'I don't think so,' I said.

'Oh you should, George,' Missy said. 'You'd love each other. Really you would.' She took a sip of her Martini. 'He has horses and dogs and handlers and beaters and, and corn fields and pine trees and God knows more birds than anyone could believe – quail and dove and wild turkey and he has shooting brakes and, and ancestral portraits and Louis Quinze furniture and Aubusson rugs and a Lear jet and really everything in the world a man could want except friends close by to talk to. So he's delighted to send his plane up for them.'

'Who'd you go with?'

'My pretty cousin Belinda and her storm trooper husband.'

'Did you hunt?'

'I went out on the wagon, but I didn't shoot. It was really all so lovely. Like one of your old hunting prints. You must meet Barney. When he comes up to New York we'll have you to dinner. It would be so much fun. The only thing anybody talks about in New York now are money, rudeness, money and sex – and bad marriages,' Missy added, 'which tend to also fall into the category of sexual catastrophes. But I'd like to hear you and Barney discuss old family portraits.'

'I was thinking about ancestral portraits the other day,' I said.

'Really.'

'Why?' Missy asked. 'What about them?'

'Well my mother has a few and I'll probably inherit them and I was thinking it was a shame how little I knew about the men and women portrayed. I mean unless your ancestor was somebody famous it's difficult to have the portrait mean anything to you. I can look at them and scrape up some residue of an anecdote I had heard about them, that so-and-so was Governor

Talmadge's son-in-law or that he was the one who broke the ladderback chair over his daughter's suitor's head. And in so many cases generations have known no more about the person portrayed than that. It would be so much better if instead, the family had saved his letters – they're the old turkey himself talking, not some artist's version of how he looked all dressed up.'

'Do you save letters?' Missy asked.

'Much to my regret,' I laughed. 'I used to have some written by my old girls and Alice found them.'

'Do you skip through letters first to find the parts about yourself?'

'Do you?' I asked.

'Of course!' Missy laughed. 'I can't wait. In prep school the first thing I turned to was how the boy ended the letter. The last paragraph was always the juiciest and – Hi, Mary.'

I looked up.

'She's gone,' Missy said. 'It was Mary Fielding. She just poked her head around the door. She's gone now.'

'Probably looking for Toby,' I said.

'Toby's playing backgammon, remember? If I know Mary, she was looking for trouble. God, these women –' Missy smiled. 'They're like jackals, really. There's nothing they like better than to salivate over someone else's wounds. They even hunt in packs.'

'Do you remember the hyena in Hemingway's *The Snows of Kilimanjaro?*'

'Sure,' Missy said. 'I loved that story.'

'Do you remember where he took that whack at Fitzgerald?'

'Oh, hey, speaking of Fitzgerald,' Missy said, 'do you remember that evening last summer when we all sat around the pool at the club and talked about Gatsby?'

'Sure,' I said. 'You and me and Alice and Walt and the Crosbys. I remember it very well, why?'

'Well, I went back and reread again *The Great Gatsby*,' Missy said. 'Just out of curiosity, really. I couldn't understand why that book meant so much to you. I mean, Gatsby was a *crook* – everyone who's ever read the book seems to have known that except you.'

'Of course he was, Missy, I knew that. But it wasn't Gatsby that I loved about the book. It was the feeling of the summer. The magic, the style. Gatsby's line, "Well, he's no use to us if Detroit is his idea of a small town," I mean, that's such a marvellous things to say. And I loved Fitzgerald's descriptions of Daisy's house and Gatsby's parties. They were so pretty, you know?'

'Gracious living,' Missy smiled.

'It's more than that. It was the celebration of illusion.'

'Gatsby's and everyone else's. I can remember before Walt and I were married how I used to dream about how our life together would be. I pictured us living in some huge old ivy-covered Tudor tower with a long, long winding driveway of crushed gravel. And a huge lawn shaded by huge old oak trees. And we'd have a pond with weeping willows and wild ducks would come into it. And sunsets would find Walt in some handsome linen suit and I'd be wearing something cool and flowing and pastel-coloured and ... and it's all such utter crap. And now,' Missy continued, 'and now I think I'd like to be somewhere all alone on the coast of Maine in some isolated farmhouse with hundreds of acres leading down to the sea.'

'You'd get awfully lonely.'

'No, I wouldn't,' Missy said. 'I'd invite you up. You'd stay with me, wouldn't you?'

'I'd love to.'

'See? Mine is only a different sort of nostalgia, really. "Nostalgia" is such a good word. It's so appropriate. It sounds like a type of small, delicate flower. A bouquet of nostalgia. People feel nostalgic about so many things – old cars, old towns, old houses, old woods and fields, old things. I mean, why else do we fill our houses with antiques that need restoring, oriental rugs that need reweaving, ancestral portraits that need repairing – none of which can we afford to have done and none of which can we afford not to do, you know what I mean? We hold on to them like we hold on to our illusions that good times and happy days will return. Somehow there's always a style we aspire to. And we pursue our illusions with such vigour I suppose in a way we're no different from Gatsby.'

'Or Gatsby's children,' I said. 'What illusions do you pursue, Missy?'

'I want to be happy,' she said. 'And you, George? What about you?'

'What about me? I just spent most of yesterday with a friend of mine, who wants to change the world ... Me?' I shook my head. 'I don't have any desire to change it, or conquer it, or anything. All I want is to have some feeling that there's a place still left somewhere in it for me. I'd like things to be nice.'

'And what about Alice?' Missy asked. 'How does she fit in? When you picture yourself ten, twenty years from now, what is Alice doing?'

'I don't know, Missy,' I said. 'I honestly don't know. I guess I just don't think about us being together for that long.'

'Well, doesn't that tell you something about your marriage?'

Not as much as it tells me about myself.'

'Ah, now George – you should have heard what my mother said after she spent a particularly gruesome evening with Walter and me. She said, "My dear, first marriages always seem so important."'

'And what did she mean by that?'

'That divorce isn't the end of the world. It may have seemed that way to her generation, but it wasn't then and it certainly isn't now.'

'It sounds as though you've made up your mind about you and Walter.'

'Does it?' Missy asked. 'I guess I have.'

'Would you get married again?'

'Probably. If the right person asked me. I'd like to have children,' Missy said. 'And so, yes, I'd get married again. And so would you. But I'll probably marry someone like Walt and you'll probably marry someone like Alice and we'll make the same mistakes all over again.'

'If we didn't repeat the same mistakes there would be no need for God.'

'And on that cheery note,' Missy laughed, 'let's have another drink. What time is it? Should we search out our mates? Let's make one tour of the ballroom and then have a drink, okay?'

'Okay,' I said.

We found Walt in the bar with Chauncey Halpert and Betty Hamlin. Betty was trying hard to be gay, to be liked, and the more she drank the more desperate she became.

'But everybody loves you here,' Chauncey was saying. 'Everyone is talking about how you throw the best parties in Winander. That you're one of the most amusing people around.'

'Do you think I'm fun, really?' Betty asked.

'I think you're a really *fun* person,' Chauncey said. 'Don't you, Walt? Don't you think Betty's a *fun* person?'

'I had a good time at her party,' Walt said.

'It was a fun party,' Chauncey said.

'Do you really think so?' Betty asked.

'And you're a fun girl,' Chauncey said patting her thigh. 'Now how about that drink?'

'Sure,' Betty said, 'I guess so.'

I didn't want to watch so I asked Missy if she would like to dance.

'Love to,' she said. 'Walt, do you mind?'

'Me?' Walt asked. 'No, of course not.'

And so I led Missy on to the dance floor. We danced in silence and then I asked, 'Why don't you and I have lunch together Monday in the city?'

'You *do* know, George, that when a gentleman invites a married lady to lunch in New York that it's an invitation to go to bed together.'

'Is that so?'

'That's what I've been told.'

'Will I see you for lunch?'

'Call me in the morning. On Monday,' Missy said.

There was a sudden terrible scream. It came from the front entrance of the club by the long, sweeping staircase that went to the powder room and guest rooms on the second floor. There was absolute silence except for the shuffling of feet as everyone crowded towards the front entrance to see what had happened. The orchestra was quiet and the doorway leading from the ballroom into the front hall was jammed. At somebody's order the orchestra abruptly started playing again, a very loud and dissonant 'Days of Wine and Roses' which faltered then shifted into a ragged 'Embraceable You'.

Missy and I made our way to the edge of the crowd and met Charlie Baker on his way out of the middle.

'What happened?' I asked.

'Betty Hamlin,' he said. 'She fell off the banister.'

'Oh God,' I said, 'is she –?' But even before I could finish my question I could see the answer in the way old Mr Neill had pushed himself back against the wall, his face ashen with memories.

'She was on top,' Charlie was saying, 'and it looked as though she suddenly, as a lark, decided to slide down. And she threw a leg over the banister and something happened, lost her balance, or something, she just kept going. She'd been ... well, I guess she'd had a lot to drink ... and I guess she ...'

'Then she's dead?' Missy asked.

'I think so,' Charlie said. 'She hit awfully hard.'

'Has anyone called an ambulance?' I asked.

'Doctor Fowler's with her now,' Charlie said. 'And what's-his-name, Betty Hamlin's husband.'

'Is somebody with him?' I asked.

'Chauncey's there. And Paul Thayer.'

I asked Charlie if he had seen Alice.

'Your Alice?' he asked me. 'I saw her leave about thirty minutes ago. She left after the backgammon game with Toby Fielding. Toby said he wanted to get his house ready for the party.'

And as I turned away Missy asked me where I was going.

'Away,' I said. 'I'm getting the hell out of here. The party's over.'

'Will I see you on Monday?' she asked.

'I'll call you,' I said.

The Fieldings lived on the other side of the lake from the club. It took me at least fifteen minutes to get to the house through the snowy roads. I was reaching for the buzzer at the front door when I noticed the grey flickering light on the living-room wall.

Even from the angle at which I was standing I could tell it was one of Toby Fielding's skin-flicks. I pushed open the door and Toby called, 'We're in the living-room.'

I went in and saw Toby and Alice standing now with their backs to the screen on which was now being projected the scratched and grainy image of an over-exposed blonde-haired girl writhing beneath a giant Negro.

'Oh hi, George,' Toby said. He flicked off the projector. And when Alice turned away from me I saw the bunching at the back of her dress where her bra strap had been undone.

'Alice,' I said, 'it's time to go home.'

She didn't answer.

'But you'll miss the party,' Toby protested.

'I don't think there will be any party,' I said. 'Betty Hamlin's dead. She fell off the banister at the club.'

'She what?' Toby asked.

And Alice laughed. She laughed and laughed and Toby Fielding looked first at her and then at me and a dribble of laughter escaped his lips as he looked first at Alice and then at me. 'George, are you serious?' he asked.

'Call the club,' I said. And I left the two of them right there. I simply didn't want to look at them any longer. To get to my house I had to drive along the lake road back past the club. Most of the automobiles had left the parking lot, but farther on there was a crowd of cars at the curve leading to the western approach to the lake. Caught in the automobiles' headlights like an insect impaled upon a pin was a small, red MG which had slid sideways off the road and into the ditch. Gazing with stupid wonderment at his left front wheel which was spinning lazily was young Tom Edmunds. And standing beside him in boots that barely covered her ankles and a fur coat which scarcely reached her thighs, was Jennifer his beautiful red-haired girl. As soon as I turned on to the lake road she recognized my car and ran towards me. I stopped and rolled down the window.

'Where are you going?' she asked.

'Home,' I said. 'Are you both all right? Nobody hurt?'

'No we're all fine, except that I'm freezing.'

I pulled the emergency brake and struggled out of my overcoat. 'Here,' I said, pushing my coat through the window to her. 'You can drop it by my house tomorrow.'

'I won't be here, tomorrow,' Jennifer said as she pulled my overcoat on over her fur.

'I won't either,' I said. 'But you'll get it to me somehow, don't worry.'

Jennifer made a 'V' with her fingers. 'Peace,' she said.

'Survival,' I said.

I made it home in another few minutes and parked next to the baby-sitter's car. I paid her, sent her home, and went upstairs and checked on the children. They were asleep and I went directly into the back room and got a suitcase out of the closet. I was just putting my shirts in on top of my folded suits when I heard the front door slam and Alice running up the stairs.

She took one look at my suitcase and shouted, 'You son of a bitch, where do you think you're going!' She swept my suitcase off the bed and spilled its contents on to the floor. I patiently picked up my suitcase and put it back on the bed and put the shirts back into it.

'Well, say something!' Alice said.

'I'm leaving.'

'I can see that,' she said. 'Why?'

'Because I've had it,' I said.

'I wasn't doing anything at the Fieldings,' she said. 'Toby was just showing me a film.'

'Is that why your bra was unfastened?'

'Is that why you're leaving? Jesus!' Alice said. 'Just because my bra strap was undone? Didn't you know the bras you wear with evening dresses can be very uncomfortable?'

'It's been a long time since I've worn one,' I said.

'Very funny!' Alice said.

I looked at Alice and her face was all pinched and white. 'It isn't just because of Toby Fielding, Alice I couldn't care less about Toby Fielding, you know? What I care about is what is happening to you, to the children and to me. And you and I are through. That's what I finally realized tonight. And that's what you don't understand. You keep thinking that everything's all right. And for so long now, *too* long! For too long now I've been trying to convince myself that even though everything wasn't all right, that some day it might be, that it could be. But it won't. Not between the two of us. Not any more. Not ever again, and I'm getting out.'

'And what about the children?' Alice asked. 'You're just going to desert them?'

'I'm not deserting anybody,' I said. 'I'll be in the apartment in New York. You have the phone number, the address, how to get in touch with me. I'll be –'

'– You're just going to go back to all those little girls aren't you,' Alice said. 'You're just going to go from girl to girl to girl and you'll never be able to give them anything. Nothing! You've never been able to give to anybody,' she laughed hoarsely. 'You're never going to be happy, George. You'll just wander from girl to girl.'

I didn't answer.

'You're going to get in touch with Lynn, aren't you! You're going to back to that girl you fucked in that apartment. You'll go back to Lynn, that's what you're going to do, isn't it!'

'She isn't even in New York, Alice. I don't want to see her, I don't want to see anybody, that's what you don't understand, Alice. I'm not leaving for something, I'm leaving to get away from something.'

'From what?' Alice asked.

'From you. From me. This. Winander. All of it.'

'And the children?'

'They'll be all right,' I said 'Once I can get settled then maybe I can provide them with at least some sort of alternative, a better life than the one we've had together.'

'Oh, why don't you grow up!' Alice said bitterly.

'I just have,' I said. I went into the bathroom and changed out of my dinner jacket and pants and put on a pair of grey flannels.

Alice came to the bathroom door, 'You even took a copy of *Playboy* into New York your last trip. The one from your bathroom.'

'I thought you had finished with it,' I said. I was putting on one of the new shirts I had had made and which had just arrived yesterday, and Alice started telling me how I would be able to wear all my new shirts with all my 'new little girls', and I stayed quiet.

'You're just running away,' she said.

'Alice, I'm not running anywhere except into New York. And you know exactly where I'll be.'

'You're going to throw everything away,' she said. 'All the good things we have. The children, the house, the pets, the – the –'

'Alice, I'm not throwing anything away. I'm trying to hold on to what I've got left.'

'"I'm trying to hold on to what I've got left",' Alice said, mimicking my voice. 'That's such shit, George.'

I didn't answer.

'Up in the air junior bird man!' she sang.

I was collecting my shaving gear and Alice kept handing me things. 'Here!' she said. 'Here's your toothbrush.'

'Thank you,' I said and put it in my shaving kit.

'Don't forget your nailbrush,' she said. 'Here!' she poked it at me, 'You'll want your nailbrush.'

And I put it in my shaving kit. 'Thank you.'

'And here's your after-shave,' Alice said. 'You're going to want it, you'll need that. You'll want to smell all rugged and masculine for all your little girls.'

'Thank you.' I put the after-shave and what was left in my shaving kit and carried it back to the bedroom and my suitcase.

'You're just going to run back to New York, aren't you?'

'Yes.'

Alice picked up my pyjamas and threw them at me, 'Here! You'll want these until you find some new little girl.'

'Thank you,' I said and put them in my suitcase.

'Why? Why are you doing this, George? Why?'

'Alice, you know why,' I said. 'We've been through it over and over again. You know why.'

'But it was so pleasant tonight.'

'Jesus Christ! Tell me, if you can, one pleasant thing about tonight?'

'I didn't hate you. It was the first time at a dance I didn't hate you. I wasn't jealous. I was having such a good time, and now you're spoiling it.'

'Alice, the last thing I mean to do is spoil your good times. If you want, why don't you call Toby back up? They're probably having the party without you. I wouldn't be a bit surprised. Honest to God, Alice, don't you see how rotten this place is?'

'Honest to God, I think you're crazy. I've never seen you behave like this. I think you're crazy, really!'

'Not any more,' I said. I zipped shut the suitcase and lifted it off the bed.

'And that's it? You've packed and now you're off like some astronaut?'

'Alice, I'm sorry ...' I said. 'It's such a goddam inadequate word, but I am truly, honestly sorry. I wish I didn't have to go. If you want to tell people I'm just going away to work for a while it's okay with me.'

'Fuck the other people,' Alice said. 'What about *us*? What am I supposed to tell myself? What am I going to tell the children?'

'Tell them I love them.'

'And is this how you show it?'

I went down the stairs, picked up a heavy sweater from the hall closet, then let myself out of the house through the kitchen door. I opened the door on the passenger side and put in my suitcase and my sweater, then went around to the driver's side. Just as I was about to climb in, Alice opened the door on the passenger side and threw my sweater and suitcase out into the snow.

'Alice, please...?'

She stood there in her evening gown and slippers in the cold.

'Alice, please?'

She wouldn't move. I got out of the car and went around to the other side. She lifted my suitcase out of the snow, brushed it off and handed it to me. I placed it in the car, picked up my sweater and tossed it into the car, too. As I was going back to the driver's side Alice said, 'This is for real, isn't it? You're really leaving, aren't you?'

'I'm trying to,' I said. I paused next to the door. 'You shouldn't be standing out here. You'll get pneumonia.'

'George . . . ?'

'What?'

'Have a cup of tea with me before you go?' Alice said. 'I'll make you a fresh pot. Grind the beans. You can take it in a thermos with you.'

'I really have to go, Alice.'

'Don't you want to look in on the children?'

'I did. They were asleep.'

'I could wake them up so you could say good-bye to them.'

'I'll see them very soon.'

'Just one cup with me? Please?' Alice asked and smiled sadly, 'For old times' sake?'

I shook my head. 'It's for old times' sake that I'm getting out of here.'

'Please, George. Just one cup. It won't take long. I can make instant coffee. I don't want you to fall asleep on the road.'

'All right,' I said, 'one cup.' I followed Alice back inside the house.

Just as the water was coming to a boil the telephone rang. Alice and I both glanced at the kitchen clock. It was almost two.

Alice answered the phone. 'Who? Just a minute. Who's calling please?' Alice let the telephone dangle by its cord. 'It's for you, George,' she said tonelessly. 'It's one of your little girl friends. Jennifer somebody.'

I picked up the telephone and Alice stood with her arms crossed watching me. Her face was becoming white and pinched again.

'Hi, Jennifer,' I said. 'What's up?'

'Listen, I'm sorry to call you so late,' she said, 'but I figured you probably weren't in bed yet. I'm down at the Police Gate.'

'What are you doing there?' I asked and Alice suddenly left the room.

'Well, I decided to catch a bus into New York and what I'm calling you about is –' (there was a faint click as Alice picked up the extension in the library) '– your coat. I'll leave it with the guard at the gate, okay? There's a bus leaving for the city in a few minutes, so I'll be all right.'

'Well, that's fine, Jennifer,' I said. 'I'll pick it up there. Perhaps I'll see you again.'

'Hope so. That'd be groovy,' Jennifer said. 'G'bye,' and she hung up.

And into the phone I said, 'C'mon Alice, let's have that cup of coffee.'

Alice came storming out of the library and stopped at the kitchen door. In her hand was a pistol. 'YOU SON OF A BITCH!' she was screaming, 'IT DIDN'T TAKE YOU LONG!'

'Where'd you get that?'

'From your WORDSWORTH, you son of a BITCH! From where you so stupidly thought you'd hidden it. That's what's so STUPID about you and your stupid secrets! They're *never* secrets! I always know exactly what you're doing.'

'You're very clever,' I said. 'And now if you don't mind, I'm going to get myself some coffee.'

'Don't be smart with me!' Alice said. She was holding the pistol in both hands now, pointing it straight at my stomach.

'Who is Jennifer? Some little girl? Some new little girl of yours?'

'She's an eighteen-year-old California girl.'

'Eighteen! Isn't that a little young even for you? And what about Missy Carlyle? Have you forgotten about her? Or is Missy Carlyle too old for you?'

'Alice,' I said. 'You're upset, I know, but that doesn't give you the right to be stupid.' I took the pan of boiling water and added some to my cup. 'Do you want some?'

'You're not leaving me for some eighteen-year-old California girl. Where'd you meet her? What is she, some sort of hippy?'

I smiled and told Alice that I didn't think we even knew what a hippy was. Alice was still standing at the kitchen door, pointing the pistol at me. I went to the icebox and got some milk for my coffee, then I sat down at the kitchen table and the whole time Alice just stood, pointing the pistol at me.

'Are you sure you wouldn't like some coffee?' I said.

'If you leave me, I'll pull the trigger,' she said. 'I'll kill you, George.'

'No you won't.'

'If you leave me, I will.'

'Either way I'd leave you now, wouldn't I?' I said. 'It's the same to me.'

'Not to *you*!' she said.

I finished the cup of coffee and rinsed the cup and saucer then walked to the door that led outside. 'Good-bye, Alice. I'll be in New York if you want me,' I said. I opened the door and paused for a moment looking across the room at my wife. 'I'm sorry, Alice,' I said. 'I am *truly* sorry.'

And Alice pulled the trigger. There was a slight ping and a rod about eighteen inches long sprang out of the barrel, unfurled, and became a small gold-fringed, blue silk flag with red lettering on it. The lettering spelled: 'BANG!'

'Alfred sent it to me,' I explained.

I closed the kitchen door and walked out to my car. When I opened the door on the driver's side I looked back through the kitchen window. I could still see Alice standing where I had left her, still holding the prop pistol with its silly damn flag.

It took me a moment to start the cold engine, and then I backed the car up and turned it around. Just before I left, I looked back in the rear-view mirror at the kitchen. Alice had come to the door and was watching me. And I'm not entirely sure this is true because it seems so patently absurd, but I think ... I *think*, that as I left, I saw her wave.

More about Penguins and Pelicans

The Great Gatsby

F. Scott Fitzgerald

No one ever really knew who Gatsby was. Some said that he had been a German spy, others that he was related to one of Europe's royal families. Despite this nearly everyone took advantage of his fabulous hospitality. And it really was fabulous. On his superb Long Island home he gave the most amazing parties, and not the least remarkable thing about them was the fact that few people could recognize their host. He seemed to be a person without background, without history, without a home. Yet the irony of this bright and brittle façade was that he created it not to impress the world and his wife, but to impress just one person – a girl he had loved and had had to leave, a girl who had loved him but was now married to a rich good-for-nothing, a girl whom he had dreamed about for over four years. This dream had long ceased to have any substance or any connection with reality – and for that reason he could not wake from it. He had doped himself with his own illusion. And only death could dispel that dream.

'It has interested and excited me more than any new novel I have seen, either English or American, for a number of years' – T. S. Eliot in a letter to the author in 1925.

Also *available*

The Beautiful and Damned

The Last Tycoon

Tender is the Night

This Side of Paradise

Collected Short Stories (*in five volumes*)

Not for sale in the U.S.A. or Canada